About the Author

Marisa Mackle is the author of the *Irish Times* bestseller *Along Came a Stork*. She works as a newspaper columnist and is also a children's novelist. Her books have been translated into a dozen languages. She is the mother of a little boy called Gary and they live in Spain. Visit her on www.marisamackle.ie.

Acknowledgements

I would like to thank God, St Jude and St Anthony for their constant love and guidance.

I would like to thank my friends and family for their patience and understanding, especially when I disappear off to write my books for weeks at a time!

I would like to give a special mention to the late, wonderful Maeve Binchy who put me on the right track when I was starting out on my writing career and was my biggest inspiration, and also to my late grandmother, Sheila Collins, who believed in me from the start.

Thanks also to the ever-supportive Rosanna Davison and Alison Canavan, and to Liz Dunne who has never missed a book launch!

Final thanks to my dedicated editor, Gaye Shortland, for her Trojan work, and to Paula and the wonderful crew at Poolbeg.

This book is dedicated to my darling son,
Gary Eamonn Mackle

1

Okay, so it's never fun being dumped. It's horrible. In fact I would go as far as to say that dumping somebody is probably one of the crappiest thing in the world that one human being can do to another human being. When you're the dumpee, the shame, the humiliation and the constant 'What did I do wrong?' questions swirling around in your head for ages afterwards are just awful. Rejection is never nice but when somebody you want doesn't want you, it's pretty terrible.

I mean, if somebody rejects your CV at least you can console yourself by thinking, well, they didn't ever give you the chance to show off your people skills, your unique innovation, or get to hear your witty public speaking. Likewise, if you're an actor you can come to terms with rejection by presuming they wanted somebody shorter or fatter, or somebody of a different sex or something. But in relationships it's much worse because they *know* you, they have spent quality time with you, and shared intimate moments with you, and you've poured out your heart to them. They've met your family, your dog, seen your bedroom in a mess and they've featured prominently in your dreams for a better future. So when they leave, they don't just leave empty-handed. No, they leave taking your dreams away with them. And then you have to start all over again.

And so I was single again. Back on the shelf I thought I'd left for good. My new-found relationship status wasn't one of my choice. God, no. I was still coming to terms with the abrupt split but I was too busy to keep analysing it to death. As my mother says: 'It is what it is.' And I must accept that. No amount of trying to make somebody change their mind will actually make them do it. Besides, it's exhausting. My baby son needed my love and energy far more than my ex did. Besides, he didn't want it anyway.

Some break-ups are less heartbreaking than others, of course. Like when you're young, you break up with people all the time for silly reasons, like they stuck you for the cinema tickets, or you don't like their new haircut, or they wanted to go a bit further than you wanted to, or you caught them eyeing up your best friend. But when you're older, and hopefully more mature (although age and maturity don't necessarily go hand in hand), you need a better reason to break up with somebody.

My boyfriend, or rather ex-boyfriend, Clive, gave me my marching orders the day my baby was born and still to this day I have absolutely no idea why. I mean, I knew he did not want me to have the baby and I knew that he was drifting further and further away from me as my pregnancy progressed but I really thought he would change his mind as time wore on, and I was convinced that after the birth he would fall madly in love with his kid, his flesh and blood. I guess I was so madly in love and so desperate for us to be together that I was blindly clinging on to the hope that he would realise that having a baby would be something wonderful. So, when I was dumped while giving birth and told to sling my hook once and for all, I was in serious shock. Of course he told me in a rather indirect kind of way. And not in front of the doctors and nurses. No. He did it on the phone. Just a couple of hours before they pulled the baby out of me.

It wasn't 'It's not me, it's you'. Rather it was, 'It's not me, it's you two'. I'll admit the timing wasn't the best. After all, anyone who has ever been dumped knows it's pretty awful when you're given a final goodbye, but when you're just about to deliver your first baby you can multiply that dreaded feeling of rejection by a thousand.

Usually when a relationship ends, there's some kind of an uncomfortable 'talk' which is rarely fun and where at least one party is dying to make an escape. But at least it's some kind of closure. It's better to know for sure than to keep wondering why somebody isn't returning any of your calls. Or texts. Or letters. Or faxes. Okay, okay, you get the picture.

I don't think I'll ever forget the 'talk' I had just before I gave birth. I had phoned Clive because I was in agony with labour pains. I was crawling around on the kitchen floor when I looked at my watch, which had just hit midnight. I was wondering whether he was still up. I was also pretty worried that he might have gone to bed already. Somebody needed to take me to the hospital and I didn't want to call an ambulance.

But no, he was up all right. In fact, he was at a party and couldn't hear very well over the music. I told him the baby was coming. He sounded surprised. Shocked, even. Then he said that it wasn't a good time for him. And hung up.

I phoned back of course. He took the call again and this time went outside to talk to me in private. He still insisted that it wasn't a good time for him. I said it wasn't a particularly good time for me either. I asked him if he could by any chance drive myself and our bump to the maternity hospital so that I could bring our baby into the world.

"I can't!" he practically snarled own the phone. "I've had a few drinks. Can you not phone your mother or a friend?"

I was stunned into silence.

"Any other time," he said.

Actually, I'm joking about that last bit. Even he wouldn't have said that. But he did suggest someone else, anyone besides him really. Surely my friend Sally would give me a lift in if she wasn't doing anything? And then he hung up once more.

I rang back a third time. This time he wasn't even polite when he answered abruptly. He said that if I called him again that night he was going to report me for harassment. He said that he could no longer tolerate the constant drama and that I needed to give him a break.

From now on he wanted a nice, peaceful life. Without me and the baby annoying him.

"You're on your own now," was the last thing I heard him say before he hung up for the final time. *Click. Beeeeeeeep.*

Of course it all seems like a lifetime ago now. Even the night of the birth itself is a bit of a blur, which is good. I don't want that unpleasant memory clearly in my head forever. But some parts of the night are hard to block out. Like the memory of going to the hospital in a taxi that I'd hailed outside my apartment on the street because I actually felt I couldn't phone one and wait ten minutes for it to arrive. The driver was terrified that my waters were going to break on the black-leather seat of his shiny Mercedes. His knuckles were white as he gripped the steering wheel and kept looking anxiously at my enormous belly. In fact, come to think of it, he even stopped off at a petrol station to buy me some kitchen roll, just in case, and presented it to me free of charge. Ah, bless.

I clearly recall admitting myself into hospital alone in the dead of night, walking up those lonely steps and explaining to the administrator in the welcoming office that no, I had no partner or anything like that to accompany me, and that no, I wasn't a private patient either – just a public one so, you know, it didn't really matter where I gave birth. I think I might have even apologised for inconveniencing her.

As it turned out, there was no room for me in any of the wards anyway. There had been an overwhelming amount of admissions that evening apparently, and so I was left out on a trolley in a brightly-lit corridor for a while, crying quietly to myself. I remember thinking how terrible it must have been for the poor Virgin Mary all those years ago when she, like me, found herself with no proper bed for the night in which to give birth. But at least she had Joseph with her, which must have been of some comfort. I bet Joseph wouldn't have hung up on Mary if mobile phones had been around back then. I bet he wouldn't have left her on her own in the stable with the ass and donkey, while he went off partying in Bethlehem.

Anyway, the baby came pretty quickly so I wasn't left in the corridor for too long. Obviously, as bad as the health system is in Ireland, they still don't allow women to give birth in the corridor with people walking about chatting on their mobile phones or discussing their holidays. And at least it was just me in the delivery room on my own. Well, me and a few other people. Actually, quite a lot of people now that I cast my mind back. There was the doctor of course, an anaesthetist, a couple of midwives, a trainee doctor, a trainee nurse and another man who I think was also a nurse. At least I hope he was. I hope he wasn't just some random spectator or something.

They say when you give birth you must be prepared to leave your dignity at the maternity-hospital door before you go in. Well, they're so right about that. It's hard to be cool and nonchalant when you're lying spread-eagled naked from the waist down on a bed before a group of uniformed strangers you met only a few minutes previously. However, the whole birth thing wasn't quite as horrendous as I'd imagined it would be. I know I didn't scream my head off but I do remember thinking at one stage that I couldn't go through with the pushing any more because I was too hot and exhausted and the sweat was pouring out of me. As ridiculous as it may seem, I remember telling the medical team that I'd have to stop, that I couldn't possibly continue with this. My body was at breaking point. I mean, what was I thinking? Did I honestly think they'd let me go off for a coffee and maybe check my Facebook to update my status and come back later? Anyway, hats off to them, they kept me going with endless words of encouragement and they were super-kind. They made me feel like I was the only mummy giving birth in Ireland that day when in reality there must have been hundreds.

The staff rolled me out afterwards on a trolley to the recovery room where I drifted into a deep, deep sleep while they looked after my newborn child for me. When I woke up it suddenly hit me that I was somebody's actual mother. Imagine, a real-life mummy! But that initial euphoric feeling was followed by one of panic. What now? I knew nothing whatsoever about babies. I hadn't even had any baby-sitting experience. I hadn't done a course in parenting or even read a book about it! Jesus, you needed a license for a dog but you could just walk out of here with a real-life human being? I was petrified!

I didn't sleep all night in the ward. The other mummies were coughing loudly and some were talking loudly in foreign languages on their mobile phones. Whenever one baby stopping crying, another would start. They never turned off the lights in the ward all night, making sleep impossible. Then just after I had finally dozed off, having breastfed my little bundle of joy for about forty-five minutes, I was rudely woken up by two nurses pushing my bed into the side of the wall. I sat up with a jolt. What the hell was going on?

"We're bringing another lady and her baby in to share your cubicle with you. We're very overcrowded tonight and just don't have enough space for everyone. I'm really sorry about this."

I could feel the tears welling in my eyes as the nurse was talking to me. I honestly didn't think I could take any more. I was so exhausted it was torturous. I wished I'd had earplugs to drown out the noise, but you can't wear earplugs in case you can't hear your baby crying. I just felt like I was in the middle of a living nightmare. The final straw was when the partner of the new mummy in my cubicle sat down at the end of my bed and started talking loudly to her. I couldn't believe it. I couldn't sleep with a strange man sitting at the end of my bed. When the nurse came around the next time, I asked to see the doctor on duty. When the senior house officer came around (a junior doctor despite the grand title – she was a very pretty little thing who looked around twelve), I told her that I needed to leave immediately.

She raised a perfectly plucked eyebrow. "Oh, but you can't leave," she said politely but firmly. "You must wait until the registrar does his ward rounds in the morning and then he will decide if you can leave or not."

"I am leaving," I said, fighting back the tears. "I can't sleep here. If I need to come back I will, but I have to go now. I'm not a prisoner and I can't be detained here against my will."

I packed up my belongings and my baby and, still in my nightie and dressing-gown, I asked the porter to phone me a taxi.

It took about forty minutes to get to Bray but the relief to be back in my own little rented apartment was enormous. It was a wonderful feeling that I didn't have to share a bathroom with six other women and their visitors any more.

"Welcome home, little fellow," I said to my little baba before feeding him, cuddling him and then putting him down to sleep in a little yellow Moses basket beside my own double bed. He closed his eyes and then I went to the fridge where I retrieved a snipe of champagne. I sat back on the bed, so relieved to be home and away from the hospital noise and its clinical smell. I toasted myself. "Here's to me and my little man," I said with a smile. "We did it. And we survived!"

The next few weeks were a bit of a haze. I know people warn you about the lack of sleep that follows the arrival of a baby but nothing could have prepared me for the sheer exhaustion. I remember thinking that if I got five hours' interrupted sleep it was like winning the lottery. In fact I became totally obsessed with getting some kip, unable to think about anything else but resting my head down on a pillow. I didn't feel great about myself and I felt guilty for not feeling great. After all, there I was, the mother of a perfectly healthy baby boy and I would often cry myself to sleep because I felt so lonely and alone. Friends said they would visit and then didn't. People often offered to baby-sit but then balked whenever I tried to make a specific date. I very quickly began to realise who my real friends were. I could have counted them on half a hand. All the party people had vanished into thin air.

I don't know what I was expecting exactly. I mean, I knew it would be hard work. I understood that it would be particularly challenging raising a kid all by myself. Clive had told me, "You're on your own, now." And he meant it.

Things were very tight financially. For the first time in my life I started to make out grocery-shopping lists. I saved on formula milk as I was breastfeeding but I had to buy special ointment for my sore, cracked nipples. The cost of nappies in particular was a huge shock to me. Thank goodness I had given up smoking when I was pregnant because the money that I used to spend on cigarettes was now needed for nappies. Sometimes my baby would go through seven or eight in a single day. I swear, they ate money.

Looking back it's hard to know how I coped at all. I remember one friend phoning me up to see if I wanted to meet her one evening. I asked her if she wouldn't mind terribly calling over to mine instead of going out somewhere. The truth was that I didn't want to be seen out and about in public. I was ashamed of the fact that I was still wearing my maternity jeans with my muffin tummy hanging out over the top, and I was embarrassed that I hadn't simply 'pinged' back into shape after six weeks like all the celebrity mums who post photos of themselves on Twitter seem to do. I actually don't have any really decent baby photos of myself and my son because I hated the way I looked during those first few months. Anyway, my friend thankfully came over and I was grateful that I didn't have to go out and could stay in my tracksuit. Besides, I wouldn't have been able to afford a baby-sitter anyway. Do you know that before I became a mum I had absolutely no idea how much baby-sitters charged? I mean, ten euro an hour just to sit on the couch helping themselves to tea and biscuits and watching DVDs by the fire as little baby slept soundly in the other room? Who could afford ten euro an hour for baby-sitting? Imagine spending that even before you paid for the bus into town, your drinks for the evening and a taxi home again? I despaired that I would never have a night out in Dublin again for the next eighteen years!

On one occasion my mother was away and I was so desperate to get someone to mind my baby that I phoned Clive. Call me sad and pathetic if you like but a tiny part of me still hoped that he might have slowly come around to the idea of being a dad by now. But no chance of that unfortunately. He was very cold with me on the phone and told me that if I thought I was going to start treating him like a free baby-sitter I had another think coming to me. I was so upset by his tone of voice that I burst into tears. I mean, it wasn't like I was even going out that afternoon. I had a pain in my gum that wouldn't go away and I just wanted him to mind our son for an hour or two while I went to the dentist. I couldn't believe how nasty he was being. I mean, surely minding your own child couldn't be classed as baby-sitting? I was so desperate that I asked the woman who lived in the apartment across the corridor from me. I had only met her a few times in the communal yard at the back where we sometimes sat in the rare sunshine. She was a single mum too from Slovenia and her baby was probably about six months older than mine. I told her that I would repay the favour any time, and she said there was no problem at all looking after my child for a little while. Oh God, I was so grateful.

Clive did eventually come and see his son. Yes, he came with a DIY kit that he had bought on the internet – a DNA test-kit – arriving one day unannounced with it in his hand saying he wanted to prove once and for all that my son was his. I have to say I was extremely insulted by this. It would never have even occurred to me to cheat on Clive when we were together. I had been absolutely head over heels in love with him, even though I realise now that the feeling wasn't at all reciprocated. I was so shocked by his unspoken allegations that I was lost for words. I think I just stood at the front door of the apartment with my mouth opening and closing. He pushed past me and went to where our baby was lying in his cot and put a stick in his mouth to swab his cheek. The little mite started to bawl and I was so upset about the whole thing. I'd say Clive wasn't there for two minutes. He didn't even ask me how I was, just slammed the door on his way out.

Of course when the online results came back about ten days later Clive didn't even have the decency to apologise to me for his behaviour. Sometimes I wished so much that I'd never met the creep, but then I'd look at my darling boy and I realise I'd go through all the hurt and the pain again. My life began the day he was born.

It was weird but I kind of looked back on my single life and thought it must have been kind of boring and shallow. I used to feel sorry for people with kids, thinking they had no life. Now I was sure people pitied me. How the tables had turned!

Anyway, I didn't have the mind-space to worry too much about Clive. My beautiful boy was thriving and I was a besotted single mummy. I found myself staring at him for ages when he was asleep and thinking: Is he really mine? I kept expecting some woman, like his real mummy, to come along and take him away, and that I'd go back to my old single life when I thought going out and getting a free glass of sparkling wine was fun.

I wasn't as shattered as I was in the beginning – at least I felt like a normal human being sometimes despite my apartment always being covered in baby clothes that I was trying to dry. Honest to goodness, my washing machine never stopped turning and I thought I should buy shares in washing powder at the rate I was buying it. A box of washing powder used to last me a year before becoming a mum. Now I was flying through it. It seemed that every time I changed John he immediately either soiled himself or puked. Especially when he was wearing white. But I couldn't be cross for long because he was just so damn cute.

By the way, the reason I called my boy John was because he was a non-celebrity, and I didn't think it was fair to call non-celebrity babies after a fruit or a sports star. Also, I didn't want him to spend his whole life trying to get people to pronounce or spell his name properly, which can be rather a tiresome and frustrating experience. My mum called me Kaylah because she thought it was very exotic and she didn't want me to have the same name as everyone else. Her own name is Ann, you see, and there are quite a lot of Anns about the place. She thinks Ann is rather common so she called me Kaylah. Kaylah with a H to make the name even more unusual. And ever since I could talk, I've been pretty much driven around the bend pointing out to people that no my name is not Kylie or Karla or Katia or Kate. Honestly, people some people can be very rude sometimes. They seem to think they can call me anything at all as long as it begins with a K. Hmm. Maybe they're just lazy. Or could care less.

I called my son John because it's simple. I don't care if it's boring. Think of the time and energy I'll save him in the long run. Mind you, you're not going to believe this, but straight after he was born the nurse asked me his name. "It's John," I said proudly, still unable to contain my joy of becoming a mummy for the first time. A real mummy with a real baby. Imagine! Yes, I remember telling her, with tears in my eyes, that my bundle of joy was called John. Then I recall the silly woman looking up from her clipboard and smiling back at me. "Is that John with or without a H?" she asked. Oh for God's sake!

Anyway, to get back to my story, I guess it's time to explain how I met Clive and landed myself in my present state of single-mum-dom.

2

Pre-Clive, life was one big party. Myself and my friend Sally both worked (and still do work) in town for a glossy monthly fashion magazine. I was the in-house stylist when we met, and she worked in the sales and marketing department, mostly selling ads and running promotions. We bonded almost immediately, became firm friends and I moved into her city-centre apartment. It was a time when everybody was enjoying the roar of the Celtic Tiger and nobody could see the recession coming. Every night of the week there was something exciting happening in town and we were in the thick of it all. We would go to fashion shows, film screenings, cocktail parties and after-work drinks, later staggering home from nightclubs without even having to take taxis because we lived in such a centrally located place. On the weekends we could casually walk around Grafton Street which was just a leisurely stroll away, and stop off somewhere for coffee. We literally had every amenity right on our doorstep, which was great for convenience if not so fantastic for our credit cards!

I went on quite a few dates back then. When I was thinner and not pregnant and had no ties, I believe I was fairly attractive. Some of the guys I met were cute, some weren't. Some of the men had no hair but were funny; other men had hair but no humour. I know I was fussy but I wanted to hold out for Mr Perfect. I didn't want to just have a boyfriend for the sake of it. I wanted it all. And the night I met Clive – two summers ago – I thought I'd finally found him.

He was a writer for a national newspaper – bright, quick-witted and attractive. I met him on a last-minute press trip to sunny Croatia that my boss Creea had offered to me in a moment of rare kindness because somebody else couldn't go. At the time I had no ties, so didn't think twice about jumping on a plane and heading off.

I don't know whether it was the gorgeous climate or the copious amount of cocktails taken while dreamily looking out at the sun going down on the Adriatic Sea, but I fell in love with him the first night of our trip. He was tall, handsome, tanned and brooding, and he fixed his attentions on me from the start like there was no other woman in the room. I didn't want to fall for him of course. News reporters have reputations and huge egos so I was on my guard and determined not to be just another notch on this handsome man's bedpost. I played it cool the first evening as we sat on the hotel veranda among the group of Irish journalists and foreign tour guides. I laughed at his jokes and was delighted when he seemed to think mine were funny too. I didn't even budge when he casually placed his arm over the back of my chair, but I was first to excuse myself to go to bed even though I could have stayed up all night.

The next day in the pool he swam up right beside me and I couldn't help but marvel at his perfect tan even though we'd only been in the country for less than twenty-four hours. He explained that his mother was Italian and that's where he got his dark skin colouring from. He said he got his green eyes from his dad's side of the family. He said he liked my freckles but I thought he was probably just being nice.

That afternoon after lunch where Clive sat beside me charming me with his wit and easy banter, we went on a boat trip down a river. Clive started jokingly taking photos of me on his mobile phone and teasing me. I asked him why he needed so many photos of me and did he not think it would be better to take photos of the stunning scenery all around us?

"I can buy postcards of the scenery," he shrugged, "but I want these on my phone so that I never forget this press trip for the rest of my life."

Everyone on the trip kept telling me that Clive had the hots for me. I didn't really need them to point out that rather obvious bit of information because he wasn't exactly playing hard to get! On several occasions he let his hand rest on my arm as he was talking to me. The touch of his skin on mine felt sensational.

The trip was amazing. Croatia is probably the most beautiful place that I have ever visited. We dined in

Dubrovnik on the third night of our trip. "Those who wish to visit heaven on earth should come to Dubrovnik," the famous Irish playwright George Bernard Shaw said of this city, and he was right. It is truly spectacular. We dined down a little side street off the main bustling square. It was very warm and I was wearing a white sundress with a light-blue cotton jumper draped loosely over my shoulders. On my feet I wore Swarovski-encrusted flip-flops. We started the evening with Prosecco as the sun went down on the city and the rich aromas from the restaurants filled the warm Mediterranean air. As I sipped my Prosecco the bubbles seemed to swim right up to my brain, making me feel light and dizzy. I cannot remember what I ate, or who said what. I just remember gazing into Clive's green eyes, mesmerised. He looked out of this world in his black linen suit and open white shirt. His sandy wavy hair was pushed back from his face with a pair of tortoise-coloured sunglasses. People were chatting amiably, eating, drinking and smoking cigars. As it grew dark the street lights came on and candles were placed on the white tablecloths of the tables outside the restaurants. I remember thinking that tonight was the night. I would no longer hold back. When Clive made his move, I would succumb to his advances. If I could have leaned over the table there and then and kissed his lips I would have.

I think there were about eight to ten other people sitting at our table, but I can't remember the exact number or even who many of them were. I was intoxicated with Clive and had eyes only for him. I longed for us to leave the restaurant. But the dessert menus were being passed around and nobody was making any moves to leave. I wondered if we would be able to lose the others and go for a stroll arm in arm around this intoxicating city, just the two of us.

Afterwards, some of the more mature journalists headed back to the hotel and the rest of us party animals made our way to an open-air bar with music. Once we had settled at a table and ordered our drinks, Clive took me by the hand and led me onto the open-air dance-floor. He wrapped his arms around me and our bodies swayed to the music. I could smell his strong aftershave as I nuzzled my cheek against his chest. His fingers played with my hair as I clung to him. I never wanted to let him go. We slipped off without telling the others where we were going and made our way back barefoot to the hotel beach. Clive and I sat at the water's edge, not caring whether we got wet from the gentle waves lapping at our feet. We kissed each other hungrily and passionately. I don't think I ever wanted anyone that badly in my whole life. We kissed and we talked and we laughed until sunrise and then we went back to Clive's hotel room where we made wild, abandoned love with the window open, listening to the sound of waves lapping against the seashore.

Our affair lasted for the rest of the week, and continued after we landed in Dublin. For the next eight months I spent practically every free moment of the day and night with Clive in his bachelor pad in Grand Canal Dock with its magnificent views of the water and the city-centre skyline. He cooked for me and rented my favourite DVDs and played my favourite tunes on his iPod. I loved everything about him from his mind to his body. I knew he had the slightly ruthless streak that most newspaper reporters seem to need to survive in the cut-throat world of hacks, but I never thought that ruthlessness would one day be directed at me. He told me he that he loved me over and over and over again. And like a fool, besotted, and in love, I believed him. Eventually (and not before time, I thought) we started to look at houses in order to move in together.

Life with Clive was exciting. We dined in some of the city's best restaurants and took impromptu trips to London and Paris. As Clive was very well-connected in the media, we often got complimentary stays in some of the country's top hotel suites, always with a couple of bottles of champagne thrown in. The managers would always greet Clive by name, seeming to know him well. It was as though he had stayed before, with some other lucky lady. I often wondered about Clive's exes and what had become of them but he never spoke about his past. He didn't seem to care about any of his exes once they were history. It was that ruthless streak he had about him.

But my heady days of carefree partying and shopping came to a sudden halt when I discovered the following May that I was late and a single thin blue line confirmed that yes, I was pregnant. Once I found out, and the shock had sunk in a tiny bit, I phoned Clive. I had a feeling he wouldn't be overjoyed with the news but I was completely flabbergasted by his ice-cold reaction.

"Can you not sort this out?" he said, leaving me in no uncertainty about how he felt.

He didn't exactly break it off with me there and then, but he made it clear that I couldn't stay with him during my pregnancy. I hoped and prayed that I would be able to win him over, and that he would eventually warm to the idea of us being a little family. He said he needed a bit of space as well as time to get his head around the new situation so I moved all my stuff from my room in Sally's apartment into my Mum's house the following week and Sally got a new flatmate up from the country who was super-excited about the dizzy new life she was going to embark on in the city, and I started to prepare for the momentous change that was about to take place for me. I thought it would be less stressful living with Mum because I wouldn't have to be worrying about rent and all that. Also, I didn't want to be in the city walking around heavily pregnant in case I fell, or somebody bumped into me when they weren't looking where they were going. Anyway, I didn't want to be a burden on Sally. Sally was young, free, single and still searching. It might be weird for her to be living with a pregnant flatmate who had to be up flushing the loo every two hours, day and night. And myself and my big bump lying on the couch every night certainly wouldn't have helped her to meet a guy. Imagine if she'd brought someone back and I was sitting there with my slippers and massive hippo-bump sipping cocoa! Sally was lovely, but young and terribly image-conscious. Of course she pretended that she would miss me like hell and that I should think twice about moving out, but I could tell she was secretly relieved when I announced I was going. I think she was actually delighted to have a new flatmate

remember walking out of her house in a daze with my hand on my bump and my head held high, vowing never to darken the woman's doorstep again. I mean, what era did she think she was living in? Did she honestly think people were that narrow-minded in this day and age? Sure even a priest wouldn't have spoken to me like that. In fact I had always been quite friendly with the parish priest when I lived with Mum. Father Francis was a good old soul and had worked in Africa as a missionary for many years. I kind of felt sorry for him when all the abuse stories came out about the priests in the Catholic Church. Father Francis wouldn't harm a fly. Even when I told him what my mother had said to me, he said not to take any notice of her and that I was to rise above her and forgive her.

But I wasn't ready for forgiveness yet and I moved myself, my bump and all our stuff into a two-bed ground-floor apartment in Bray which I found through an ad in the *Evening Herald*.

3

So myself and Baby John are now living in that apartment in Bray, Co Wicklow, which is just outside of Dublin and near the sea. It sounds like it's a very nice place to live, especially in the summer, but it isn't as glamorous as you might think. I suppose it's okay but to describe it as any way exciting or upmarket would be terribly misleading. I mean, it's hardly Monte Carlo – no yachts or fancy cocktail bars or anything like that. Having said that, it's a very popular spot with un-sporty types who like to wear tracksuits (vest top underneath: optional). The area tends to get very crowded on hot sunny days (not that we have them here in abundance, I might add!) because half of Dublin takes the train to Bray and they spend all day on the beach and then go home leaving their rubbish, including empty beer cans and soiled nappies behind them. So even though it's cold and rainy in the winter, at least all the blow-ins are gone and it's nice and quiet in Bray. I prefer it like that.

Our home is in a small modern-ish, safe complex, not too far from the sea or the main street of Bray. The main bedroom is big enough for a double bed and a cot, and the spare room is just a little bigger than a box-room. It doesn't have as much storage space as I would like because John's stuff takes up so much room but it has a bath which I love. You can take away all my comforts but I would be lost without my daily bath. I just love to lock the door, fill the tub with bubbles and relax with a book, some candles and a nice glass of wine. When I put John down every night it is the one thing I look forward to. Baths are the cheapest form of relaxation in my opinion and I make sure every night is spa night. Complete with bath oil and nice-smelling body lotion for afterwards. Showers, although quick and easy, are not the same at all. I could never live in a place without a bath. Mind you, when I was pregnant, baths weren't as much fun at all. The bath water was never enough to cover my bump and although I'd be nice and warm underneath the water, my poor bump would feel the cold! And of course when John was smaller it was no fun at all to lie there constantly on edge, an ear cocked to hear him cry, and then have to leap out causing a tidal wave to swamp the bathroom.

Now that I live alone with my baby I feel kind of isolated. He is six months old and I am back working part-time but I work from home. So I am in contact with my colleagues by phone and email and so on, but I don't actually meet them in the flesh. Then, apart from some ladies in a local book club that I joined while I was expecting John, I don't really know anybody locally and the neighbours in my complex keep very much to themselves. I don't know many other single mums to hang out with.

Single mum. Those two words are two words that I don't like. It's like a stigma. Those two words give an unwanted image of a greasy-haired woman with a fag hanging out of her mouth and a baby hanging out of her arms, somebody that wears her pyjamas to the post office. Or is that just me being ridiculous? In the children's story books nobody grows up to become a single mother. Everyone finds the perfect partner, gets married and lives happily ever after. The frog turns into a prince, Sleeping Beauty wakes up, and the Ugly Sisters get their marching orders. Real-life isn't like that, however. Apart from Kate Middleton, the rest of us must come to terms with the fact that we're never going to marry a prince. Or, in some cases, even get married.

Nobody teaches you how to become a mum. And what's more, nobody teaches you how to cope as a single mummy. The baby doesn't come with a rule book! As a single mummy you constantly worry. Am I doing this right? Or am I totally useless? Can somebody please help me get some sleep! You are also bombarded with advice (most of it unwanted!) by well-meaning friends and family. Friends offer to help out but then find every excuse not to. It's lonely, but it's also fun. It's exhausting but so rewarding. The only person who has been consistently nice throughout all of this is Father Francis. He has a heart of gold. I bumped into him the other day and he offered to christen John whenever I felt the time was right. I felt so grateful I almost cried. He is so kind.

Now that I live in Bray, I don't go to Mass any more. I suppose I should really, but it's a lot of hassle getting the baby up and washed and dressed, and myself up washed and dressed too. I can't bear the thought of us sitting in a draughty church for almost an hour with people coughing and sneezing all around us. I do say my prayers though and I bless myself every time I pass a church, an ambulance or a hearse so I'm not anti-religious at all. I'm just kind of taking a break at the moment.

At the moment I am so broke it isn't even funny. It's so true what they say about single mummies having no money. Babies cost so much. It's mad because they're so small and don't smoke or drink, drive fancy cars or want to go on holidays and wear designer clothes, so you'd wonder how on earth they whittle away all the money, but they do. The frigging nappies are the worst. Like I said, they cost an absolute arm and a leg. Even the own-brand ones don't come cheap. At this stage I'm considering towelling nappies. No, I'm joking. How did they do it in the old days? How did they spend half their lives hand-washing nappies and still get their husbands to fancy them? It must have been a nightmare . . . all that scrubbing . . . *ew*!

Look, I know it's not good for the environment to be using disposable nappies, but until they come up with a better solution, I'm afraid I'm going to have to keep using them. Gosh, they're so handy, especially when the baby has only done a little wee and I can whip the nappy off and replace it within seconds, and with only one hand while chatting on the phone at the same time. (Can you imagine a man being able to multi-task like that? Eh, I don't think so.)

These days I think back in horror to how I used to fritter money away. You know, when Ireland was supposedly rich and we were all milking it? At least that's what we were being told? Anyway, in those heady days I had no problem spending a fortune on a pair of 'must-have' shoes. I once spent a whopping seven hundred euro on a pair of gold peep-toe heels that dug into my heels painfully and almost rendered me a cripple after a night on the tiles. I can't believe I parted with my hard-earned cash for something that hurt me so much. Okay, they admittedly looked fabulous as they glistened in the sun-drenched shop window, but even after all the money I spent on them, only a handful of women admired them and not one man did. Not even one. Men don't understand why women spend a fortune on shoes and I'm beginning to side with them on this one now. I mean, think of all the nappies I could have bought for the price of those killer heels! I could have bought a whole mountain of them. And now I don't think I even like those shoes. They look, dare I say, a little tacky. They're just a bit too *Big Fat Gypsy*-type for me now.

So yes, I'm broke. Completely smashed, actually. The proverbial wolf is at the door. I am struggling to pay the rent on my miserable wages. The middle of the month is definitely the worst when I start wondering whether I can hold out until the end of the month. I get paid a little at the end of every month but it's hardly enough to survive. I have to say I do really look forward to the Child Benefit on the first Tuesday of every month, and although it's not much I really don't know what I'd do without it.

As I told you before, I work as an in-house stylist for

a fashion magazine, which sounds very glamorous but really it isn't at all. In fact it's bloody hard work dealing with uppity PR types all the time. I work from home two and a half days a week at the moment and Mum takes Baby John on those days. I really am grateful for the time she does take him because honestly I'd be like a prisoner otherwise. The only thing is that Mum is very busy with her golf and her bridge and her committee meetings (she's goes to loads of committee meetings!), and although she doesn't complain too much I can definitely see her becoming a little resentful about becoming a free baby-sitter. If I push her any more she's in danger of snapping and I can't afford to let that happen. If she goes I'll be lost. Everyone else has already gone. She's the last one left.

So I decided a few days ago that I had no choice but to get an au pair to come and live with us. I cannot afford to pay somebody an hourly wage so the cheapest option is to give somebody board and keep in exchange for baby-sitting and pocket money. The girl can stay in the second bedroom and help me mind John. Then I can do my styling work in peace and also have the odd night out too. I miss going out and I miss not feeling like part of the human race. Of course I know that I will never be a party animal again and that I now have serious responsibilities but I would love even to be able to walk along the seafront in the evening without the pram, just getting my thoughts together.

Later on that day I was in Spar getting a few groceries when I just happened by the noticeboard. Normally I wouldn't even bother reading the handwritten notes that people living locally stick up on it, but this time one ad did catch my eye. In nice neat handwriting there was a short note by somebody looking for a job working with either children or elderly people. It had a number and a name on it. I jotted the number down on the back of my grocery bill. The following morning I rang the number and asked for Samira.

Samira sounded quite serious on the phone. Her English wasn't great but it wasn't terrible either. I asked her whether she could start pretty much immediately and she said that she could. I gave her directions to my apartment block and she said she knew where it was and that she would be looking forward to meeting myself and John the following afternoon.

True to her word, Samira turned up on my doorstep the following evening bang on time. Her rather glamorous name turned out to be misleading. She was an earnest-looking girl with small eyes, a big mouth, thin and gaunt with slightly protruding teeth and her long mousey hair scraped back into a ponytail. She was casually dressed in skinny jeans, Uggs, a white T-shirt and a loose grey cardigan. She told me she was eighteen years old, from Bosnia, and that she was working for a family locally in Bray. But the hours didn't really suit her, she explained, and she was looking to move. She also told me that she was attending English classes nearby but that she kept having to miss them as her boss wouldn't allow her time off in the afternoons. She seemed perfectly fine and polite and she told me she wasn't afraid of hard work. She told me that she had looked after plenty of children and young relatives in her home town before she came to Ireland and that she had lots of experience. I asked her if she had a boyfriend and she said that she didn't. Neither did she smoke or drink. She said she liked to read in the evenings or listen to music on her iPod. She seemed to tick all the boxes, and she was polite if a little distant. I thought I would give her a start and offered her the job.

She's moving in tomorrow. I'm all excited now. It's as though I'm about to get a 'Get Out of Jail' card.

4

This morning, after I got John up, bathed, fed and dressed and took him for a little walk, I decided to do some de-cluttering because my apartment was kind of messy right now. My wardrobe was still brimming with all my pre-pregnancy skinny clothes, as well as my awful unflattering maternity clothes (some of which were just large-size regular clothes). I was going to take the maternity clothes to one of Bray's many charity shops but then I thought I might make a bit of money by listing them on eBay. I mean, there's a baby boom on right now so there must be lots of women looking to buy maternity clothes, right?

Seriously though, everyone seems to be pregnant. At least all the women shopping in Bray seem to be anyway. I kind of look at them and feel glad it's not me any more. I'd say that the recession and the bad weather last winter has probably contributed to the vast number of babies due this year. After all, people need to stay warm and when funds are low and it's wet and cold outside, staying in becomes the new going out. But I'm honestly glad I'm not pregnant any more. I can't bear flicking through magazines in waiting rooms and the like because all the expectant celebrity mummies are all blooming. When I was pregnant I just looked like a blooming mess! And it's not just the celebrities – I mean, have you seen how depressingly gorgeous today's mummies-to-be in general are? I remember, when I was a young child and lots of my friends' mummies were expecting, they wore hideous flowery smocks that made them look like they were expecting baby elephants. And who could forget the God-awful denim dungarees that should have been banned from the market? They made every pregnant woman look like a fat Farmer Joe! But nowadays it's glamour all the way to the labour ward. But me, I don't know why, I found it enormously difficult to find maternity clothes that looked flattering on me. That's why I ended up buying some ordinary large-size clothes, which looked more appealing than the regular maternity clothes. I think I might have even bought a few man-size tops too. In the end my saving grace was a wine-coloured, velvet Juicy Couture tracksuit which I bought in Nelo maternity shop for a small fortune. But I reckon I didn't take it off me for the last three months of pregnancy so it was well worth the money.

I remember also buying one black going-out dress to party in. Nice designer maternity dresses cost so much you wouldn't want one in every colour! When you buy gorgeous clothes you expect to get years out of them, but you never want to see maternity clothes after you've given birth so it doesn't make sense to splash out on a whole wardrobe. The black dress served me well. I wore it every time I wasn't wearing the maternity tracksuit. It was fairly nondescript, knee-length with sleeves, but I didn't exactly wish to draw attention to myself when I was that large so I was happy to hide behind it. I still have it hanging in my wardrobe. Don't ask me why because I don't intend having another baby. I had one for the experience, I love him more than life itself but now I'm looking forward to reclaiming my life. At least the mornings, anyway.

But hats off to those who do manage to look perfect during pregnancy. I envy them. There was nothing elegant about my pregnancy. I carried a plastic bag around with me to get sick into and during the snow I wore an extra-large fake fur coat that made me look like a moving mountain. Oh my God, I was a disgrace!

Okay, moving on . . . after taking photos of my clothes laid out on the bare wooden floor of my bedroom, I listed the items carefully and hoped that I made the clothes sound at least slightly attractive and not at all as hideous as they really were.

Then Samira arrived in the afternoon to live with us and the first thing she did was remove all the bedding from her bed. I was mildly insulted as I had spent the day before ironing it all for her. But she said she had a phobia about sleeping in bed linen that somebody else had once used and that she would prefer to sleep in a sleeping bag on top of the bed.

I thought that it was a bit odd. I mean, what would she do in a hotel? But I decided not to make a major fuss about it. It was no big deal. Once she had finished unpacking, I made her a toasted sandwich and some tea, and I asked her to tell me a bit about her old job and her duties.

Samira made a face. "I didn't like the family one bit. They were hard work." She sighed heavily. "The father was a stay-at-home dad who would boss me around all day. He would never get dressed and would be in his dressing gown all day barking orders at me."

"Like what kind of orders?" I asked, intrigued.

"Well, for example, every morning I would have to hoover and dust the entire house," she began, "and then I dunno, I might be expected to wash the walls. Or clean the toilets."

"Clean the toilets?" I was astonished. Some people had an awful cheek! "But an au pair is supposed to be like a family friend and treated as such."

"I thought that too but this family treated me more like a slave than a friend. They would order me to deep-clean the oven, or maybe clean the carpets, polish the silver or do some digging in the garden."

I let out a long whistle. "Goodness me, that's unbelievable. Seriously, I just think it's shocking that he expected he could get away with that," I said, scandalised. "That's slave labour if you ask me!"

"I agree. Au pairs often find themselves open to abuse from their employers because they are vulnerable, being so far away from home."

I shook my head. Samira's story made me feel sad. "If he was a stay-at-home dad then why couldn't he do the heavy work himself?"

Samira shrugged. "I think he thought those tasks

were beneath him. Men, huh?" She scrunched up her face.

"Well, I should certainly hope that not all men are like that. I mean, I couldn't imagine my own father behaving like that when he was still alive. He was a true gentleman."

"And what about the father of your child? What's he like?"

I opened my mouth to say something but I couldn't find the right answer. To be honest, I was a bit affronted by the question. I mean, I didn't think I was going to be interrogated by the new au pair. My love life was absolutely none of her business and I thought she was being a bit too familiar.

"He's fine," I said with a hunt of coolness, making it obvious that discussions concerning Clive were not going to be on the cards. "Hey, why don't you put on your coat, Samira?" I asked, quite obviously changing the subject. "It seems to have stopped raining now and I'd love you to take little John for walk as he hasn't had any fresh air at all today."

She got her coat and buttoned it up to her neck. Then she put John in his little raincoat and put him in the pram. He smiled up at her innocently and my heart melted a little bit. I didn't want to share him with Samira or indeed, anybody, but I couldn't think of any other option for the near future besides having a live-in au pair.

Although I was lonely these days being a single mum, I knew that it was not a good idea to become too friendly with Samira. If you became too friendly with your au pair they wouldn't respect you as much. I didn't want to encourage her to pry into my personal life. I wondered if there was some way of introducing her to other foreign au pairs so that she could have people of her own age to hang out with in the evenings. The last thing I needed was for Samira to stay home every night and be under my feet. I need a little bit of breathing space for me and the apartment was rather small. Maybe I could join one of those mummy-and-baby forums and see if any other mums were thinking along the same lines as me.

The next day I logged into one of those mummy sites. When I was pregnant I would visit them a lot, trying to get pregnancy tips about diet, hospitals etc. When your own friends are not pregnant they don't want to chat about pregnancy-related stuff so it was nice to have these sort of online support communities at my fingertips. But then once the baby came along, I kind of lost interest. Anyway I didn't even really have the time now for internet surfing. But I went into one of the sites and searched for an au pair community. I met a lady called Sheelagh who lived in the Bray area and had just started a French au pair. She was dying for her to meet new friends, and she invited myself, Samira and John over to her house the following afternoon for tea.

Samira didn't show much interest in the idea and simply shrugged when I told her where we were going.

"Sheelagh's au pair, Claudine, is eighteen too, and she's from France," I told her, trying to inject some enthusiasm into my voice.

Samira just shrugged. "Oh."

I pretended not to notice her complete lack of interest

and continued talking. "So, anyway, Sheelagh's little girl is nine months old and she lives nearby. I'm thinking it would be lovely for you and Claudine to take the prams along the seafront together if the weather is nice."

"Yeah, okay," she said, examining her nails with a look of boredom on her face.

I felt like giving her a shake. She just wasn't showing any enthusiasm. I hoped things would get better when we got around to Sheelagh's. I found directions to her house on Google maps. It was a nice terraced house that had been newly painted and carpeted. Sheelagh was a short, lovely bubbly woman of around thirty-eight years of age with a big welcoming smile on her face. She gave myself and Samira a hug and then cooed over John, telling me what a gorgeous, bonny baby he was. I was surprised to hear her Scottish accent as I had just presumed she was Irish.

"No, I'm from Aberdeen and I've been living here four years now," she laughed.

"Your house is really cute, like something straight out of an interiors magazine." I looked around in appreciation.

"Thank you!"

"Where's your baby?" I then said. "Is she asleep?"

"Yeah, Lisa's asleep at the moment and Claudine has gone out for a jog. She loves running by the sea as she is from inland France. Living by the sea is a huge treat for her. She tells me it's like being on holiday all the time."

I couldn't help but feel a tiny bit envious of Sheelagh with her sprightly au pair. It would be lovely to have somebody positive looking after your child. I was already becoming tired of Samira's permanently gloomy face.

We sat down in Sheelagh's homely kitchen as she made us tea and produced a homemade carrot cake. I was very impressed.

"*Mmmm*. I'll have to get the recipe for this cake from you," I said after taking a mouthful and savouring it. "This is truly delicious. You could give that one Nigella Lawson a run for her money!"

Beside me, Samira slowly ate her slice of cake but didn't make any comment about it.

"I used to be a full-time pastry chef before I moved to Ireland," Sheelagh told me. "Now I work four days a week part-time in a café in Dún Laoghaire. I bake scones and cakes in the back kitchen and the café sells them to the lunchtime crowd. They're quite popular even though I say so myself!"

"You know, you should really think about selling these to a few places. You could make a fortune."

Sheelagh gave a little smile. "I might do that. People have said before that I should start my own business, but I've never really had the confidence and then . . . well, with my separation and everything . . ."

"I'm sorry. I didn't realise you were separated."

A flicker of hurt seemed to flash across her face. Just for a split second. I hoped I wasn't making her feel uncomfortable. After all, I'd only just met the woman fifteen minutes ago. We were interrupted by somebody coming through the door.

It was obviously Claudine.

She rushed over to me and shook my hand. Then she shook Samira's hand. "It's a pleasure to meet you both," she said, brimming with goodwill. She was a little out of breath from her run and her cheeks were slightly rosy. She was tall and slender with glossy hair tied back in a high ponytail and looked the picture of good health.

"Have some cake," Sheelagh offered.

"Thank you, but maybe later," Claudine answered sweetly. She went to the sink and poured herself a glass of tap water. "I think I might have an apple instead."

Sheelagh and myself exchanged glances. It was obvious the lovely Claudine minded her figure well. No wonder she was as slim as a whippet!

As Claudine was drinking her water we could hear Lisa starting to cry in the next room. Quick as a flash she put down her glass. "You stay there," she told Sheelagh, "and I'll get her up."

She was so different from Samira, I thought. So far, Samira was always looking to me for direction – it was rare that she showed initiative. The next moment Claudine was back in the kitchen cradling little Lisa in her arms. I couldn't take my eyes off the little girl – she was so beautiful with huge blue eyes underneath long black eyelashes.

"Wow! She's going to be such a stunner when she grows up! A supermodel in the making!" I laughed.

"Aw, thanks. She gets those Irish blue eyes from her daddy. I wonder if she'll be a charmer like him too?"

John seemed delighted to see somebody else as small as himself and reached out to little Lisa.

"Why don't you girls take the babies into the playroom?" said Sheelagh. "There's lots of cuddly toys on the play mat for them, and you can get to know each other too."

Claudine said she thought it was a great idea. Samira stood up and I handed John to her.

Once they were gone I turned to Sheelagh. "Claudine's a star," I said. "What a find!"

"I know. I'm so lucky to have her. I hope she stays with us for a good while longer. I'll have to bribe her if she ever tries to leave! So, how long have you had Samira? She seems quiet. Is she shy?"

"Only a few days. It's hard to read her. I mean, she's being very quiet here but maybe that's because she's shy in front of you and Claudine. But she does keep to herself a lot to be honest, and yet she is always asking me unnecessary questions. I don't know whether that's her trying to practise her English, or whether she genuinely is a bit clueless."

"You should read to her in the evenings, maybe even for a half an hour or so. Just to help her with her English. I do that with Claudine and I explain the words she doesn't understand. She really appreciates it."

"I did try that once but she wasn't very bothered. I don't think she really enjoys being a childminder to be honest. She was working for another family before she came to live with us and she didn't get on with them. Mind you, I'm not really surprised about that. They sounded absolutely awful."

"Well, remember you're only hearing her side of the story. They might not have been that bad."

"I know, but they really seemed to have been taking her for granted. I don't agree with abusing au pairs. We were all young once, and it can be scary moving to a new country without your safe network of friends and family."

Sheelagh sighed. "It's difficult to find the right girl. Before Claudine came along I had an American girl who ran up huge phone bills and ate me out of house and home. I couldn't afford to keep her. I'm so lucky I found Claudine."

"Did you go through an agency for her?"

"Well, no, actually – my sister-in law told me that her au pair had a friend in France who wanted to come to Dublin and learn English so she asked me if she could forward Claudine's CV to me for consideration. I have to say her CV was more than impressive. Claudine was head girl in her school, played junior tennis at national level and is studying child psychology."

I gulped. Suddenly I felt absolutely awful. I had never asked Samira for a CV. I didn't even know if she had ever gone to school or had a single hobby. Oh, God, did that make me the worst employer ever? I sensed a sort of shame creeping over me. I should have demanded a CV from Samira. Then again, she was only eighteen. I doubt she'd ever had a real job before coming to Ireland.

"So I liked the look of her CV," Sheelagh continued, now getting up to put the empty teacups in the dishwasher, "and then when I checked with both her referees, I was absolutely convinced that this girl was going to be the right one for our family."

Okay, now I felt sick. I hadn't asked Samira for any references. Sheelagh had phoned two people. She had obviously wanted to be doubly sure of who she was hiring. Sheelagh was a good mother and I was not. I really did feel bad about myself. Samira could have been a school drop-out or a social delinquent, yet I had chosen to put her in charge of the person I was supposed to love more than anyone else in the whole world. I was not fit to be anybody's mum.

Sheelagh then looked over at me. "So how did you find Samira?"

"Um . . . she had put up an ad in the supermarket and I just happened to come across it."

"Oh. Okay. Well, at least you didn't have to pay an agency fee. They can be pretty hefty."

"Yeah, I know."

I squirmed in my chair. Suddenly I wanted to get out of there and hide away somewhere I could mentally give myself a kick. This woman obviously thought I was too stingy to go through a proper nanny agency that would probably have produced a golden girl who had won all sorts of medals and could speak five different languages and maybe was in her final year of medicine or something.

"Gosh, I never even asked you if you would like another cup of tea! I just cleared the cups away without even thinking. That's my baby brain at work now. I'm sorry for being rude. I can put the kettle on again if you like?"

"Oh no, I'm fine honestly. Actually, is it okay if I use your bathroom, please?"

"Sure, it's just in the hall under the stairs."

As soon as I closed the door behind me I took a deep breath. Sheelagh's little cloakroom, like the rest of this house, was immaculate. The floor looked like it had been polished, the white handtowel was soft and luxurious, and a brand-new Molton Brown liquid soap and hand lotion perched on top of the sink. How did she have her house so perfect? Why did she have the nicest au pair ever? And why was I being so pathetic as to compare myself unfavourably to a practical stranger? Stop it, I chided myself. Seriously, get a grip. You can only do your best. Samira may never be runner-up for best au pair in the world but there's nothing wrong with her. You make it work.

I splashed some cold water on my face and then washed my hands. I was almost afraid to wipe them on the fluffy white towel afterwards.

"Well, the girls seem to be getting on great," beamed Sheelagh when I came back into the kitchen. "I just popped my head in the door and they're laughing and chatting like old friends."

"Really?" I was surprised. I'm not sure if that small revelation was supposed to make me feel better or worse.

"You must come over again. Or maybe we could go over to you? What do you think?"

"Yeah, brilliant, any time!'

"Maybe Claudine can take Samira and little John to the mummy and baby yoga classes in the town?"

"Mummy and baby yoga?" I raised an eyebrow.

"Yup, the classes are held twice a week there on the main street above that café that recently opened. I've gone a couple of times but half the grown-ups that attend are au pairs as the mummies don't have time to go. I'd say Samira would love it!'

I wasn't so sure about that but I said I'd suggest the idea to her anyway. To be honest I wasn't really sure if herself and the bubbly Claudine would become pally, but I hoped that Sheelagh and myself would become firm friends. I admired her and I wanted to know her more. Hopefully she would be a positive role model for me.

5

You know when you're so tired you can't even speak
properly, never mind being able to remember things or
even think of anything besides crawling back to bed?
Well, that's what it's like having a new baby. It's like
working through the night, only worse. Because if you're
a shift worker, or indeed if you've even been out all night
partying, you know that sleep will be yours soon. You
count the hours until you can crawl under the duvet and
block out the world. When you've a newborn, that much-
anticipated moment never comes. Night after night is lost
in a fog of tiredness. And there is no overtime pay. No pat
on the back. Just more of the same for the next few
months.

And now I have no Samira to help share the load. She's
gone.

Yes, Samira left citing homesickness. Even though I
was little taken aback when I realised she was going, it's

a sort of relief to be honest. Don't get me wrong, she was a nice enough girl, and I could have done a lot worse, but she really hadn't made any effort to integrate with myself and John and she wasn't able to use her initiative at all. I mean every couple of minutes she'd be knocking on my bedroom door, asking questions. Where are John's nappies? Where is the sweeping brush? What time are we having tea? Have you seen my phone? It was enough to drive me around the bend! And she seemed to have quite a bad Facebook addiction too. She was never off the frigging laptop. I mean, what was she writing about all day? Me? I dread to think. Maybe she was telling her friends that she was having a really boring time in Ireland with an overweight single mum. Who knows?

She completely surprised me too. After all, I had no idea she was unhappy. And then one night after I had retired to my room she pushed a short note under my door telling me she would be leaving the next day.

Anyway, she has gone now. And once more I find myself without any childminder. The first thing I did when she left was open the window in her room as she had never once opened it during her stay. Now I've completely cleared out her room and given it a good scrubbing and an airing. I want it to look nice and cosy and welcoming before the next girl arrives. Of course I would really love to keep it as a nursery for Baby John and fill it with cute bunnies and teddies, and paint it sky blue, but I am broke, and anyway I don't even know if the landlord would allow me to paint the walls. So the way things are we have to manage the best we can with John's cot in my room.

I need to get another minder so the search goes on. I'm going to go for an older girl this time. An older girl will be mature and should have experience with children. Samira was only eighteen years of age and I felt she was a bit nonplussed with Baby John. She sometimes even sighed when I asked her to do simple tasks like putting out the bin or hanging the washing on the drying rail. She wasn't the tidiest of people either and a few times I had to reprimand her for leaving her dirty dishes in the sink for me to wash up. Sometimes I used to think she'd come to Ireland for a rest!

An older girl will hopefully not be moping around the place waiting for something exciting to happen, and not be addicted to using social-networking sites. Maybe I could get an Irish nanny-type from down the country that would go home every weekend? I think a situation like that might suit better actually. First of all, an Irish girl wouldn't be homesick and, second of all, I wouldn't mind having the place to myself at the weekends just in case I ever meet a man again. I know, I know, but miracles do happen sometimes, and I don't think I could get too passionate if I knew the au pair was in the room next door.

I actually have an ad running on the internet right at this minute. I put it up a while ago and included a small photo of myself and John. So, yes, the ad is live. I'm so short of cash right now I can't even afford to go through an agency. The ad is up on one of those free buy-and-sell sites. I hope it doesn't seem too dodgy to be looking for Miss Right online. I have all my fingers and toes crossed that I get somebody compatible with us, and also fun.

Samira wasn't fun but she was very trustworthy which of course is the most important thing. And at least she didn't go out drinking like other girls do. I mean you hear some horror stories. Young Brazilians, apparently, party until dawn when they come over here to mind children!

I made a list in advance. I wanted to be clear about what I needed this time. So here are my ten commandments. My wish list for my very own Mary Poppins is that she must:

1. Smile a lot. I feel this is important. If you smile at a baby he or she will naturally smile back. Anyway, I don't want a grumpy puss around the house. It's bad enough being broke without someone glaring at me all the time in my own home.

2. Have shortish hair. Okay, I know that sounds bizarre but Samira had hair way down her back and insisted on washing it every morning. It meant she was hogging the bathroom for at least forty minutes every morning using up all the hot water. Then, to add insult to injury, she'd leave long dark hairs in the bath for me to retrieve from the plughole after she was finished. That's why this time I'm looking for somebody with medium to short hair. Preferably a skinhead!

3. Be thinnish. Now I know this is quite an un-PC thing to say and, believe me, I am quite a large lady myself, but I'd like the new girl to be slim and fit. If she's slim she's probably watching her weight and won't eat me out of house and home. She will also

have plenty of energy to take John out for long walks in the pram which will be nice because at least then I'll have some 'me' time to read a chapter of my book or take a warm bubble bath. These are two treats that I used to take for granted in my pre-baby days and now I miss them both like hell! You wouldn't catch me out clubbing on a Saturday night off. Hell, no! A bath and a book and I'm as happy as Larry. So anyway, I don't want a huge au pair. If she's thin she might inspire me to lose the baby weight of which I have lost none so far. At least if there's a skinny bitch walking around the house, I might be shamed into not devouring a packet of chocolate biscuits all in one go.

4. Not be mega-popular. I don't mean she should have no friends at all in a weird, loner/loser type way. But she shouldn't have hundreds of giggling pals coming and going. I don't want the baby waking up with strangers ringing the doorbell all hours of the day and night wondering whether the au pair is coming out to play. She can have one or two friends, that's no problem. Preferably nice, quiet girls who like knitting or something. Oh God, it really is such a big undertaking to have a complete stranger come live with you in your own home! The last thing I need is to be worrying about somebody who's out clubbing until all hours in a pair of hot pants. No party animals need apply.

5. Must be independent. I'd like a girl who takes initiative and isn't asking me all day what she should be doing next. I'd like her to get the baby up, bathed and dressed in the mornings without me having to

tell her to do it. I'd like her to surprise me with a nice cup of tea now and then.

6. Clean. Okay, so I'm not going to be asking her to scrub the floors or clean the windows but she needs to be neat and tidy and not leave dishes in the sink. A friend of mine employed a girl recently who would leave the dishes in the sink on her day off expecting my friend to wash up after her. Honestly, you couldn't make it up!

7. Non-smoker. I confess I used to be a smoker. I had a filthy twenty-a-day habit. I would wake up in a fog of smoke and go to sleep in one too. There were at least two or three permanently overflowing ashtrays dotted around our old flat as myself and Sally chain-smoked the evenings away. I remember once waking up at 3.00 a.m. and panicking because I couldn't find a cigarette. I actually rang a taxi to go down to the local garage and pick up a packet for me. Of course when I got pregnant I gave up immediately. Now I'm one of those really annoying non-smokers who shoo other people's smoke away if they're standing smoking in a bus shelter beside me. That's how anti-smoking I am now. I couldn't bear to have a smoker in the house.

8. Quiet. Oh, how I do love the sound of golden silence. Of course I am very much aware of the impracticality of longing for a quiet, noise-free home with a six-month baby, but when John goes to sleep at night I like to curl up with a book and get lost in another world. Before I had my baby I'd say I read three or four books a week. Now I find it hard even

to get the book for my monthly book club read. Reading is probably the last form of entertainment I can afford so, therefore, if somebody was listening to a loud TV or radio in the next room I think it would drive me crazy. Maybe I should seek an au pair who also likes to read and we can swap books or something? Now, there's an idea.

9. Calm. She must be the yin to my yan. Sometimes I can get so worked up about things. I panic if I find myself running out of nappies and milk formula. I fret when I've done a huge wash of baby clothes and its pouring rain outside and I can't dry them. Most of all, I lie awake at night worrying about money and ignoring the small pile of official brown envelopes stacked on the table beside the front door. I need to stop stressing so I think that a calm person could be a very good influence on me. Maybe we could do yoga together.

10. Friendly. Now this might seem like a really obvious one, but I don't want somebody who makes me feel like a stranger in my own home. I don't want to dread hearing another person turn the key in my front door and wonder what uncomfortable small talk I should start engaging in. An au pair is supposed to be part of the family, but not so close to me that we are living in each other's hair. I want to just click with somebody.

I am looking for Miss Right. Surely that isn't too much to ask?

6

My son got his first two teeth this week. Or maybe it was last week. I'm not too sure. You see, I was over in Mum's at the weekend and she looked at me crookedly and said, "You never told me!"

"Never told you what?"

"About Baby John's teeth! He's got two of them. Why didn't you tell me?"

I was genuinely surprised. "Oh, I didn't know. Nobody told me."

"But you're his mother!"

I felt a bit guilty then. I mean, I should have known. I should have been the first to discover them as I knew he had been teething for some time and his gums were sore, but the truth is that I'd been looking in his mouth and there was no sign of them. Like buses, two came along at once with no warning.

I sent a text to Clive to tell him the good news and as

usual I got no reply. Then I spent a bit of time wondering what other parents do. Do they celebrate occasions like this? Do they stick a camera down their baby's gob and post the pics on Facebook? Isn't that a bit OTT? Other people don't really care, do they? Just because they feign initial interest in your tot doesn't mean they've given you the green light to bore them to tears every time they meet you for the next few years.

I saw these really cute baby books in a stationary shop recently. They were selling them in pink and in blue. Inside you could stick all kinds of things onto the pages such as a lock of your baby's hair or his painted handprint, and record all important dates like baby's first tooth arrival etc. I wouldn't really be into that though. I don't want to become too obsessed. It's unhealthy. Mind you, my mother thinks I'm the other extreme. My baby isn't even christened yet because I can't decide on godparents. I am trying to think of two people who will be generous and remember him on his birthday and at Christmas-time, unlike my own godmother who gave me zilch. But I'd need to get a move on. At this stage he'll be making his Holy Communion before his christening. He'll be walking up to the church himself and maybe even pouring a jug of water over his own head.

It's a difficult time though. The teething thing is so frustrating for both of us and it makes me feel so helpless. Nobody likes to see their little one in visible pain. John's gums are sore and sometimes he screams so loudly I have to check to see nobody's torturing him. I've tried everything from rubbing Bonjela on his gums, to sticking his teething ring in the freezer and I sing 'Hush-a-bye, Baby' from morning to night. All of it helps but there's no miracle cure.

I met an old college friend of mine at the supermarket recently and told him I was wrecked because of my baby's teething.

"He's not sleeping, poor mite, and neither am I," I told him bleary-eyed.

"Tell me about it," he said, commiserating with me, and shook his head. "I remember my own son's teeth coming down. But," he went on, "it's much worse when they lose them."

"That must be painful too," I agreed.

"Painful on the pocket," he said gloomily. "Recession or no recession, the Tooth Fairy demands to be paid. And she hasn't brought his prices down in line with the current economic climate!"

I'd never thought of that. The Tooth Fairy! Oh my goodness. I guess she'll be making plenty of visits over the coming years, as will Santa Claus. I hope I have enough money to grease the palms of their hands. I need to get back to full-time work and fast.

As soon as I get home I switch on my computer.

It's a real sign of the times. My inbox has been overflowing with replies from eager au pairs looking to come to work for my little family. Some of the applicants seem highly qualified with tons of experience and degrees and diplomas, although unfortunately a lot of them don't seem to be able to read. Like that barman from Dublin who explained that he wanted a career change after a few years in the hospitality industry. He was so enthusiastic he even sent a photo. And in case you're wondering, yes, he was very cute! But suitable? Not really. Mind you, he'd be handy for making me a vodka cocktail in the evening after a hard day's work. I'm joking!

Anyway, I got literally hundreds of CVs from all sorts of applicants. In fact I got so many that I really began to regret the fact that I'd advertised myself. If I'd gone through a nanny agency they'd have been able to sift out all the riff-raff. I can't tell you how exhausting it was trying to read all the CVs, some of which were completely illegible i.e. I like you children. We make very good fun.

I had asked applicants to include photos too because, you know, you can tell a lot from a photo in my experience. Like if somebody was scowling at you, and their photo looked more like a mug shot than a friendly snap, you wouldn't really choose them to be your au pair. You wouldn't be keen on somebody too glamorous either. Somebody very glamorous might find herself a rich man and then she might decide she'd rather live with him in a fancy penthouse than in a two-bedroom apartment with a single mum and her snotty kid.

I got one rather odd CV from a couple of Scandinavian girls. Yes, a couple, even though I had specifically said I wanted one female. They said in their email that they were willing to work for free as long as they could be together. They also sent a photo. They had nice smiles, but all the facial piercings were off-putting. Besides, I really did want just one girl. There isn't room in my humble abode for more than that. After all, I only have one child and how many females does little John need?

Then I got a call from a woman who said she was also a mum and that we could meet up with our kids and have fun in the park. She seemed so nice and enthusiastic but I'm really hoping to get a girl who doesn't want to become best friends with me and will see me as an employer rather than somebody to hang out with. Somebody calm, who won't mind doing the ironing and tidying John's room while I get some shut-eye if I'm exhausted. Besides, I never see my own friends as it is, never mind trying to make more online!

Then I got a CV from a girl called Katia who had never looked after kids and wanted to eventually become an engineer and hoped that I would speak English to her all day so that she would be fluent in a couple of months. I had to reread that one a couple of times just to make sure it wasn't a piss-take. Like, hello? Did she think I was running a language school or something? Of course I don't mind speaking English to a foreign girl who is here to learn English – but all day? Give me a break!

Maybe I could get an Irish girl. A nice local girl just out of school maybe, somebody who wants to move out of home for the first time. If I had an English-speaking girl then I wouldn't have to speak slowly all the time and if I had a local girl staying with me she could go home every weekend and then I could have the place to myself. Also a local girl wouldn't miss her family. A friend of mine told me her sister got a girl who missed her family so much she was on Skype non-stop talking to them and, when she wasn't on either Skype or Facebook, she was sobbing her heart out because she missed them so much. After three weeks the girl told my friend's sister that she had booked a one-way ticket back home and she had to go and interview a whole set of new girls again.

I really think it wouldn't be fair on John to have a whole lot of girls coming and going like some kind of train station so I hope our girl stays and becomes part of our little family. Mind you, I don't want somebody to stay forever. Like, suppose she never wanted to leave and twenty years down the road she was still with us? Hopefully I'll get somebody who wants to stay for a year. A nice normal girl with no piercings or strange eating habits or dodgy boyfriends. Surely that's not too much to ask, is it?

Oh gosh, please, please, let me find somebody suitable soon. I am desperate!

7

Who's that girl? I thought the other day, glancing in the mirror and shuddering. That girl had dark roots, dry frizzy hair and was wearing an old T-shirt with baby sick on the front of it. She also had unfamiliar circles under the eyes. I didn't recognize her. But sadly it was me. Something drastic had to be done. So I called on my mother to mind John and took myself off to the hairdresser looking for a miracle (and intending to claim my usual press discount).

"Make me look like this," I demanded, waving a dog-eared picture of Kate Moss in her prime. "I'm willing to pay whatever it takes."

Actually I did nothing of the sort. I'm not that delusional, not yet anyway! I just explained that I'd like a bit of colour in my hair to make it look not quite as dull as it did. The hairdresser offered to do her best.

"Would you like a few magazines to look at with your

coffee?" she asked cheerfully when we got to the drying stage.

I said I would. Anything rather than discuss a holiday that I wouldn't be taking, which she was bound to ask me about. Anyway I was looking forward to enjoying catching up on some celebrity gossip. The only time I ever got to read magazines nowadays was when I went to the hairdresser.

The girl handed me a pile of reading and I was all set to read about Angelina and her brood when I came across a very sad article about a pair of Siamese twins. One had survived but the other had died six weeks after being operated on. Tears formed in my eyes and I tried fighting them off. But it was no use. I'd already been in a tearful mood that day. My mother had told me she'd visited a friend's daughter with leukaemia in hospital a fortnight ago. The girl was a mother of three, her youngest seven months old. As the girl lay in her hospital bed my mother had chatted to her about everything, including the current economy. She said how worrying it was that house prices were falling and people were losing their jobs. The friend's daughter had smiled and said, "Myself and my husband used to worry about stuff like that. Not any more. Now all I want to do is live." She died a week later. When Mum told me I couldn't stop bawling. "I want to live," she had said. But that didn't happen. Her wish hadn't come true.

Thinking about that girl again as I read about the Siamese twins, it suddenly made me realise that if my hair didn't look great, it didn't really matter. Or if I couldn't afford a sun holiday this year, that didn't matter either. Baby sick down the front of my top just means my baby is alive and well and the sound of his cries in the middle of the night should be reassuring rather than frustrating. The more I thought about it the more the tears flowed and I could no longer stop them. I felt so guilty for secretly moaning about minor mishaps going on in my life.

"Is everything okay?" asked the bubbly hairdresser, turning the dryer off for a second. "Is the coffee not okay?"

I looked down at my full, untouched cup and then looked at her in the mirror through my tears. She seemed fairly alarmed. It probably didn't look good for her to have a crying customer.

"Oh, it's not the coffee," I sniffed, dabbing my eyes with a tissue. "Honestly, the coffee is lovely. Sorry, I was just having a little moment."

Later on that evening I was still feeling a bit down. I couldn't understand why. I wanted to snap out of my bad mood. I should have been feeling all positive after getting my hair done. Usually that put me in great form!

After I had put John to bed after his bath, I started googling stuff on the internet about hiring nannies and au pairs. I came across a newspaper article which made the hair on my head stand up. It was quite shocking. The article was about money scams and it was entitled: NANNY FRAUD.

It read as follows:

She looks like a nice smiling, honest girl. She wants to learn English, is caring and adores kids. She doesn't mind helping out with the housework either and is

60

happy to baby-sit in the evenings also. She particularly wants to come to Ireland because she has heard many wonderful things about our country and she is anxious to work with kids of all ages and hopes to become a nurse one day.

So you write back to this girl, let's call her Maria. Maria emails back immediately, full of gratitude. Becoming an au pair is a dream of hers and she comes from a huge family and has lots of experience looking after babies and toddlers. You, of course, are a harried overworked mum so you write back asking how soon can she come?

She's on her way, she says. But there's just one problem. Maria has no money and her parents are struggling financially and can't help out. Can you transfer over the money for her flight? She would be most grateful. You are a little surprised, but because you are hiring her yourself and not through an agency, therefore avoiding high agency fees, you agree to send her the money. After all, you need someone yesterday and she's on stand-by to fly into Dublin. You agree to meet at Dublin airport.

Only Maria never arrives. Why? Well, because Maria never existed. That lovely smiling girl in the photo is probably not even aware that her photo has been posted on the Internet. And that girl has never had any intention of becoming an au pair in a foreign country.

I was shocked when I found out this was happening to vulnerable mums and dads across the world but apparently it's rampant. So do be careful. You can be very lucky. I myself found a fabulous girl online but it took me a couple of months of talking to people online before I finally found her. If you need a girl urgently, it's probably best to go through an agency that has already done the initial interviews for you.

Alongside the article were lots and lots of comments from angry parents who had been caught in this internet scam. I was cross-eyed reading them all. I am glad and relieved that I hadn't wired money abroad to some stranger who might never show up! You'd be sick with yourself if you'd been caught, wouldn't you?

The next morning I was feeling a lot more positive about my nanny search. I had scheduled five back-to-back interviews with girls who all sounded almost too good to be true. They all absolutely loved kids, apparently, and it was their dream to work with them. I had wonderful visions of Mary Poppins herself landing in my garden, complete with umbrella. Within minutes she'd be singing to Baby John and we'd be all trooping off to the park linking arms. Or so I had envisioned.

Anyway, I had got up extra early and wakened John who was in a deep sleep after a restless night and was none too happy about being aroused from his dream, which probably featured lots of cute bunnies and teddies. He yelled and screamed as I struggled to put on his best Burberry outfit which was a present from Sally. It is white so he's never been allowed wear it for obvious reasons but he looked adorable in it. Please God he wouldn't start throwing up everywhere just as I began my interviews.

The first girl was due to show up to my apartment at eleven. I had sent everyone texts with directions just in case, but the block is easy to find anyway. I had made fresh coffee because I read somewhere that if you are trying to sell a home it's a good idea to greet potential buyers with the smell of coffee. Now, I know I'm not trying to sell a house but I am trying to entice somebody to live with us, so why not use the same tactics with prospective childminders? I had full make-up and new clothes on to convince the new au pair that she would be living with a glamorous yummy mummy and not a complete slob, and I had my hair swept back into a chic chignon. I had even sprayed a dose of Chanel No. 5 perfume behind my ears and was wearing smart high heels (something I rarely do since having a baby) for a bit of extra effect.

Now that myself and my son were looking fairly presentable, I began to feel both excited and nervous. It was almost as though I was going on a blind date or something. I felt myself peering out the window at everyone walking down the street to see if I could spot the first candidate.

I waited and waited and waited. I even opened the front door of my ground-floor apartment and looked up and down the street to see if I could spot Mary Poppins but all I saw was a very elderly woman hobbling on a stick, and a dog cocking his leg on the gate of the house three doors down. There was no sign of the girl who was supposed to be coming. She had not kept her appointment and hadn't even had the courtesy to send me a text to say she was cancelling. And then I realised to my horror that I had been stood up! Oh my God, she'd got a better offer.

She found a nicer family. We had been rejected before we'd been given a chance to even sell ourselves as a lovely little family. I can't even begin to describe how deflated I felt. It brought me back to my childhood years when my best friend decided she wanted to be friends with somebody else, and then my teenage years when the guy I fancied at the school disco asked another girl to dance. I fleetingly felt a wave of despair. Had she decided to go to another family? Did she feel another family would be more fun than myself and my son? Maybe the other family had offered foreign holidays and a huge bedroom with an ensuite and a flat-screen TV? I looked at John on his play mat gurgling away to himself. He was so cute. How could somebody not want to mind him?

I boiled the kettle again. I had to stay positive. I would find a great girl eventually. All hope wasn't lost and another four girls were due to come. I couldn't beat myself up over one little no-show. I made a strong coffee, changed John's nappy for the third time that morning, washed his face, re-applied my make-up, dusted the sideboard, rearranged a few framed photos and waited. And waited. It was now ten past midday and no sign of anyone. I began to feel deflated. What was going on?

The sound of the front-door buzzer startled the life out of me. I put John down on his play mat and anxiously checked my appearance in the mirror to make sure no bits of John's mashed banana was left in my hair. I took a deep breath and patted down my skirt. I didn't want to come across as too anxious, did I?

I opened the door with some trepidation.

"Hello, I'm Karena." A small, slight girl with jet-black

frizzy hair, carrying a folder, gave me a tight smile. She was dressed in a green parka jacket, jeans and sneakers.

"Hi," I held out my hand and gave the girl my best firm handshake. "Did you find us okay?"

"Yes."

"Well, do come on in. I do hope it's not going to rain. The clouds are a bit gloomy, aren't they?"

"Yes."

"They predicted sun but those weather forecasters always get it wrong, don't they? No need to get out the sunshine lotion yet, haha."

I knew I was babbling and I should just shut up.

"So, have a seat," I said, showing her into the small sitting room which was so clean you could have eaten off the floor. "Would you like some coffee?"

"No, thanks."

"Or tea? I have all kinds of herbal teas. Or perhaps you'd just like plain old Barry's tea with milk?"

I was greeted by a blank face.

I sat down in the chair opposite her and crossed my legs.

"So, do you love kids?"

"Yes." Her facial expression belied any sense of emotion. She had barely glanced at John since she'd entered the room.

"And do you have any experience with small babies?"

"No."

I was struggling now. I really was baffled. Why was she here? Seriously, what was she doing in my sitting room, staring at me like I was some kind of alien and making me feel uncomfortable in my own home? It didn't take a genius to work out that this wasn't the start of a beautiful, healthy relationship. I wanted to show her the door immediately but found myself glued to the chair.

"So," I tried again with a smile, hoping to get some kind of reaction, "are you enjoying Ireland?"

"It's okay."

"How long have you been here in Ireland?"

"Just one week."

I relaxed a tiny bit. A-ha! If she was only here a week she probably had very little English. It wasn't fair for me to be so judgemental. It must be scary to come halfway across the world to another country, looking for a job with a strange family. And besides, maybe she was shy as well.

"That's not very long," I said gently. "It takes a while to get used to new cultures and traditions. So, have you any questions for me?"

"Yes."

I waited patiently, expecting her to ask me about what exactly I would need her to do or about her time off.

Instead she looked me straight in the eye and said, "How much you pay?"

8

I keep forgetting I'm no longer pregnant. Yes, I know, how sad does that sound? But seriously, when I'm out for lunch and asked by the waiter if I fancy dessert, I still say I'd like to try everything on the menu. Then I suddenly check myself and order just two or three things instead. I'm getting there. A lot done, more to do, as they say. I really am trying but it's just so hard to come to terms with the fact that I'm not eating for two any more. I miss eating six doughnuts at a sitting or sinfully smothering my croissants in butter. I hanker after the days I could easily polish off a tub of Ben & Jerry's, or a sack of coal. Ah, no, I'm joking. I always drew the line at coal, although I have heard that some pregnant women love it!

My point about all of this is, a couple of years ago when I wasn't pregnant and was a size eight, I attended the magazine's annual summer party at the Grafton Lounge. I wore a chiffon pink-and-lime-green dress, which sounds hideous, but actually it was lovely. But fast forward and the summer party is next week. I've told them I can't attend. I didn't tell them the reason was because I can't afford a baby-sitter and that nothing fits me now anyway. I'm probably more like a size fourteen this year which means that absolutely nothing fits. Oh God, why can't I lose weight? If anyone has a miracle solution, suggestions on a postcard please. And don't say I should try sit-ups or anything because life's too short for that. Even Mum wiped me off the tennis court last week and after just one set I nearly collapsed with exhaustion. Blast you, Posh Spice, for making it look easy! You too, Julia Roberts! I hadn't thought I was too bad really until I recently spotted a photo of mum-of-three, Julia Roberts, running on a beach in her bikini in one of the papers. It really put the pressure on. I mean, if she can do it, we should all be able to do it, right? Dammit!

I interviewed all day without any luck. After Karena left, another girl arrived with her boyfriend. I didn't think this was a good sign. She didn't speak any English and her boyfriend was going to be her translator. I was dumbfounded. I couldn't accommodate a couple. The flat was tiny. I explained this to the boyfriend who then turned to his girlfriend to explain what I just said. The two of them looked so disappointed that I felt guilty for turning them away but what could I do? It would never work with a couple.

Then two girls came at once. One said her name was Inga and the other girl was an Irish girl called Diane.

I smiled at them both and thanked them for coming.

I asked Inga if she wouldn't mind waiting outside for about ten minutes while I interviewed Diane.

Inga gave a great big sigh and looked at her watch. "I haven't got all day, you know," she said sullenly.

I have to say I was a little shocked. "Right," I said, trying to keep my voice even. "I do understand but you're a little early for the interview. Please wait."

Then I took Diane into the kitchen. "It's nice to meet you," I said.

Diane had long thick dark hair which she wore in a plait. She was wearing a long wine-coloured maxi dress and a wraparound cardigan. She wore sandals on her feet and she had a brown satchel hung over her shoulder. She was polite but didn't smile.

"What hours would I be expected to work?" she asked outright.

"Well, I work two and a half days a week so I'd like you to work those days at the very least but ideally I'd like you to work every day with Saturday and Sunday off."

"Right. What do you do? I mean, what do you work at?"

I gulped. Just who was supposed to be interviewing whom? "I work as a fashion stylist for a magazine."

"Oh, very nice."

Funny, that's mostly the reaction I get from everyone when I say what I do for a living. If only they knew the reality!

"It's okay," I said, "but it's really not as glamorous as it sounds."

"But it's better than minding babies, right? I mean,

cleaning poop and wiping away vomit isn't glamorous either or well-paid, but hey, we all need to earn a crust somehow!"

To say I was stunned by her answer was an absolute understatement.

"Don't you like childminding?" I asked.

"Oh, I do," said Diane. "It could be worse, I suppose, but like, nobody grows up thinking they'd like to be a childminder when they're older, do they? But with the tough economic times we're in now, you'll take whatever you can take, hey?"

I was appalled. Did she really think I'd entrust with my son with somebody who was minding him because there was nothing else to do? My God!

"So are you looking around at other jobs?" I asked, although in hindsight I should have wrapped up the interview immediately rather than prolong the pain.

Diane shrugged. "I guess. The right job hasn't come up yet so childminding will have to do until it does. Anything to pay the bills, you know? Is there much money in styling? How would I get a job as a stylist? I don't suppose you could give me a list of contacts, could you?"

I didn't know whether to laugh or cry. "There aren't many jobs in styling right now," I said truthfully. "In a recession, styling jobs are usually thin on the ground and the pay is awful."

"That's a bummer. If the pay is bad I wouldn't be interested." She paused for a moment as though deep in thought. And then she started up again, "Hey, not meaning to be rude or anything, but if stylists don't make much money are you sure you can afford me?"

I heaved a huge sigh of relief when Diane finally left. "Will I call you?" she asked at the door.

"Eh . . . I'll call you," I said. "And if you don't hear from me, then you'll know somebody else has filled the post."

"Fair enough," she said as if she didn't really give a damn either way.

I looked around to introduce myself to the other girl, Inga, whom I'd asked to wait outside. She was gone. Oh, well, good riddance. Jesus, what a day!

I was pissed off with myself and with the world in general. To think that I had wasted the whole day and found absolutely nobody! I couldn't understand it. Why did nobody suitable want to work for me? Wasn't there supposed to be a recession on? Weren't people glad to look after a child in return for board, keep and pocket money and lots of free time?

It wasn't like I had five brats all running around making lots of noise or I lived in the middle of the country, miles and miles from anywhere. I basically lived five minutes from the train station and the sea, and I had one very good little boy to look after. Unlike in some homes, I didn't have a sleazy partner who might be coming on to the au pair when he came home from work, nor would I be forcing anybody to be doing heavy-duty chores. But nobody I had seen had fitted the bill and I needed to find somebody fast. Still, there was no point giving up hope just yet. I'd just have to renew my ad again in the morning.

The following evening I had another fifty or so eager-sounding applicants waiting for me in my inbox. It took me ages to sift through them all. Over half of the applicants were Brazilian girls. I'd heard Brazilians were lovely, kind and warm people but they also had a reputation for being party animals. I didn't know if I needed a total rave-loving party animal minding John. If she was going out all night, how would she be able to stay awake during the day? Somebody else had told me that Filipinas were ideal because, not only were they sweet and good-tempered, but they weren't afraid of hard work.

Yvonne from my weekly book club had told me how her wonderful Filipina woman even used to darn her socks until she stopped her, as well as doing all the ironing, cleaning and childminding.

"Wow!" I retorted. "She sounds amazing."

"I know! She flies around the house, tidying everything away, scrubs the place spotlessly clean, gets the baby up, dressed and fed – and that's all before she brings me breakfast in bed every morning."

I admit I was jealous. Dangerously so. It even crossed my mind that I should kidnap this Wonder Woman and keep her in my house. Or failing that, maybe I could bribe her to come and work for me by offering her a higher wage than Yvonne paid her?

"She sounds too good to be true," I sighed. "I want to marry her. Has she any shortcomings at all?"

Yvonne frowned as though she were racking her brains. "Not as far as I'm aware. She's always smiling unlike the last lady we had from East Berlin who never smiled. She didn't have much of a sense of humour. But then again I think she may have had a hard life living behind the Iron Curtain so maybe she wasn't used to smiling. But our new Filipina girl is just wonderful. She even runs me hot bubble baths in the afternoon so I can relax for a while."

I found myself fantasising about long leisurely midday baths with scented candles and trashy magazines. To hell with the sense of humour – if I wanted to laugh I could always hire a funny DVD. I didn't want someone funny but I did want someone kind.

Yvonne promised she'd ask her au pair whether she had a twin. Or failing that, any relation at all.

"I pity you though," she said after we had all analysed *A Thousand Splendid Suns* over a glass or two or three of wine. "Before we got our East Berliner who never smiled we had a lassie from South America who would put odd socks on our children, regularly forget to comb their hair, and leave her own dirty dishes in the sink for us to clean up after her. One day she even forgot to collect the kids from school. Total nightmare!"

"Our girl was from Scandinavia and used to walk around in her underwear," another lady from the book club, Heather, said with a disgruntled sniff. "I swear she did it on purpose just to tease Jimmy."

I said nothing. I've met Jimmy a couple of times and he is no oil painting. I mean, I'm sure he's very nice and everything but he's bald, bespectacled and pudgy. Why on earth would a young Scandinavian set her sights on him? I didn't believe it for a minute. Honestly, some women can be far too paranoid when it comes to their other halves.

Then some of the other women joined in our discussion on childminders and the stories became more hair-raising as more wine was consumed. I heard about one girl who left her vibrator in the family bath and another girl who regularly shaved her legs with the daddy's good razors and destroyed them. I heard about the girl who was so hungover she threw up in the kiddies' paddling pool, and another who set the kitchen cooker on fire while trying to light a cigarette from one of the rings.

And worse was to come. I was told about a girl who left used sanitary towels on the bathroom floor, the girl who 'borrowed' condoms from her employer's wardrobe before nights out, and another girl who watched X-rated movies on the family DVD player while the parents were out.

By the time I finally arrived home to relieve my mother of the evening's baby-sitting duties, I had convinced myself to be a stay-at-home mum. How could I possibly ever go back to full-time work and leave my pride and joy at home at the mercy of some crazy au pair?

9

Being a mum is tough. I don't care if you're single or happily married with a wonderfully devoted husband who puts you on a pedestal and helps out with daddy duties, it is not easy for any of us. That's why I hate mums who are just unbelievably competitive. I mean, come on, it's not a race!

"My son is almost walking," said a smug-looking platinum-blonde mummy in the park the other day. Her little cherub, dressed head to toe in Ralph Lauren, was roughly the same age as mine. "What about yours?"

I looked down at John in his little pram playing peacefully with his teddy, and I then looked back up at the woman with a sort of half-smile on my face. "Almost walking? My baby's practically running marathons!"

She laughed.

I laughed back, a kind of hysterical high-pitched squeal. "Oh, and he's already throwing the javelin," I boasted. "Like, hello?"

Actually no, I didn't say anything that obnoxious. Instead I just smiled through gritted teeth and merely congratulated the woman on her wonderful child. I also neglected to mention to her that my child wasn't even crawling. Let her think she was the world's best mummy if she wanted to.

Mind you, I don't know why John isn't crawling yet. Maybe he just can't be bothered. I leave him on the floor and he chooses just to stay in the same position. Anyway, it's not a flipping race, you know. I feel like telling this to all the competitive mums out there. Haven't they anything else to be doing other than making out their children are more advanced than other peoples' kids? I wish I'd all the time in the world to get John walking and singing, tying his own shoelaces and shouting 'Mummy, I love you' from the rooftops. But I'm a busy woman trying to get back to work and trying to find an au-pair to help me, so my baby son will just have to develop in his own good time. Look, we all get old way too fast so why should I be pushing my child to get ahead and grow up before he's good and ready? I'm already dreading the day he doesn't want a kiss from me because he finds it too embarrassing. Apparently it's heartbreaking the first time they push you away and say, 'Mummy, stop!' I'm really enjoying the fact that now I can place a big smacker on his cheek whenever I feel like it and he has no choice in the matter because he is firmly strapped to his highchair with no chance of escape.

I'll let you in on a little guilty secret. At the moment I'm trying like mad to train him to say 'Mama' before he says 'Dada'. If his first word is 'Dada' I'll see it as the ultimate betrayal. At the moment all he can say is 'Wub' which isn't a word I've ever heard of and I don't think it means anything but he says it a lot for some reason. Maybe it's a slang word in Babyland. I, on the other hand, only ever say one word back, and that's 'Mama'. I say it at least a hundred times a day and point to myself in the hope that somehow I am managing to brainwash him. If he says 'Mama' first I'll be the happiest parent alive and also I really think I deserve that credit after all I do for him.

You could go mad urging your children to grow up quickly, but it's best not to panic if there are delays en route. Here's an interesting fact: Einstein didn't start to speak until he was four. That gives me hope for John. Maybe he'll be a genius and people will say, "Is that your son, the famous inventor?"

Anyway, I'm digressing here, so back to the au pair search. At long last I'm finally seeing a light at the end of the tunnel, albeit a dim one. After viewing countless more CVs online where the childminding hopefuls could neither spell nor make any sense, I opened up an email attachment containing a very well-written, concise CV from an Irish girl. Her name was Bernadette (very sensible name, don't you think?), she lived near Limerick and she was twenty-four years of age. According to her resume she'd had a couple of years of experience minding children, had worked in a nursing home as an aide and was now doing a Montessori course at night. When I read her CV I nearly cried with joy. This girl sounded like a real gem! And she was one-hundred-per-cent Irish so she would understand perfectly when I asked her to pick up Barry's

Tea or Heinz Baked Beans or Cadbury's Dairy Milk or Tayto's Cheese and Onion crisps in the supermarket. She certainly seemed to have a lot going for her. I mean, she was obviously caring (named after a saint and all that!), she had tons of experience, was studying at night (which meant she wouldn't want to be joining me on the sofa watching TV around the clock) and she was even first-aid trained. Was this my dream woman? I wanted her to move in yesterday!

When I phoned her she sounded so nice and friendly. She was articulate, polite and almost too good to be true. I offered her the job on the spot and she in turn accepted my offer without even the slightest hesitation. *Hurrah!*

She is arriving on Monday and I'm so excited. I am going to paint her room this weekend with kind permission from my landlord, and I'm going to give her my Laura Ashley cushions that I bought on eBay for her sofa. I've also got her a new duvet and pillow covers to go with her curtains. They're pink and white and very feminine. I think she'll love living here. I have a really good feeling about this. Hopefully Bernadette will be worth the wait!

Unfortunately John is still teething quite badly and my heart goes out to him. He's having a hard time sleeping. If I have five hours solid sleep I am over the moon with joy. I don't know what I did with my time before he came along. I can't even remember the last time I had a lie-in. My life is passing by in a whirl of nappies, bottle feeds, heaps of laundry, Bonjela, soothers, and exhaustion.

Sometimes I feel guilty for the way I'm feeling. I should be overjoyed to have a baby when I know there's thousands of women out there who would dearly love one but can't conceive but I'd love it if now and again I could have some free time. I'd relish even half an hour to myself during the day. I dream about being able to walk along the promenade in Bray without the pram for once, listening to my favourite iPod tunes. Am I a bad mother for craving those simple little life luxuries? Before I was a mum I wouldn't even have considered any of those activities a treat. I mean, what on earth did I do with all my free time before Baby John came along? I can't believe I took it all for granted.

All my friends have practically disappeared. It's like they all disappeared into a big black hole together, never to be seen again. The ones who promised to baby-sit never did, not that I blame them really. It's no fun looking after a six-month old, especially if he isn't even theirs. But, for example, Sally, whom I considered a very close friend before, keeps posting messages on my Facebook page telling me publicly that she misses me so much which is weird. I mean, I've only moved out to Bray, not the Bahamas. Bray is really only a few minutes on the DART so it's not like I'm based in the middle of nowhere. And anyway the views from the train are fabulous when you're coming out to Bray so it's not a boring journey at all. I wish more people would make the effort to visit me. I mean, it's so much easier for somebody without a pram to travel on public transport.

The first time I took Baby John on the bus I was terrified. There is only one space on the bus for a pram so I was wondering what would happen if another mummy with one got on the bus? Then I found out that it's first come, first served. Because I was on the bus with my pram, the driver told the mummy at the next stop that she couldn't get on the bus with hers because I was already on the bus with mine, and I felt so guilty as I looked out the window at her crestfallen face. Especially as it had just begun to rain.

But the nice thing about travelling with a pram is that most people are very decent about helping you get the cumbersome vehicle on and off trains and buses. Men are especially gallant about helping, and opening doors, and that kind of stuff. I think seeing a helpless mummy with a baby brings out their kind nature.

Okay, I'm in the chemist's now so I must concentrate. I don't know if you've ever heard of baby brain but I have an extremely bad dose of it at the moment. Even yesterday I went to the Spar shop specifically to get nappies and I came back with bread and milk and no Pampers. When I came home and discovered that I was nappy-less I nearly cried and had to go all the way back to the shops again. My poor aching feet didn't thank me a jot! So now I need Bonjela for the teething, nappy-rash cream and aspirin for myself.

I pay for my goods, shake my head sorrowfully when I'm asked if I have a customer loyalty card (no, because I never seem to have the time to fill out the application form) and then I head for home.

Monday really can't come quickly enough. I just cannot wait to meet the real Bernadette in person. She seems so lovely and nice and normal. I placed fresh flowers in her room today on the windowsill and they smell divine. I really hope she likes them, and that she's not allergic to pollen or anything. Now that would be just my luck!

Tomorrow first thing I'm going to bake a cake so when she arrives we can have tea and cake and it'll be a nice welcome for her. I'm not going to ask her to do any chores or anything when she first arrives as I intend to allow her settle in but, hopefully, if the weather permits she can come for a nice walk with myself and John and get a feel for the area.

This evening, once John is put down in his cot, I'm going to do something I haven't done in a long time, and that's watch a girlie DVD with a generous glass of red wine. Well, why wouldn't I celebrate? It's been the toughest six months of my life raising a baby all by myself and soon part of my life will be my own again. I haven't been this excited since I was expecting Santa as a little girl.

10

I was woken up this morning, long before my alarm clock went off, by the seagulls calling out to each other as they circled above our small apartment complex. As it was a nice and bright morning with clear skies I got up with a spring in my step, washed and dressed myself and then went to wake the baby. He was none too pleased about getting up so early however. John isn't an early bird. He definitely likes a lie-on in the mornings. So many people tell me I'm lucky to have a baby who doesn't wake at five demanding to be fed, but John is the complete opposite. He never feels like rising until at least eight and sometimes later than that. Mind you, he's a bit of a party animal at night. He often refuses to go to sleep before ten which can be very annoying, especially if there's something that I want to watch on TV. But overall he's a good sleeper.

"Come on, baby! Up you get now! This is going to be a very special day for us today."

He lay still. Not budging. In his little opinion it was just another morning and he wasn't ready to embrace it yet.

"Come on, pet! Let's get up. We'll get you some yummy breakfast and then put you in the bath so you'll be lovely and clean for Bernadette. Won't that be nice?"

A groan indicated immense displeasure at being woken from his dream. He turned away from me with a little sigh. I briefly wondered what babies dreamed about. Did they dream about bunnies and teddies and other babies? I often saw John flinch in his sleep and he tossed and turned an awful lot. He seemed to dream a lot. Did he dream of me? I'd love to have known.

John cried a little when I lifted him out of his wooden cot. Not a sorrowful cry, more of a cranky one. It didn't last long. Once he was in the bath, he forgot he was cross, and started to play with his yellow toy duck. I wanted him to be nice and clean for Bernadette. I badly needed to create a good impression. I was going to dress my baby in a little cream-coloured outfit with matching hat – a present from an auntie which I had always thought was too good to use before now.

John, as always, loved his bath. He has this white plastic bath seat which he can sit in and chuckle and gurgle and splash all around him, playing with his rubber duck and his bath storybook. He was a picture of contentment now. For a fleeting moment, I felt guilty. I only had this one little boy and couldn't cope. Did I really have to pay another woman, a stranger, to share these precious moments with my beloved son? Could I not be bothered myself? But then I chided myself for feeling guilty. Most women felt slightly guilty for hiring a childminder, didn't they? I wondered how my own mother had raised us with no help at all. How did she do it? My dad had worked in England on building sites until I was ten years old and then had to come home due to a back injury. My mother, who is an ex-nurse, had held the fort all that time. No childminders, au pairs or nannies in sight. I really wondered how she and all the other hardworking women of her generation managed to raise large families. Raising children was still considered a fairly thankless job. In society anyway. Yvonne, one of the ladies from the book club, had once told me that she could literally see the light fade from people's eyes when her answer was 'I'm a stay-at-home mum' to the pertinent and oft-asked dinner-party question 'What do you do?' In reality raising kids was the hardest job of all. At least in an office you got your coffee-break and your lunch break and in many cases you clocked out at 5.00 p.m. With motherhood there was never a clocking-out.

Still, I wasn't complaining. It had been my choice to have a baby. Nobody had forced me into it. I was right there at the conception! And although I had never envisioned being a single mum struggling financially, the reward of seeing John smile for the first time or hearing him babble back at me was more exciting than any work promotion or fancy cocktails on a Friday evening with work colleagues, and worth more than all the millions in the world.

I'm doing this for you, darling John, I thought silently as I dabbed my son's head gently with a sponge. I'm doing this so that I can go back to work and provide for you and – I won't lie either – I'm doing it to keep myself a little sane.

John was clean, fed, bathed and changed and was happily playing on his play mat wearing his best outfit when the front door bell rang. I felt my heart lurch a little. So this was it! Bernadette was here. It was almost like welcoming a brand-new member to the family.

I stood up and looked at myself anxiously in the hall mirror. I looked fine despite the dark circles under my eyes. I wiped away a bit of smudged mascara with the tip of my finger. My heart was beating a little faster than usual. Good God, this was as bad as going on a date! With slightly clammy hands, I opened the front door with a big smile. There she was. Bernadette. She looked exactly like she did in her photo. Fresh-faced, friendly and very Irish-looking with a smattering of freckles on her pale face. She wore navy jeans and a belted white bomber jacket and had her brown hair tied back in a ponytail. She held out a hand, but I reached out and hugged her instead. Shaking hands was too formal for somebody you were welcoming in to be part of the family.

"Did you have any trouble finding the place?" I asked, picking up her very large suitcase and heaving it in from the porch. "Wow! This is heavy."

"I know," she laughed. "It is a bit. I have my whole life in there! I'd no trouble getting here at all. I just took a taxi from the train station."

"Take off your coat and sit down in the sitting room and relax. John is in there on his play mat. I'm sure you're dying to meet him."

"Eh, yeah," Bernadette said awkwardly, following me into the room. "Oh, he's cute."

I put down the suitcase and picked John up. He was dribbling onto his best outfit.

"Would you like to hold him?" I asked Bernadette.

She shrugged non-committedly. "Sure, why not?"

I felt myself flinch. Something wasn't quite right here. There was no light in Bernadette's eyes. She had only been here less than five minutes and looked bored already. What was wrong? But I then decided to banish my negative thoughts. After all, it was only normal to be cautious when meeting another woman to whom you were about to entrust your only beloved child. It would take more than a few minutes to properly break the ice.

I smiled at Bernadette who gave me a stiff smile back. She held the baby awkwardly in her arms. For one who had clearly stated on her CV that she adored babies, it didn't look like it now.

"Would you like a cup of tea?"

Bernadette shook her head.

"Or coffee? Or even a glass of water, perhaps?"

"No, honestly, I'm grand."

"Okay, if you're sure," I said amiably, reclaiming my baby. "Come on, I'll show you to your room. I'm sure you're looking forward to getting settled in."

She followed me wordlessly. I showed her the wardrobe I had bought for her in a closing-down sale in Bray, which had been delivered the day before. "I'm sure you'll have enough space there for your belongings, but if not let me know."

The girl had a nonchalant look on her face. I took a

deep breath and said nothing else. Maybe Bernadette was just painfully shy. Or perhaps she was a bit overwhelmed about moving to the city from a small country town. She might have said a teary goodbye earlier to her mum and dad. A boyfriend, even? I thought it was best to give her a bit of space to gather herself together.

"I'll be in the kitchen with John if you need me."

"Okay," said Bernadette. "Eh . . ." she began again but then hesitated.

"Yes?" I asked eagerly.

"I was just wondering, eh . . . is it just yourself and the baby here?" She looked around the room as though she was expecting some madman to jump out of the closet any second.

"Yes, it's just me and John," I smiled. "I'm not married," I added with forced gaiety.

"Oh. Okay, fair enough."

I forced another over-the-top smile and then left Bernadette to unpack in peace.

Back down in the kitchen again, I strapped John into his baby seat and put on the kettle. I needed a strong mug of coffee after that not-so-smooth getting-to-know-you moment. Or maybe a stiff vodka. No, I'm joking. But I did feel a little uneasy for some reason. There was something funny about Bernadette's demeanour and I just couldn't put a finger on it. Then again, what had I been expecting? A really life-like Mary Poppins, complete with big black umbrella landing on the chimney and singing songs at the top of her voice? Get real, Kaylah, I chided myself, you've seen one too many Disney films as a child.

I sat down on a chair and switched on the TV to drown out the sound of silence. Bernadette didn't seem to be making too much noise as she was unpacking. In fact . . . there wasn't even a sound coming from her room. Maybe she had decided to lie down for a while. She was probably tired after getting the train up to Dublin. Maybe she hadn't been able to sleep very much due to the excitement of starting a new job this week. I settled into watching a BBC programme, one of the ones I loved so much about people buying rundown properties and then doing them up to sell for a profit. They always gave me lots of ideas about the things I would do one day if I was ever lucky enough to get a foot on the property ladder. I sincerely hoped I wouldn't be paying rent all my life. It was money down the drain really. If only it wasn't so damn difficult to save a deposit! Anyway, even if I did have a deposit, would I ever get a mortgage loan? Everyone was saying the banks still weren't lending. I wondered how much hope I would realistically have, being a single mum with no savings and no permanent job. It was kind of depressing thinking about it.

Just as I was reaching for my first chocolate biscuit of the day to satisfy my sweet tooth, a rap on the kitchen door made me jump.

Bernadette was standing at the door. She was still wearing her coat. Odd, I thought. It wasn't that cold in here, was it? I had made sure to leave the heat on high so that Bernadette would feel warm and comfortable.

"Hey!" I gave her a warm smile. "Are you all unpacked?"

Bernadette shifted from one foot to another. "Well,

actually no. I'll probably have to unpack later." She looked at her watch somewhat dubiously. "I'm kind of under pressure right now . . ."

"Pressure?"

"Yeah, sorry. I know it sounds bad, but . . ."

"But what?" I frowned, feeling utterly confused. What was Bernadette talking about? Pressure to do what?

"Is everything okay?" I pressed her gently. "There's nothing wrong, is there? Can I help you with anything? Would you like a cup of tea?"

"No, thanks. Honestly no. But, eh . . . I wonder would you have the number of a local taxi firm? I'm meeting another family in Foxrock in half an hour and I don't want to be late."

I gulped, feeling momentarily stunned. I needed clarification. Bernadette was happy to offer it.

"You see," she began, as I listened in bewilderment, "I need to meet a few families this week. I am not one hundred per cent sure I will take this job, although I am very grateful for the offer . . . you and your son seem very nice."

I opened my mouth to say something but remained speechless. I think I was in mild shock.

"So," Bernadette continued, in a breezy manner as though she were merely discussing the weather or something, "I intend to meet up with a few families this week, and then by Friday I will have made the decision regarding what I feel is best for me. I'll give all the families my answer on Friday. Is that okay with you?"

I was so flabbergasted I couldn't speak. I held John in my arms and remained silent.

Bernadette glanced at her watch again. "Yeah, so I'd better run. I'd probably be quicker getting a taxi at the rank at the train station. Sorry about this. I hope you don't think I'm rude."

And then she was gone.

11

I must have stood looking at the slammed door without moving for at least a minute, although it felt like much, much longer. I was completely and utterly bewildered. What had just happened there? Had I just imagined that totally bizarre scene or was it for real? Baby John tugging urgently at my long straggly hair brought me back to reality. I put him down on his play mat. The phone rang suddenly and I picked it up after one ring.

"Hello, darling, it's your mum."

Mum always tells me when it's her on the phone. Like I never would have guessed otherwise.

"Oh, hi, Mum," I said.

"Is everything okay? You sound exhausted."

"Do I? Well, I am exhausted actually."

"You poor thing. Now, hopefully when this new girl arrives, she'll help you with your work load. You need someone to give you a break so that you can organise yourself a bit better. What time are you expecting her?"

"Well, see, the thing is –"

"It's just that if you weren't expecting her until this evening you could come out to Aldi with me and stock up. Are you short on supplies like nappies and wipes or anything like that?"

"I am actually, but –"

"Okay, I can't stay on the mobile, it eats money. I'll call around to you in about fifteen so be ready – I can't delay because I have an appointment with my chiropodist at two."

Before I could get a word in edgeways my mother had cut me off. I left John playing on the baby mat and took a peek inside the door of the spare room where I had left Bernadette to unpack moments earlier. The wardrobe was bare. The girl hadn't even unpacked a single thing. The large suitcase was unopened at the end of her bed. I wondered what I should do. Should I go to the supermarket with my mother? If I did that then who would let Bernadette back in? She didn't have a key and all her stuff was here.

In a sort of a daze, I put on my coat and hat and got John's little coat and hat for him.

In no time the doorbell sounded again. My mother was on the doorstep. She gave John a big kiss. He gurgled back at her in delight. "How is my favourite grandson?" she cooed, rubbing his little cheek with the back of her hand.

He was her only grandson and she doted on him as though he were her own.

"Mum, I need to ask you something –" I began.

"Well, you can ask me in the car, sweetheart. I don't

want to get stuck in the lunch-time traffic and end up missing my chiropodist appointment later. You should see the size of the corn on my left foot. No wonder I'm in pain."

I strapped John's baby-seat into the back of the car. It was an awkward task and it didn't help when my mother kept saying, "Is he not strapped in yet?" But soon enough we were ready to go. My mother talked nineteen to the dozen all the way to Aldi, spouting random nonsense about the neighbour's daughter who had just split up with her husband. I found myself zoning out. Mum was forever gossiping about the neighbours, and also relating inane trivia about the people she played bridge with to me. Only when we stopped at the car park of the supermarket did she pause for breath and that was just to ask me whether I had a two-euro coin for the trolley.

"Mum!" I burst out. "Bernadette arrived today and put her case in her room and then went out and I haven't seen her since."

My mother turned and frowned at me. "What are you talking about, darling? Who on earth is Bernadette?"

She went to open the passenger door. I instinctively grabbed her upper arm. "No, wait! I need your advice. Bernadette is the Irish au pair I was telling you about. She arrived today on the train and then she said she was going out to meet another family."

"She what?"

"She just came and then left and said she'd be back later. She said she would choose a family at the end of the week."

My mother pushed her sunglasses back on top of her

highlighted head of hair. "Well," she said calmly, "let her stay with one of the other families then while she's deciding."

I felt a wave of relief wash over me. Thank God! At least another human being had just confirmed that the feeling I had in my heart was right.

"So what do you think I should do?"

"It's very simple. Did you give her a key?"

"No, I'm not that daft."

"Well, then, it is very simple," Mum said pragmatically. "If this girl, Bernadette, is waiting on the doorstep when you get back you must tell her that you are not running a free hotel for job-hunters."

"And if she's not there?"

"If she's not, then . . . I presume you have her phone number?"

"Yes."

"Well, then, you ring her and tell her to come and collect her suitcase. Now come on, we don't have much time to get the groceries."

12

"Hello, Bernadette? Is that you?"

"Yeah, who's this?"

"It's Kaylah. I'm just wondering where you are?" Despite my mother's advice, I hadn't rung Bernadette when I got back to the apartment. I had waited throughout the afternoon and into the early evening – I suppose in the hope she might turn up and tell me I'd got it wrong and it was all a misunderstanding.

It sounded as though Bernadette was in a very noisy place. A crowded bar, perhaps?

"Oh hi, hang on a minute – I need to step outside so I can hear you."

There was a pause. I took a deep breath and waited patiently. Really, this girl was turning out to be something else. If I told anyone this was happening they probably wouldn't even believe it.

"Hello?" She was back.

"Hi, Bernadette. I am wondering what you want me to do with your suitcase?"

"Huh?"

"Well, you can't leave it here," I insisted.

There was a longer pause this time. "Is everything okay, Kaylah?" she then asked as though I was the one with the problem.

"Bernadette, I offered you a job based on your CV and our telephone conversation. I didn't say it was okay to just dump your stuff here and go out partying."

"Partying?" She sounded stunned. "I'm just meeting my cousin for a drink. She's just come home from Australia and I haven't seen her in over a year."

"I'm sorry, Bernadette, but your social life has really got nothing to do with me. I am tired after the long day I've had and all the messing about has left me feeling very frustrated. I am therefore going to bed early and I cannot stay up to let you in to collect your case."

"But why would I be collecting my stuff? I thought we had an arrangement?"

"So did I – I thought the arrangement was that you were coming to work for me."

"Are you saying I can't stay with you then?"

"Yes. That's exactly what I'm saying."

"But where will I stay?" Bernadette sounded outraged.

I rubbed my temple in frustration. "With your cousin? In a hostel? I don't know. And anyway it's none of my business. If you prefer I can leave your case in the porch for you so you can collect it sometime tonight at your own convenience."

"All right then. Suit yourself."

Click. She was gone. I stared at my phone, stunned. My head was spinning. Good God, the stress of it all was getting to me. I sighed in exasperation. I could feel a migraine starting. Why was it so bloody difficult to get a good au pair? Come on! I slumped down on the sitting-room sofa and put my head in my hands. I felt defeated and worn out, and if I'm being honest, a bit foolish too. That girl must have thought I was an awful eejit if she thought she could get away with behaving like that. Then John began to whimper. A sudden strong pong told me that he needed his nappy changed as soon as possible. I looked over at him and saw that he had also puked a bit down his nice new top. Seriously, if it wasn't one thing it was another. There was never any spare time as a mum. Not to even mention the mountain of washing and ironing to be done. It was all beginning to get on top of me.

Later that evening, after John and his favourite teddy had been put down in his little wooden cot and a few lullabies had been sung, I poured myself a large glass of red wine and sat down at my computer. It was time to go back to the drawing board. Bernadette had arrived to collect her case. She had come in a taxi, and removed it wordlessly from the front porch. I honestly found the whole thing very odd indeed, but it was a blessing that she had shown her true colours early on, and not in a few weeks' time when it might have been too late.

Maybe it was time to approach a proper nanny agency. Perhaps I should splash out on a fee for peace of mind. The only problem with agencies was that they had lots of strict rules like having to pay holiday pay and offer free flights and offer the use of a car and all that malarkey. With funds at an all-time low, I was barely managing to keep the roof over our heads without having to fork out a fortune on employment agencies too.

I decided to renew my ad on the internet one more time. Yes, it would mean having to read many, many more practically illegible CVs, but I couldn't just jack in all my hopes because of Bernadette turning out to be a few raisins short of a fruit-and-nut bar. I logged onto the employment section of the website and renewed my ad. Then I started reading a few of the other ads so that I could compare them to my own.

It was pretty fascinating stuff. Lots of families seemed to be making fairly heavy demands on their would-be au pairs. There was one ad from a family with five children, looking for an au pair who would be willing to do housework as well as help the children with their homework, and they expected some poor girl to do it all for a hundred euro with just one and a half days off a week. I thought that was pretty outrageous. For the same money I was offering two days off a week, a free travel pass and my girl would only have to help one mother look after one child. I didn't expect my future au pair to do much housework. Apart from a few errands down to the local grocer's and keeping little John's clothes in order and some light ironing, she wouldn't be asked to do much at all. I believed that an au pair's interest should lie with the child and not cleaning. After all, how could somebody truly look after your child properly if she was on her hands and knees scrubbing floors? I just couldn't believe some the ridiculous demands being made by some of the families. They were looking for slaves, not au pairs!

I was tired now. I was fighting to keep my eyes open. It had been an exhausting, dramatic day and nothing had come of it so far. But at least the spare room was available now and ready to move into. The flowers on the window-sill looked fresh and inviting. Well, not inviting enough to make Bernadette want to stay, maybe, but still . . .

I decided to go to bed early. If I had a second glass of wine I would surely pay for it in the morning by feeling drowsy. One glass was my limit now. God, I would be such a cheap date if anyone was offering. But sadly nobody was.

I was about to log off my computer when a new email in my inbox caught my eye. That was strange, I thought. Either it was a very enthusiastic candidate or SPAM. My eyes were closing now, and I yawned as I opened up the email.

Hello, I am just wondering when you are available. I am a recent widower, aged thirty-seven, and I have two daughters aged one and three. We live in a nice house in Sandymount near the sea. My mother also lives with us and helps out but we are looking for an au pair to help her when I am at work and also to come on holidays to Spain where we have a summer house. Please reply if you think this is a job that would suit you. Thanks, Stephen.

I read the message and then read it again. Aw, the poor man! He must have been confused and thought I was offering my services as an au pair, and not looking for one. I wondered whether I should just ignore it. I thought about it for a few more seconds and then sent a quick email back.

Hi Stephen, I'm afraid I'm in the same boat as you. I'm trying to hire help myself. Hope you will have more luck than I've been having trying to find my own Mary Poppins. It's a bit of a jungle out there. I thought it would be easy. Good luck and take care, Kaylah.

13

I packed my baby's newborn clothes in a large plastic sack yesterday. It was with a tear or two that I completed this difficult task. I mean, it was heart-wrenching folding his miniscule yellow-and-white striped Babygro for the very last time knowing that he'd never wear it again. It's hard to believe that he once squeezed into such a teeny garment as he's now a bit of a thug to be honest. Like this morning when he started yelling at five in the morning I just looked at my watch and nearly cried. I just thought: You cannot be serious, Mister!

But he was serious and he continued yelling until he got his own way and I eventually brought him into my own bed and he fell asleep cuddled into me, happy as Larry. I know, of course, that all the books say it's a bad habit to have your baby sleeping in the same bed as you, but give me a break. He seems to prefer my bed to his cot and I'm just looking for a peaceful life. To be honest all the books out there can tell you how to raise your child but ultimately you just have to use your own common sense. I mean, they say that it's best not to give solids to babies under six months. Well, try telling that to my little guzzler. At five months old he'd have eaten the hand off his arm if I wasn't feeding him solids.

Sheelagh's next-door neighbour has a baby two weeks older than mine. Her baby is still on bottles only because she is reading a book which tells her exactly what to do. The same woman can never go anywhere because her baby is always crying. I feel sorry for them both. I always think the baby is hungry and his mum doesn't realise it. The thing is that all babies are different, so what works for one won't necessarily work for another. I wouldn't have my baby starving just because I'd read some book telling me not to give solids before six months. I try my best to use the brain God gave me. The rules are always changing anyway. Our mothers were told not to put babies to sleep on their backs yet we're told the complete opposite. So who makes up the rules? In your own house you are own mistress so I need to remember that. It doesn't matter what your friends or your mothers-in-law or the nosy neighbour down the road thinks. Mums instinctively know what's right for their own babies so it's best to take no notice of women who think they are experts because they've done it all before. Nobody knows your little one like you do. How could any expert or author of a book know John better than I know him myself?

Now, tonight is the final book club night for the summer and I am really looking forward to it. I just can't wait for a bit of adult company. It won't resume again until the end of September when the kids are well settled back to school. I'm really not quite sure how I'll entertain myself without the book-club ladies to tide me over! I've been living vicariously through them and all their holiday plans. Joanne is taking her four children to Alcudia in Majorca for a week, and Heather and her husband and child are heading off to their place in Portugal. Yvonne is Connemara-bound with her brood, and Deirdre and her husband who don't have any children are going to a gourmet cookery school to learn culinary delights for a fortnight. Then they're taking their jeep to England where they plan on driving around the countryside at their leisure. Karen is off to the South of France on a camping trip. Anita seems to be the only one not to have any plans and that's because she says the hassle of taking her five boisterous boys anywhere is enough to want to make her cry. Anita is separated and her ex-husband by all accounts only takes the boys on Bank Holiday weekends but refuses to ever have them for more than two consecutive nights because they wreck his bachelor penthouse down by the docks and interfere with his love life. Apparently he has a string of young girlfriends. Well, he is rich!

When anyone asks me what I am doing for the summer holidays, I remain suitably vague. Sometimes I just say I'm visiting my sister in West Cork. It's enough to satisfy their fleeting curiosity. They don't need to know the truth and they certainly don't need to know that my sister, Ger, has never once invited me to stay in her sprawling mansion in fashionable West Cork where they have a built-in swimming pool attached to the house. Of course they always invite their well-to-do friends down from Dublin to stay in their guest rooms and they seem to have barbeques on the lawn and pop a lot of champagne corks. But there never seems to be enough room for me which is a shame. Mind you, Ger is pretty good at keeping in touch on Facebook and is always posting lovely pictures of herself and her house and her kids online, so I never feel that she is too far away. She sometimes even chats to me on Skype!

I would give my right arm to get away somewhere sunny this summer. I really would. I sometimes dream of feeling hot sun on my face or paddling at the sea edge with my baby in a cute pair of togs and a sun hat. The apartment is starting to feel a bit claustrophobic as it's quite small and confined. There's no garden, only a small back yard, and it's been raining non-stop for the last few weeks. It's getting a bit depressing actually. I mean, there have been a few sunny afternoons where I've managed to walk the promenade in Bray between showers but overall the sun has remained firmly hidden behind clouds and scorching-hot beach days have been noticeably scarce. Anyway, little John is too small to be taken on a long, unnecessary flight. Holy God, even the thought of having to pack for him, take his pram through security and then face delays, followed by a trip with him on my knee for a few hours doesn't bear thinking about. Maybe, if I get the right au pair, we can go away somewhere nice in Ireland. Maybe I'll hire a little house by the sea for a week and invite Mum down too. After all, there are so many gorgeous, unspoiled places here such as Kerry, Galway, Sligo and Donegal. There really is no need to be going away with the baby and have all that fussing at the airport over plastic bottles and having to take off your shoes. Anyway, the way the economy is going now, we need more people to holiday at home and get our once-thriving tourism industry thriving again. If only that didn't mean getting so damn wet!

I have to admit I haven't quite finished the book that we're going to be discussing tonight. Unfortunately it's one of those dreary, upsetting, but apparently highbrow reads where women are deemed second-class citizens in their own country, and their cruel husbands take younger second wives once they are past their prime, and people are brutally tortured and murdered in the name of religion. Chick lit it certainly isn't. Sometimes, just now and again, I wish we didn't take our literary endeavours so seriously. It would be nice to sit down with a chilled glass of sparkling wine and discuss one of the Sophie Kinsella shopaholic books now and then. But I just know if I suggested a chick-lit book I would face looks of complete horror from the literary ladies at the book club. So now I have to quickly skim through the book, speed-read the last chapter, read some well-informed reviews on Amazon and pretend I know what I'm talking about later. I reckon I'll be doing a lot of nodding and agreeing with everybody else's verdict on the misery-lit book.

Mum will be coming around in time to give me a chance to get in the shower and freshen up. It will be my first chance of the day to get out of my vomit-stained pyjamas, which makes me sound like an awful slob I know. It's magical having a shower and knowing that Mum is in the other room minding John. Usually I have to bring his baby seat into the bathroom with me and can never enjoy more than a quick two-minute scrub-down.

I really wonder what I used to do with my time before I had John. I mean, I must have wasted hours on Facebook looking at holiday snaps of people I didn't even know very well. I remember a time I could have easily spent forty minutes in the shower, or a couple of hours surfing TV channels with my feet up on the couch. When I lived with Sally, I never remember either of us rising before noon on a Sunday, and even then one of us would persuade the other to get dressed and go out to buy fresh croissants, coffees and the Sunday papers. Even that task seemed like a chore at the time. Now I shake my head in wonder when I remember the lazy, spoilt me. Eight o'clock is a lie-in for me these days. Eight thirty is practically a holiday!

Nobody gives you a medal for being a tired, harassed mum. There are no promotions, pay-related bonuses, or congratulations for doing a good job. And that's understandable. Nobody cares if you're up all night with a screaming baby, don't have five minutes in the day to yourself and are struggling to cope. That's right, nobody cares and why should they? They have their own lives and day-to-day worries without giving your situation a second thought. But you will not get any thanks for being a martyr. You cannot do it all and you shouldn't try. There is terrible pressure put on mums to get back in shape, look great, be fabulous cooks and supportive partners if there even are partners, and get back to work as soon as possible. Yet there are still people out there who deride mothers for hiring help when they should be doing everything themselves. "Our mothers did it so why can't they?" they cry.

Well, it was different back in our mothers' day. There were communities back then. People didn't live in apartments miles away from their families and not knowing their neighbours. They helped each other. Now we compete against each other. We all have to be doing better and coping better than anybody else. Rubbish to that, I say. No mother should try and be a saint and do everything, nor should she constantly moan about how tired she is because nobody wants to know. We're all tired.

Obviously friends and family don't like being taken advantage of, so you can't just load babies off on people every time you want to go shopping, and you can't wait for them to offer because that's realistically never going to happen. Some friends will offer to help you out "any time". This, you will soon learn, translates as "no time at all" as they think up excuse after excuse not to help you out. But others will help now and again if you really need their help. I honestly don't know what I'd do without my mum's help. I read somewhere that the actress, Anna Friel, recently revealed that she employed two part-time nannies while she worked on set. She came in for a bit of flak after that announcement from stay-at-home mothers. Well, if she can afford the two nannies, why not? I think it makes her a good parent that she is working to provide financial security for her daughter. She is a single mother. She cannot work and look after her child. It's just not physically possible. I totally get her. I just wish I had her money too!

It didn't take me too long to walk to the book-club

venue which was in a charming old Victorian house on the seafront.

"Don't drink too much," my mother had warned.

She always says that, as though I were some awkward fifteen-year-old going to her first school disco, and not a middle-aged woman going along to another middle-aged woman's house to discuss a dreadfully depressing book for the best part of two hours. Anyway, I was walking home afterwards and not driving so what was all the fuss about? Mum thinks anyone who consumes two or more alcoholic units in one evening is a raving alcoholic. She'll be sending me off to rehab if I'm not careful.

Joanne had a fire lit even though it was the beginning of July. It was fairly chilly outside though and my eyes lit up when I saw the smouldering coals in her fireplace.

"Will you have a glass of wine?" she offered, taking my coat.

Will I? Are you joking? Of course I will. That's the only reason I came!

I kept my sentiments private however. "Yes, please, white wine would be great, thanks," I said politely, taking a seat by the fire. "Isn't the weather just the pits for this time of the year?"

"Oh Lord, don't talk to me about it," Joanne sighed. "It's a nightmare having the kids in the house all day. Thank goodness we're going to Majorca next week. At least we have a big outdoor pool there to amuse the kids. It's fabulous."

I agreed that yes, it must be fabulous. Oh to be rich!

"Tanya? Tanya, a glass of wine for Kaylah, please. And bring in the canapés too."

The Secret Nanny Club

My eyes widened. Canapés? Good gracious, Joanne was going all out this evening, wasn't she? Most people just provided a few crisps and nuts out of packets. And who was Tanya anyway? I thought Joanne had only boys.

The next minute the Tanya in question emerged from the kitchen holding a silver tray with a single large wineglass on it.

"Madame?" she enquired politely.

I looked back at her in amazement. First of all I could hardly believe that Joanne had gone to the trouble of hiring caterers and secondly, this Tanya one was the double of Claudia Schiffer with sallow skin, vivid blue eyes, long dark eyelashes, wavy blonde hair cascading down her back and legs up to her armpits. Good God!

"Thank you," I said finally, when I found my voice. "That's very kind."

She gave a sort of nervous smile and scuttled back to the kitchen.

I turned to Joanne, who was by the window fixing her curtains, and raised my glass. "Cheers!"

There was a knock on the door and Joanne went to answer it. Then Heather breezed in a waft of Chanel No. 5 perfume. She is super-glamorous but married to a rather dull, but wealthy man. She has a glossy auburn bob, fabulous translucent skin and always wears designer clothes. I am in total awe of her.

"Hey, Heather," I said.

"Oh hi, Kaylah. I'm not late, am I?"

Kiss, kiss.

"No, not at all. I'm the only one here so far."

"Thank goodness. We were delayed on the golf course.

Longest game ever. I had barely time to shower when I came home. Thank God for the nanny laying out my clothes on the bed. I wouldn't have known what to wear otherwise."

"She picks out your clothes?" I was gobsmacked. Had I heard right?

"Oh, Nanny is like my right hand!" laughed Heather, showing a perfect set of pearly teeth. "What would I do without her? She even helps me apply my fake tan when I don't have time to go the salon."

"Really? She does all that? I'm surprised she doesn't shave your legs too!"

My comment caused Heather to chuckle.

"But seriously, how does she manage to do all that and still look after the kids?" I probed, intrigued.

Heather accepted a large glass of wine from Tanya, who had suddenly appeared again with her tray. "Matthew is in school. She only needs to help him get ready in the morning and help him in the evenings with his homework when we go out."

Oh yeah, I had forgotten that Heather only has one child. I was still surprised she had a nanny for her school-going son though, considering that she doesn't even work.

The next minute Tanya was handing around canapés. I took a little cracker with cream cheese and Heather helped herself to a mini-pizza.

Joanne practically shooed Tanya away before she came too close to her with the tray. I always secretly believed that Joanne didn't eat. Now I was convinced she didn't. At the moment she was sipping slowly on a glass of sparkling water with a slice of lemon in it. She kept checking her watch nervously. "I hope people aren't late."

Oh, for God's sake! I didn't know what she was stressing about. It wasn't like we were at a special occasion like a wedding or christening or anything where we were pressed for time. Honestly, it's just a get-together to discuss some crummy book, I thought. I came here to relax, so why can't she?

As I was draining my first glass of wine (*oops!*) there was another knock on the door. Next to arrive in was Karen, who owned two city-centre chemists. She arrived in wearing a comfy-looking, well-worn beige Juicy Couture tracksuit and her hair back in a messy bun. Karen is probably the most well-off among us and therefore seems to have no interest in dressing to impress anyone.

"Hello, girls, sorry I'm late. Traffic was mental. Oh, I'd love a white wine, thanks. I don't think we've met before. What's your name?"

"My name is Tanya."

"How do you do, Tanya. It's nice to meet you. Where are you from?"

"I'm from the Ukraine."

"Are you enjoying Ireland?"

Tanya glanced nervously at Joanne who gave her a stern smile in return. Talk about putting somebody on the spot! She was hardly going to say she hated the country and her job in front of her new boss now, was she? But before she had time to answer the question the doorbell sounded again.

In came Anita. Anita, with her shock of white hair, is

by far the loudest of the group. She has the most vulgar laugh. It gets louder and dirtier after a few scoops of wine. She is a separated mother of five and runs a successful bakery in Wicklow. She doesn't have a nanny and I really take my hat off to her. How on earth does she do it? Mind you, two of her children are in their late teens so they help out looking after the younger ones, I believe.

Then Deirdre arrived in, apologising profusely. Apparently the DART had stopped on the tracks for about fifteen minutes and no reason had been given for the delay. Deirdre, probably in her late sixties, is the oldest member of the book club and the most cultured. She lives in Dalkey, always sips the same glass of wine all evening and discusses whatever book is on the menu in depth. In fact, I'm convinced that if it weren't for Deirdre, our little book-club group wouldn't keep going.

Oh my God, I'll never forget the stress of hosting one of our evenings! You would have sworn I was cooking a three-course meal on *Come Dine with Me* instead of just having a few ladies over for some wine and a casual chat about a book. But seriously, I nearly had a breakdown in advance of the evening, fretting that my apartment would be too small to accommodate everyone and worrying that John would start crying and I'd have to attend to him at the expense of my guests. Deirdre had hosted the evening the week before in her adorable Dalkey mansion where she is neighbours to the rich and famous and has glorious views of Dublin Bay. Her marble bathroom alone is about the same size as my apartment, complete with Missoni handtowels and Jo Malone hand-cream. It's like a five-star hotel. I wanted to move in straight away and never leave! When she took us on a little tour of her immaculate back garden, complete with its own herb garden and a pond with a spectacular fountain like something out of Powerscourt, I couldn't help being frozen with fear at the thought of shoving all these people together the following week into my cramped little rented home. I was dreading it!

In the end I spent the whole day scrubbing and cleaning, I bought flowers to fill the sitting room, Mum took John away for the night and I overcompensated for my humble abode by buying in expensive sparkling wine. Were they impressed? Well, certainly nobody complained. At least not to my face anyway. Did I read the book on our reading list that week? You must be joking. I didn't have time. In fact, now that I think of it I can't even remember what the book was about that week! I was so relieved when they had all said their goodbyes and left. I honestly don't understand people who take great pride in entertaining other people at home on a regular basis. The stress of it just isn't worth it. I'd rather just meet people in a pub or restaurant and foot the bill any time.

"So, I think we're all here now," said Joanne in a clipped voice. She sat at the edge of her cream-leather settee now and, giving a stiff smile, said: "It's time to talk about the book now."

I sat up straight as though I was back at school again wanting to look like I was actually paying attention. Aware that I was midway through my second glass of wine now, I thought it would be best to get my rehearsed review out of the way in case I forgot what to say later.

I had no intention of debating the book – I just wanted to say what I thought of it. Or at least thought of the first few chapters and the last chapter that I hurriedly read while simultaneously trying to paint my toenails before leaving my apartment (I hadn't had time to check out the Amazon reviews). Then, all going well, I could sink back into my chair again and enjoy my evening off, chatting about more important things such as childcare.

"So," Joanne looked sternly at the group over her reading glasses. "Who would like to start?"

I put up my hand. "Em, I think I'll kick off with this one, if that's okay," I offered.

Joanne looked visibly surprised since I am never ever the one to volunteer first.

"Be our guest then, Kaylah."

I cleared my throat. "Well," I began, trying to sound like the book had deeply affected me on some level, "I found it a harrowing read but thought-provoking on many different levels. I thought the heroine was stoical in her approach to day-to-day living, trying to keep her children safe in a war-torn environment full of trauma and tumult, but it is a novel of great intricacy."

I stopped suddenly. Everybody was looking at me with great interest as though they expected me to continue but I had said my piece. That was all I had to say on a book that I hadn't even properly read. I picked up my wine and gave it a sip to let people know I was finished and it was now their turn to speak.

I caught Joanne's gaze. Her head was tilted in thought. "I do agree with you," she said. "But I find your use of the word 'stoical' interesting."

"Right," I said. "I see." Jesus, would she ever move onto the next person now? I'd had my say. I was done and dusted as far as I was concerned. It was supposed to be a book club here, not a private conversation between Joanne and myself about a book that only one of us had read!

"Well, I mean she has to be stoical in the face of adversity," I said and then quickly turned to Deirdre. "What do you think?"

I thought it was a fairly safe bet to bring Deirdre into the conversation as quickly as possible. Knowing Deirdre she would have read the book at least twice and analysed it to death. She was like the school lick!

"I do agree that the heroine was stoical in the first half of the book, but then her emotions got the better of her in the second half, especially after what happened with Ahmed."

Nobody said anything. I felt under pressure to continue the conversation since I had been the one to kick it all off.

"What happened with Ahmed was dreadful, yes," I mumbled even though I didn't know what I was taking about. Who was Ahmed anyway? It was the wine talking. I wanted to be finished with the book. I wanted to drink another glass of wine and talk about au pairs. I wanted to tell them all about what had happened with Bernadette. I was sure they'd all be shocked!

Suddenly Joanne was eyeing me again. I felt like a schoolchild who hadn't done their homework properly. It felt like being back in the classroom, you know, the one time you hadn't done your homework was the very time you would be picked out by the teacher to answer a question.

"Do you think it was right for her to go back to Ahmed though? After all, it was a terrible risk given the circumstances."

"A terrible risk, but worth it in the end I suppose," I continued spoofing. I desperately needed the ground to open and swallow me up.

Nobody else spoke. I felt a conspiracy. Had they not read the book either? Why was Joanne picking on me? It was our last night all together before the summer break – this was supposed to be fun for goodness' sake!

"I don't believe," said Joanne, in a tone of voice I didn't care much for, "that it was a good thing for a woman to take such a terrible risk when she was the mother of two small children. In fact, I would go so far as to say –"

My phone rang suddenly. Phew! Thank God for that! I never did get to hear how far the hostess would go to say.

"Sorry, I really have to get this," I said. "It's my mum. I told her to phone if there was a problem. You girls carry on without me."

I leaped out of my chair and shot outside. It was Sally. I was both surprised and pleased to hear from her. Since I gave birth to John I'd only seen Sally once. She called over for a bite to eat but she was afraid to hold the baby in case she dropped him and she was absolutely appalled when I lifted him up at one stage during our lunch to sniff his nappy. Of course she didn't say anything but she didn't have to. The horrified look on her face said it all.

"Hi, Sally," I said.

"Can you talk?"

"Yes, but I can't stay talking long. I'm at a book club."

"A book club?" Sally sounded shocked. "Where?"

I found myself smiling. Sally isn't much of a reader, although she does love fashion magazines. However, I don't recall ever seeing her with a book in her hand in all the time that we shared an apartment.

"Here in Bray. I saw a notice in my local library and I joined so I could meet nice cultured people in the area."

"Oh, excuse me," Sally giggled. "It all sounds a bit highbrow for me. Any nice men in the club?"

"Haha, are you joking me? No, it's a ladies' book club, so no men allowed."

"Jesus, that's a bit of a waste of time, isn't it? How are you going to find love if you're stuck inside reading books all the time and then when you do go out you just meet a bunch of literary-type women?"

"Good question," I answered. "Hmm, I don't have an answer for that. Listen, I'd better not chat too long. We're in the middle of discussing a book right now. We must meet up soon though."

"Yes, we must," Sally agreed. "Soon."

"How about next week?" I asked, perking up. I suddenly was realising how much I had missed Sally and my girls' nights out. It really had been way too long. Maybe I could get a baby-sitter for the evening or Mum might kindly hold the fort for a night. Or even a couple of hours.

"Well, next week isn't great as there's so much on, and the week after I'm going on holidays with Robert."

"Robert?"

"Yes, he's the new man. Actually he's not so new any more. We're together over two months. You must meet him. You would love him!"

Hmm. I think I'd love it more if he had a nice friend for me.

"So where are you going on holidays?" I asked, trying not to feel envious. It seemed like the entire population of Ireland was leaving en masse for their summer holidays.

"We're going to Sicily for six nights. Robert is treating me."

"Oh wow! I like the sound of that. He's obviously quite keen."

"I hope so! I'm dying to get away and the pictures of the hotel on the internet look amazing. Are you going away anywhere yourself this summer? Oh, by the way, how is the baby?"

"John's fine," I said. Surely she couldn't have forgotten his name already? "He's great but he's teething now so the nights are a bit restless. It's not easy, especially when you're doing it on your own."

"Oh, oh well, it's cute that he's getting a tooth. You must email me a photo when you get the chance."

"I will."

"Listen, Kaylah, I hope you don't think I'm being cheeky or anything but I am just wondering if I could borrow your lovely emerald-green dress for next Saturday? Robert has invited me to a black-tie ball and I don't have anything to wear. If you don't want me to, that's okay, I understand."

I was flummoxed. I really was. I hadn't heard from Sally in months and now she was ringing me up out the blue to ask if she could wear the most precious item of clothing in my wardrobe? I hadn't even worn it myself yet because it was given to me by one of Ireland's most famous designers just a couple of weeks before I got pregnant. It was a thank-you gift for persuading Ireland's most famous actress to wear it on a *Late Late Show* appearance. Apparently the designer in question sold out of all his key season pieces within a week after her appearance.

"Okay," I said reluctantly. I felt I was being put in a corner. I really wished that she wasn't asking this favour of me. I'm the type of person who doesn't even like somebody reading my newspaper or magazine before I do, never mind wearing my one and only couture dress.

"Oh great! Thanks," she said breezily as though she had just asked me for a lighter for a cigarette.

"Right, well, call out to me whenever you like. I'll put the kettle on. We can have a chat and you can see John."

I decided not to be small about it. Let her wear the dress. After all, it was just hanging in my wardrobe doing nothing anyway. And it would be good to see her again, I thought optimistically. I hadn't seen her in so long. She should be able to fill me in on all the office gossip. I really felt out of the loop now. It was as though I had been forgotten about altogether.

"Oh, I'd love to do that, Kaylah, but things are manic in work at the moment and Bray is so far away. It would seriously take me all day getting there and then getting back into town afterwards. I'll tell you what, I'll send out a courier for the dress tomorrow. That could save us both a lot of hassle."

And before I could say anything else, she was gone. I stared at the phone for a few seconds, not knowing what to think. Should I be insulted? Or annoyed? Or simply hurt? Then I put the phone back in my bag. Oh well, I shrugged, at least having a baby had really let me know who my real friends were. I had never felt more alone in the world. Even the ladies in the next room discussing the book were not my real friends. I didn't really know very much about them and they were all a little older than me.

To my horror, and in spite of myself, I felt tears spring up in my eyes. I fought them back. The last thing I needed to do now was start crying. But I couldn't help feeling let down. I was sick of trying to be strong the whole time and pretending that my feelings didn't count. I took a tissue from my pocket and dabbed a lone tear that had escaped. Then I went back into the room where the discussion about the depressing book was in full swing. Oh sugar! I thought they would have wrapped it up by now.

I sat down. Anita patted me gently on the shoulder. "Is everything okay?"

Oh no! I must have looked really upset. Maybe my mascara had run. I was embarrassed now. The last thing I wanted from people was sympathy.

"Is there something wrong with your little fellow?"

"Oh no, he's fine, totally fine. It was just a false alarm. My mother couldn't find his dummy but it turned up behind the sofa."

I could feel myself going red. Why did I lie and say that my mother was on the phone? What was wrong with me? I sat down and studied the cover of my book so as not to draw any further attention to myself. No such luck though.

"What about the new girl you were getting? Has she arrived yet?" asked Yvonne.

Thank you, God! A change of subject! "Well, no. Actually she did come but she has since left."

"She left already? That was quick!"

I revelled in telling them my little story about Bernadette and all the drama that had taken place. By the shocked look on their faces, it seemed that my tale was grabbing their attention far more than the book we were supposed to be critiquing. Soon I had forgotten all about Sally and her snub.

"What a cheek!" said Heather, looking aghast. "Imagine being that brazen! Mind you, it's so hard to find good help these days. I was ages looking for my girl. Thank goodness I found somebody suitable in the end. She's a gem and I'm so lucky. It's a pity I couldn't say the same for my last two girls who were an absolute nightmare. One fancied my husband and the other would eat for Ireland and then lock herself in the bathroom for hours. Bulimia is a real problem, I find, with childminders in this day and age."

"I guess you get what you pay for," shrugged Karen, who as owner of two thriving chemists obviously had no problem paying a nanny's wages.

"That's right," Heather agreed. "If you pay peanuts you get monkeys. Simple as that."

"All I can afford is a monkey," I sighed. "But at least I deserve monkeys that don't expect me to provide a free hotel room in my apartment."

The others smiled politely at my feeble attempt at humour.

Tanya was back in the room topping up wineglasses. I wasn't sure how much English she could speak because she wasn't saying anything. She still looked kind of nervous. Maybe she felt slightly intimidated by the group of strangers in the room. She really was a stunning-looking girl with full lips and brilliant blue eyes. She could have done with putting on a few pounds though. She really was scarily thin.

"I'm glad that I never had to worry about childcare," said Deirdre. "The stories my sisters used to tell me about her numerous nannies would make your hair stand up on end. You couldn't make them up if you tried. One nanny she had even crashed her husband's car when she took it out without permission. Another used to walk from her bedroom to the bathroom naked until my sister told her that it was completely unacceptable. Apparently where she came from in Iceland they do that kind of thing all the time. Or so she said."

"Filipinas are marvellous, I have to say," Yvonne joined in the conversation animatedly. "I have had two in the past. They don't mind working hard, they don't go out partying like Brazilians and they don't complain like the French and unlike Italian girls they are great with the housework. Most of them send all their money back to their families in the Philippines so they're very diligent."

My head was becoming frazzled now with all the advice. I put down my glass of wine as it was clearly going to my head now. I had started the ball rolling and now all the women were trying to outdo each other with their nanny stories. It would seem that the unsuccessful stories far outweighed the successful ones. Really, there didn't seem to be a magical solution.

Deirdre was the first to stand up and make her excuses. She had an early sailing the following morning and needed to make sure everything was packed into the boot of her car. Then Heather said she had better go to as she needed to be up bright and early to do her Pilates classes in the morning. Yvonne said she would stay on for some more chat, as did Anita. Anita's husband had taken all five of the kids to Disneyland Paris for a couple of days so Anita was under no pressure to go home. In fact, she told us, the only thing she had to remember was to attend her local spa the following morning for a massage and a French manicure.

Really those ladies seem to inhabit a different world to the one I do, I thought as I waved good-bye to Deirdre and Heather. They all seemed so organised and appeared as though they had it all worked out. In a way I wished I was more like them. I too would have liked to have plans for the following day that involved something other than a mound of washing, ironing and sterilising bottles.

Yvonne wasn't drinking (she's on a strict no bread, potatoes, sugar or alcohol diet) and had offered to give me a lift home. Anita, on the other hand, eagerly accepted another huge glass of wine. I put my hand politely over my glass when Joanne tried to top it up. I knew my limits.

As we chatted some more (mostly about childcare as it really is a hot favourite topic among mothers), I found myself no longer brooding on Sally's earlier phone call.

She could have the dress and I would graciously loan it to her. After all, it wasn't as though I would be going anywhere in it soon. Anyway, I wasn't slim enough even to get one leg into it at the moment! I'd have to do something about my diet. Before I used to want to be slim for vanity reasons but now I was a little worried about my health. I was fat, particularly around the middle. I needed to lose the lard, for John's sake at least. I decided I'd have to cut down on the bread (lethal waste of calories) and sugar (my downfall since I was a kid – why can't I say no to Jelly Tots?) and up my exercise routine. I really have no excuse not to exercise as I live right beside the promenade in Bray. How much would I love to be able to wear a beige Juicy Couture tracksuit and look like a cool yummy mummy like Heather? Although I am totally ashamed to admit it, sometimes I still wear my maternity clothes (which I didn't manage to sell on eBay!). I know, John is now seven months and I still wear trousers with elastic waistbands while sitting in cafes eating doughnuts and looking at pictures of celebrity mums prancing around in bikinis six weeks after giving birth. Oh, I know they're not like you and me and they have personal chefs and trainers and nannies to help out, but reading about them is enough to send me into the gloomiest of moods.

Finally the evening wound down, in no small part due to Joanne glancing obviously at her watch quite a few times. It seemed to me that despite the amount of effort that she had put into hosting the evening, she had remained uptight throughout and was looking forward to saying goodbye. At the door she gave me a brief air-kiss and said she hoped that I would enjoy the rest of my summer.

I followed Yvonne out to her car, a snazzy Mercedes SLK bought for her by her second husband (a senior consultant in St Vincent's private hospital). It was a close, balmy evening with only a slight breeze. I wouldn't have minded walking back to the apartment but my heels were quite high and one was beginning to rub quite painfully against the back of my heel. I slid into the soft leather passenger seat and closed the door. Then just as I was about to buckle my seat belt there was a rap on the window. It was so barely audible that I wondered if I had imagined it. But no. Tanya was at the window, her eyes wide, like a startled rabbit.

I rolled down the window. There was no sign of Joanne, who had presumably gone back inside. "Hi Tanya, is everything okay?"

She held up a white cardigan which I recognised as mine. "Is it yours?"

I opened the car door. "Oh, thank you," I said gratefully, taking the cardigan from her. "I must have dropped it without noticing."

"No problem," said Tanya, smiling for the first time since I had seen her. She really was a beauty. When she smiled her whole face lit up.

"Well, goodbye," I said, kind of awkwardly, because she was just standing there at the car and hadn't moved away. Why? Was she looking for a tip or something? It was weird.

Yvonne had already started the engine. I gave Tanya a little wave and then went to shut the window. But suddenly she grabbed the top of the window and I had to stop.

"Is everything all right, Tanya?" I asked, somewhat alarmed.

"Yes, but wait." She glanced over at Yvonne nervously, and then took what looked like a folded white envelope from a back pocket of her skirt. "I want to give you this. Maybe you can read it if you have time."

"Oh, okay, thanks," I said, completely confused now. What in the devil's name was going on?

Yvonne revved the engine of her car and we moved off. "What did she give you?" she asked as we pulled out of the driveway.

I had the envelope in my hand. It was sealed. My instinct was not to open it there and then in front of Yvonne, but to open it later in the privacy of my own home.

"I'm not sure," I said, putting it in my bag. "I wonder if she's lonely. It must be hard for a young girl to come here from abroad and try and settle in and make friends as well as learning the language. A friend of mine has a lovely au pair called Claudine. I must introduce her to Tanya. I'm sure they'd be delighted to meet each other."

"They might not want to hang around with each other if they're trying to improve their English though – they might prefer to spend time with native speakers. I wouldn't feel too sorry for them either. Sure, don't they get free board and keep and don't have to worry about paying bills? It's not a bad life."

"I suppose," I said, leaning my head back on the headrest and closing my eyes for a bit. I didn't really feel like talking about au pairs or nannies any more. I was looking forward now to going home and getting a good night's sleep without the baby waking me, which he normally did a couple of times a night. Suddenly I was completely overcome with tiredness.

I nearly tripped over one of Baby John's dummies when I came in the door. He has about ten of them because I am so terrified of running short. The last time we went out to a supermarket and he inexplicably lost his dummy, he almost roared the place down. With all the disapproving looks I was getting (especially from old people) I practically ran from the store with my 'siren' wailing until he was red in the cheeks. By the time I got home and found another soother to pop in his gob, I realised to my immense frustration that I had forgotten almost half the groceries including Fairy Liquid to wash my full sink of dirty dishes. I sat down on the sofa, put my head in my hands and burst into tears. Of course, looking back now I realise that I was suffering from severe mummy-brain which is a condition that affects sleep-deprived mummies and especially sleep-deprived single mummies.

I was putting on the kettle to make myself a sobering cup of tea when I suddenly remembered the envelope that Tanya had thrust at me. I sat down and opened it tentatively. I'm really not sure what I expected to read in the letter but I was shocked to see such a brief hand-scrawled message.

Please help me! Tanya

Her mobile number was also written on the note.

I felt my blood run cold. I sat up straight and stared at it. What was wrong with her? Was she in danger? My imagination suddenly started running riot. Was Joanne keeping her prisoner in her house? Perhaps there was a dungeon at the bottom of the house? Maybe Joanne's husband was keeping her as a sex slave? I felt my imagination running away with me. I tried to envisage Joanne's husband. I had only met him once, briefly, when he had opened the door at Joanne's first book-club hosting. He had seemed a pretty innocuous fellow, polite but nothing to write home about. He was of slim build with rather narrow eyes – and had he a moustache? I couldn't quite remember.

Steady on there, Kaylah, I said to myself. As if they have kidnapped her! Joanne and her husband were perfectly reasonable and respectable middle-class folk. They would be the last people you could imagine being involved in something sinister. Maybe this girl, Tanya, was an aspiring actress, a bit of a drama queen.

Feeling very confused, I dialled the number. It rang once and then cut out. So I tried again.

"Hello?"

The voice was barely audible. I could hardly hear it.

"Hello, Tanya? It's Kaylah here. Is everything okay?"

"Yes, but I cannot really talk right now, sorry. But is it possible for me to come to your house tomorrow afternoon? Maybe you can help me?"

"Sure," I said, feeling fairly bewildered. "That's no problem at all. I'll do whatever I can."

I proceeded to give the girl my address over the phone, and we arranged for her to come at twelve midday. She thanked me and abruptly hung up. I found myself rubbing my right temple in confusion. What in the world had that been all about?

14

I was in a baby and maternity shop in the Dundrum Town Centre one day buying John some little white vests for the summer. The girl serving me was quite obviously pregnant so I asked her when she was due.

"Seven weeks, now," she beamed. "I'm looking forward to it, although I know I'll miss being pregnant. It's such a lovely feeling."

I smiled and nodded at her but I just couldn't relate to her at all. I had hated every waking minute of my pregnancy. I was ridiculously emotional throughout the whole nine months. I remember once walking past a dead bird and bursting into tears. The poor little bird, I thought, sobbing all the way down the street. That's how silly I was. When I wasn't snivelling into a tissue I was throwing up all over the place. I even started carrying a plastic bag around because I simply couldn't walk past a petrol station, a chipper or somebody smoking a cigarette without puking.

Sometimes there wasn't even time to fish the plastic bag from my pocket and I had to throw up over the nearest wall or into the nearest bush. Now that was toe-curlingly embarrassing, especially around Christmas time when I'm sure passers-by thought I'd had one too many the night before and tut-tutted to themselves as they hurried on by.

Some women say they bloom during pregnancy and this girl behind the counter was obviously a very good example of that, but I personally found the whole experience blooming awful to be quite honest. I slept approximately two to three hours a night throughout the entire duration. My baby's head was in an awkward position underneath my ribcage which made it really uncomfortable for me to sleep. I had constant hiccups too, and awful heartburn. Also, why don't they tell you about having to wee every five minutes?

I used to look in the mirror and not recognise the creature looking back at myself (well, I still do). A couple of months into the pregnancy I remember thinking I looked like Garfield's sister. My bloated face was huge and I couldn't blame that on the pregnancy, could I? The baby grows nowhere near the face! I'd put on so much weight even my pregnancy clothes didn't fit towards the end.

They say you forget all about your pregnancy after you give birth, but don't believe all you hear. You so don't forget. Yes, I'm the happiest, proudest mother on earth but I would have preferred to find my baby under a cabbage like my mother found me, apparently.

I met an old man recently in the park who admired my little boy and asked his age.

"Just over six months," I said.

"Time for another one?" he suggested with a twinkle in his eye.

I shuddered involuntarily. "God, no. No chance of that."

As soon as I'd said it I regretted it. The man seemed shocked by my firm answer. I almost went on to explain how I'd remained celibate since my child's conception but thought better of it. Sometimes there's such a thing as too much information. Which brings me to my point. My point is that pregnancy is a very private experience, when your body becomes a safe house for a growing life. Once you conceive, this little life takes over, disrupting your sleep, your social life, your sex life, your career, everything basically. It's not easy but you just let nature take over. If you're like me you go into hibernation for a while, nesting, as you figure out how to prepare for your whole life to turn upside down as it inevitably will.

But although it's a private, personal experience, everyone else seems to think it's very much their business. Even strangers in the street. I remember being in one baby shop and the assistant asked me whether I'd had a vaginal delivery or a Caesarean in a really loud voice. Now maybe I'm a little more conservative than most people but I honestly don't think people that you've just met should be asking you those kinds of questions.

I tossed in the bed, yawning loudly. It had been a long, sleepless night. John had cried and cried and cried. I had cried too from exhaustion and from the sheer helplessness I felt at not being able to help him. I couldn't bear to think of my little angel being in pain from his teeth.

His two little cheeks were flushed bright red and he also had nappy rash. I bathed him several times during the night and I drank coffee to keep me awake as he chomped his gums on the bottle.

In the morning I woke with a sudden jolt. I had an appointment somewhere but I couldn't think where. Then it suddenly hit me. Oh yes, Tanya was coming around. God, the mysterious Tanya. I wondered what on earth she wanted. I could hardly bear the suspense!

Even though I was dog-tired and John was cross and cranky, I still made an effort to look somewhat normal for Tanya's visit. I even found myself putting on make-up – something I don't really get around to doing these days. I also half-heartedly brushed my mane of long hair and applied a coat of lipstick.

She was bang on time. I opened the door and welcomed her in. She was all smiles and fresh-looking in a crisp white shirt, fitted denim jacket, beige slim-fit trousers and black-patent high heels.

She sat down on my couch, after having bent down to give John a kiss in his cot, and then refused my offer of a cup of tea or coffee.

"Well, if you don't mind, I'll have a coffee myself," I said. "We didn't get much sleep here all night. Teething."

Tanya nodded sagely. "Bonjela."

"I know."

"And lots of it. You sit down and put your feet up. I'll make the coffee. I have the rest of the day off."

"Well, if you're sure. I think I will. I just take it black, thank you. The instant will do."

I sank into my couch gratefully for the first time that

morning and took a deep breath. I felt more relaxed now. Even John was smiling. He seemed to like Tanya. She was much friendlier today and seemed to have lost that hunted look she'd had about her last night.

She was back in a jiffy with a large mug of coffee. She sat down beside me and crossed her long legs.

"I'm sure you're wondering why I am here," she said almost casually.

"Well, I had been wondering . . ." I trailed off, watching her with interest. She was terribly slim and tall with high cheekbones and long dark lashes. Her hair which was platinum blonde was almost certainly natural. If I didn't know better I could have sworn she was a top model.

"I need to leave my employer, Joanne, as soon as possible."

"Oh?" I sat up straight and wide-eyed.

"Yes, it's very urgent. I need to get away from her and her family. I don't like living there. Actually, that is an understatement. I hate living there. This is my first day off in three weeks even though I'm supposed to have a day off every week."

I sat up straight. "Only one?"

"Yes. Sundays. But every Sunday there is something."

"What do you mean?"

Tanya turned her palms to the ceiling. "Well, there's always some excuse. Like last Sunday one of the children was sick so Joanne asked me to stay at home and mind him when she took her daughter into town shopping. The week before there was a christening down the country and they said I had to go to help them mind the children. I shared a triple hotel room with the kids. There is always something. They treat me like a slave."

"That's outrageous," I said, feeling genuinely shocked. "You should have two days off every week. That's standard."

"I know. That's what they say at the Secret Nanny Club."

"The what?"

"It's an online club where all of us nannies exchange horror stories. Even though my job is awful it's not as bad as some others. You would be shocked at what goes on in this country."

I raised an eyebrow. I wasn't sure whether I wanted to hear more. However, I found myself leaning towards Tanya quizzically.

She lowered her voice dramatically, her pupils dilating as she continued, "One girl I know worked for two accountants and their kids. They were nudists and took the girl to a nudist colony for two weeks in Greece. She didn't have to take off all her clothes but they used to force her to pay volleyball with them when they were naked and then sit down with them and have picnics. She didn't know where to look."

"No way."

"Oh, yes! And another girl discovered a secret camera in her shower room where somebody was watching her washing herself. It turned out to be the children's father!"

"What? You are joking!"

"I certainly am not. And do you know something else? Another girl's passport was taken from her and locked in the family safe so she could not go home until her full year was up."

"I'm sure it must be illegal to do that!" I found myself gasping. "Are you sure all these stories are actually true?"

"Well, of course I am not one-hundred-per-cent sure," said Tanya with a shrug. "And I have no proof. But why would people tell lies? I have shocking stories of my own after all! I tell them about Joanne and her husband Willie. Willie walks around naked except for socks and a purple G-string."

"A G-string?" I was shocked and suddenly I didn't want that image in my head. How would I ever look him in the eye again?

"Yes, he always wears G-strings. He even has a leopard-print one. It's disgusting."

I put my hands to my ears. "Enough!"

"I have to leave that house before I lose my mind," Tanya urged. "You need to rescue me. Joanne has me working day and night – even on my hands and knees scrubbing!"

I shook my head. "I can't believe anyone would be that uncaring. I mean, she never struck me as a particularly warm person but – but really, that kind of behaviour is selfish and even cruel."

"Listen," said Tanya, gazing at me with huge imploring eyes. "I know you don't know me and I'm forcing myself into your home here. But I heard you say last night that you don't have childcare and that you need it. I am not looking for much money and I work very hard."

I gulped. This had all come about so suddenly. "Well, it is true that I –"

"Can you please give me a chance? I promise I won't let you down and I will keep your place so clean you will be able to eat off the floor. You can trust me to look after John safely when you are in work. I really need to stay here and learn English so I can be a translator and earn a good wage and be happy. I can't afford to pay rent somewhere and I need to save money. Please consider me. If you hate me you can fire me after a week."

I said nothing for a few seconds, waiting for all of this to sink in. Tanya did seem like a nice girl and I had no doubt she was a hard worker. She seemed to have had a very rough time working for Joanne and her husband. To think people like them could get away with treating a poor foreign girl like that! I worried that if I took Tanya on it would be very awkward at the next book-club meeting. The other ladies would be curious to know whether I had found the right au pair. I would probably have to choose between Tanya and the book club. I decided that I would cross that path when I came to it. I didn't want to lie to anybody, especially not Joanne.

I fiddled with the ring on my little finger. Okay, so what did I have to lose? Well, nothing really (except the book club). It was a bit of a no-brainer when I thought about it. After all, I was looking for somebody to mind John and Tanya was looking for a live-in au pair job. I had everything to gain, hadn't I? I took a deep breath and then stood up.

"Okay, come on then, I'll show you the spare room. I hope you like it."

15

I found myself sitting in Sheelagh's homely kitchen the following morning having tea and a freshly baked muffin. I couldn't wait to tell her all my news. Sheelagh was such a good listener and her house was so cosy, warm and welcoming. She was predictably shocked when I told her that Samira had left suddenly, and that I already had moved in a new au pair.

"That quickly?" she asked, all agog.

"Yes, I know! Can you believe it? Probably not. I can hardly get my own head around it myself. The whole thing is very surreal. You couldn't make it up."

"So what's this new girl like then?"

"Okay, where do I start?" I was delighted to have somebody else to talk to. Sheelagh was in the same boat as myself being a single mum, and unless you're one yourself it's hard to imagine how difficult it is coping on your own. "Tanya is from the Ukraine and she is absolutely stunning. I don't know why she wants to be an au pair to be honest. She should be on the screen. But she's lovely and I'm sure she'll be kind to John."

"We must introduce her to Claudine."

"Yes, I do hope they can meet up and become friends. It's a shame that Claudine and Samira didn't get to become friends, but hey, such is life . . ."

The door opened at that minute. In came Claudine with little Lisa, who looked as cute as a button, in her arms. She came straight over to me and air-kissed both my cheeks.

"It is so nice to see you again, Kaylah. Your hair is lovely. Did you get it done?"

Actually I had just got it blow-dried and I was delighted that somebody had noticed. Now that Tanya was there I could start doing 'me' things again.

"Thanks for noticing, Claudine. I actually got it done this morning to give me a bit of a lift. It's not like I'm even going out anywhere to show off my blow-dry."

Sheelagh sighed and ran a hand through her own curly hair. "You're making me feel guilty. I really should do something with my unruly locks. I might treat myself on my birthday."

"When's that?"

"Next Monday. Actually, speaking about my birthday, I was thinking of going out for a couple of drinks. Would you be interested in joining me?"

"Of course!" I brightened. That sounded like a good idea. It seemed like ages since I'd gone out anywhere besides the book club.

"Excellent! I was thinking of Finnegan's in Dalkey? I

haven't been there in ages and it's one of my favourite pubs. I'll rope in a few of the girls. Does Saturday week suit?"

"Yes, that sounds great. I'll need to ask my mum to baby-sit though because I give Tanya the weekends off."

Sheelagh gave a little sigh. "You're lucky to have your mum to help out."

I found myself shifting a little uneasily in my seat. I didn't like to probe but I wondered if Sheelagh's parents were still alive. She had never mentioned them.

"Mum's okay," I said, "and I'm very grateful for her help." I wasn't about to tell her how I had to flee my mother's house during my pregnancy after the 'illegitimacy' slur.

At this point Claudine excused herself, saying she felt that Lisa could do with a nap. I accepted another cup of tea from Sheelagh and sank back into my cushioned seat.

"Were you always close to your mother?" Sheelagh asked.

"Truthfully, no," I admitted. "But I had a happy enough childhood. My father lost his labouring job through injury when I was a kid and my mother got a nursing position in a hospital in another part of the city which meant we had to move and myself and my sister had to leave the school that we attended. That was hard, you know, saying goodbye to all my friends. My parents sold our nice house and we rented another house near her work which wasn't as nice, and I found it quite difficult to make new friends in my new school. I just threw myself into my studies then and got enough points to study science at UCD."

"Is your father still alive?"

"Sadly he passed away five years ago. I miss him every day. I chat to him late at night and I hope he's up there listening to me. I believe that he is always looking out for me. I would have loved him to meet little John. John looks a bit like him. He has the same big brown eyes."

"I'm sorry for your loss."

"Thanks . . . and how about you? Are your parents around?"

"I don't know," said Sheelagh matter of factly. "I know that sounds strange but I haven't had any contact with them for two years now. I presume somebody would have contacted me if they were dead, but I honestly don't know where they are or what they're doing. Nobody has been in touch and I'm an only child."

I was completely stunned by her answer. I looked at her and suddenly she looked different. The bubbly smile had disappeared and I could see the sadness etched in her eyes.

"Sorry," she said. "I'm sure you find that shocking, but I was left with no choice. My mother abused me all her life and my father was an enabler. I was fond of my dad like you were of yours but he turned a blind eye to the abuse and he's devoted to my mum so when I went no-contact on her, I had to include him too. Sad, I suppose, but I've moved on now."

"No contact at all?" I said in a small voice as I tried to imagine no contact whatsoever with my mother. For all the friction there was often between us, I think I would be lost!

"No contact at all. No birthday cards, Christmas

cards, phone calls or texts. No nothing. I never even told her that she has a granddaughter."

"That's very sad."

"It's sad but you reap what you sow. She beat me every day of my childhood so she can't expect me to forgive and forget. It's not simple to just banish painful memories like that. The beatings stopped when I was sixteen but the verbal abuse, the constant put-downs and the belittling comments continued right up until my mid-thirties. But I'm in therapy now and things are getting better."

I sipped my tea. Sheelagh had knocked me for six. For such a bright, friendly woman, she seemed to have endured a rotten past. You never knew with people, did you?

"My friend, Sally, once went no-contact with an ex of hers," I said. "He dumped her on a whim and instead of trying to win him back or get answers from him or obsessing over him like she'd done with other boyfriends, she just deleted his number, and blanked him every time she saw him. She wouldn't respond to any form of contact with him and even blocked him on Facebook. It really worked I have to say. He came crawling back."

Sheelagh grimaced. "But I'm not doing this to win my mother back or to have her crawling back or whatever. This isn't a game unfortunately. I don't want her in my life telling me I'm not a good mother and that I couldn't hold onto my husband, because that's exactly what she would say. I was never good enough and I wasn't allowed have an opinion of my own. My feelings were always simply dismissed. I had to let her go, to save myself. You can never change a narcissist and it's a waste of time to even try."

"Wow, and I thought I had an overbearing mother. I mean, mine can be an awful pain and downright nasty sometimes but I couldn't imagine just shutting her out of my life like that. My sister, Ger, doesn't have much to do with my mum though – she just gets on with her own life."

There was a pause for a while. Not a prolonged pause, but a pause as we both dwelled on our own thoughts.

Then Sheelagh spoke up again. "You know, I'm sure most people couldn't imagine just cutting a family member completely out of their life, but it is an awful shock when you finally realise your mother doesn't love you and never did." She said this with no kind of bitterness whatsoever. There was just a resigned acceptance about her situation. "However, I decided a while ago not to continue being a victim. I didn't have a childhood but I want to enjoy my life from now on. My aim for the future is to be the best mother I can be to Lisa and not let the destructive cycle continue."

A lot of what Sheelagh was saying was making sense. I admired her strength. Here she was in strange country with no contact from her parents and an estranged husband, and in spite of her harrowing childhood she was so fantastically strong. Her outlook was so positive and she radiated goodness.

"By the way," she brightened suddenly, "you'll be glad to know that on your excellent advice I contacted three local shops to see if they would take a small order from me to try my cakes out, and guess what?"

"What?"

"Two of them agreed! I'm over the moon about it!"

"Oh my God, that's fantastic news, Sheelagh. Well done, you!"

"Well, I might not have done it if you hadn't suggested it. Now the orders are very small – just some cupcakes, scones and muffins, but if they sell the shops have promised to re-order so that's exciting."

Her enthusiasm was intoxicating. I was so delighted for her. She deserved the business and I was sure it would take off. Sheelagh's baking was to die for.

Claudine was back in the room. "Are we celebrating Sheelagh's good news?" she asked with good humour.

"Yes, isn't it exciting?"

Sheelagh smiled. "I couldn't do it if I didn't have Claudine to help me with Lisa. You know what it's like trying to do everything yourself."

"I do indeed," I nodded. "It was so hard before I got Tanya. When Samira left us suddenly I was rightly stuck. But what could I do? She was homesick and wanted to go home so that was that."

Claudine turned to me with a look of surprise on her face. "But Samira didn't go home," she said. "She's still in Ireland, working for another family. I'm in touch with her on Facebook."

She could have knocked me down with a feather with this startling news. I was dumbfounded. Samira hadn't gone home to Bosnia? She was still here? God Almighty, I felt like a right fool.

"I had no idea that she went to another family," I said in a small voice. "Wow, okay. That's a revelation." I was stumped. "But no worries, I hope she's happy where she is now. It might have suited her to work with older children."

"Yeah, maybe," said Claudine, blushing slightly. "I'm sorry. I thought you knew. She met a lady at the mummy and baby yoga classes who offered her a job and promised to pay her a little more than you."

Sheelagh gasped. "Oh my, I can't believe somebody went and poached your au pair! How brazen of them! And it's all my fault for recommending the damn yoga classes."

"No, it's fine, honestly, it's just fine. Nobody is to blame. She wasn't right for us and Tanya's with us now so it's all worked out fine for everyone."

I forced a smile but deep down I was stung. Samira had made me look like an idiot. Why couldn't she just have been honest and say she was going to another family instead of feeding me that complete bull about homesickness?

When I got home later Tanya had the place looking spick and span and had even put flowers on the kitchen table to brighten the place up. I felt like hugging her and planting a big kiss on her cheek. It was like I had died and gone to heaven the day Tanya came to live with us. I was sure that my guardian angel up there or maybe my dad had sent her to me to help me get my life back on track. She was up first thing every morning, had the kitchen polished, the floor swept, the bathroom spick and span, and John up, dressed, fed and watered before the postman had even arrived.

She had an abundance of enthusiasm and fun.

Nothing was ever too much for her. Baby John adored her and she doted on him too. Tanya would skip off to the park with him before noon every day, and then pick up the groceries on the way home. She had a permanent smile on her face, always looked fresh and as pretty as a picture and was unfailing in her goodwill. What amazed me even more was that she was always thanking me rather than the other way around. As though I was doing her some kind of favour!

There was no tension in the house whatsoever. If I needed some time by myself Tanya seemed to instinctively know and would take John out for little walks or else play with him on his play mat in the sitting room. She kept telling me over and over again that she was so grateful for her new job and that she was no longer exhausted from having to mind Joanne's children, tiptoe around her cranky husband and slave away with the household chores. She even said she didn't need Saturday and Sunday off but I insisted. I wanted to treat her as well as possible. I think if you treat people well you get back what you put into the relationship . . . well, unless you're dealing with the likes of Samira . . . or Bernadette . . . or Sally . . . or Clive . . . But one thing's for sure, nobody stays somewhere where they are undervalued. Not in the long run anyway.

I asked Tanya if she would like to go to English classes. Her English was really good as it was but lots of au pairs go to classes and it's a nice way to meet friends in a foreign country.

But Tanya seemed surprised at the question. "Classes?" She looked at me blankly.

"Well, yes, I mean, you won't learn any English from

John and I know you said your dream was to be an interpreter one day. I'm sure you were learning a lot more from Joanne and all her kids. You would probably find the classes sociable too."

But despite my encouragement Tanya didn't seem that keen. "I have my own friends already," she said. "I always meet the girls from the Secret Nanny Club when I'm out and about. So I'm not at all lonely. Honest!'

I decided to quietly drop the matter. If she didn't want to go to classes she didn't want to go to classes and it was none of my business. However, I did think it was strange for somebody who wanted to become a professional translator not to want to go to English classes. I decided not to dwell on something that didn't really concern me. It was time to focus on my own life now and try and get back into some kind of routine.

I took a deep breath and phoned my boss, Creea, to say I was ready to come back to work part-time in the office, in addition to working from home. I had thought she'd be pretty pleased to hear from me as Sally had emailed me on Facebook several times to say they were snowed under with work and extremely short-staffed at the moment. But I was disappointed to find her response was lukewarm at best.

"When exactly are you coming back?" she asked without even enquiring about me or Baby John. She sounded harried and fretful.

"I was thinking of next Monday?"

"Monday, *hmmm*, well, that might be a problem because we have two interns here at the moment filling in for you and they take turns at using your desk and computer so we don't have a desk for you right now. Monday week would suit better. Then we have our monthly meeting and you can get straight back into things."

"Oh, okay!" I tried to sound upbeat.

"By the way, did you get the group email I sent this morning?"

"This morning? Oh no, I'm afraid I haven't even opened the laptop at all today. Was it important?"

"Well, it's not great news to be honest, Kaylah. Everyone here at the magazine has been told we need to take a five-per-cent pay-cut with immediate effect. I hate to be the bearer of bad news but the orders come from the top. We're all in the same boat . . . magazine sales are way down . . . you know yourself . . . it's tough out there."

"I know," I said in a small voice, feeling crushed. "I know it is."

Then I thanked Creea for her call even though I was the one who had called her and I said goodbye. I think I may have also said that I was looking forward to coming back to work but I'm not sure. It's all a bit of a blur now. I remember feeling dizzy anyway. I was really struggling as it was. How on earth was I going to be able to pay Tanya and buy nappies and food for the three of us? How was I going to afford my electricity bills and health insurance bills which were already crippling me? Winter was looming and it was going to be a harsh one, there was no doubt about that.

"Is everything okay?" Tanya asked, looking concerned. She had Baby John in her arms and her head was slightly cocked to one side. How did she know I had just got bad news? That girl was able to read my mind so much it was uncanny.

I sat down on the sofa. I was almost shaking. "Not really, but it will be fine."

"Would you like a cup of tea?"

I smiled in spite of myself. Tanya may have been foreign but she had already grasped the Irish way of life. No matter how bad things are, or how many problems we have, we always manage to find the solution in a nice hot cup of tea.

"Thanks, Tanya. I would love one."

She handed my baby to me and I cuddled him close. He smiled at me, so full of trust and love. I knew I had to cope with this bad news.

But I was already stretched to the limit financially and there was no point asking John's dad for any maintenance as when I had phoned him to tell him we were having a boy after having my twenty-week scan, he told me that he wasn't interested, and that he had a lot on his mind after being forced to take a fifty-per-cent pay cut at work. He also told me that he was now sharing a bedsit with his brother as he could no longer afford the rent on the swanky bachelor pad.

Everybody that I knew was up to their neck in debt and there didn't seem to be any shining light at the end of the tunnel. Tanya was back with the tea and a biscuit which she placed on the coffee table in front of me.

"How bad is it? Or should I not ask? Tell me to mind my own business if you like."

I gave a wry smile. "It's bad but it could be worse," I said. "I have a lot to be thankful for. I have my health and I am mother to a beautiful boy. I shouldn't really complain. It's just that things have not been good for me financially since I went part-time in the magazine and now they're looking even worse. I've been asked to take a significant pay-cut."

Tanya didn't bat an eyelid. "I see," she commented without any emotion whatsoever. "But you won't starve this winter, will you?"

"I'll try my best not to," I sighed. "But the price of everything is going up and wages are going down. I don't know how the government expects us to keep going like this."

"At the village where I come from people survive on very little," said Tanya thoughtfully. "When I was growing up the only designer clothes we saw were in foreign magazines. I wore my sisters' clothes and never got anything new. We got one pair of shoes a year if we were lucky."

"I suppose we were spoiled here in Ireland the last few years," I said, putting John back down on his play mat. "We all thought we were rich. Everyone was telling us that we were rich. And we weren't." I sipped my tea. It was comforting.

"Some people are rich, or else they act like they are very rich. Take some families in America or England for example," Tanya continued. "I talk to the girls in the Secret Nanny Club online and they tell me about the huge houses they work in and how the ladies wear something once and then they bin it because they don't want to be seen wearing the same thing twice."

"Well, I didn't know anyone pre-recession who was that extravagant myself. But it's true that for a while in this country we all went a bit crazy spending money that we never actually had. And the banks are mostly to blame because they gave money they didn't have to people who could never afford to give it back. We couldn't stop spending on the never-never and now we're broke. I am thankful I have a job to go back to. Some of my friends who had great jobs a couple of years ago are now on social welfare."

We sat in silence for a while. I lost myself in my gloomy thoughts and Tanya cradled John, rocking him until he drifted off to sleep. I wondered if I could possibly do anything – anything – to boost my income. But unfortunately fashion stylists weren't exactly in hot demand in the middle of a recession. There was a time I could have demanded a fee of a couple of grand just to take out some clothes from a shop and dress models for a day in a fancy location. Not any more. Now the same clients wanted you to do the same work for half the amount they used to pay. Even very big clients such as major clothing companies now approached you and asked you to email them your fee. They would get all the known stylists around town to put in their respective fees and then, in most cases, choose the cheapest one. It really was dog eat dog in this industry. Or stylist eat stylist.

I hadn't seen many of the stylists since giving birth to my son. We weren't friends as such but we all knew each other socially of course because we would bump into each other regularly at press days, or be seated next to each other in the front rows of prestigious fashion shows. The older stylists who were well established and had their own clients for years always seemed standoffish and reluctant to welcome any new kid on the block. The stylists guarded their clients like trained Rottweilers. You could almost see them baring their teeth if you stepped onto their territory. Most of the stylists were female although you did get the odd male who was as bitchy as or even bitchier than them.

When I started out as a freelance a few years ago there were only a handful of stylists on the scene but now it seemed like every second woman in the country was a stylist or at least had aspirations to become one. The market was getting saturated and the competition for clients was fierce. You needed to network like hell to remain at the top of this cut-throat industry and I was at a big disadvantage living out in Bray like a hermit.

You see, anyone can be a stylist. You don't need to have a qualification. All you need is a phone and an email address to get started. I have a degree in science which is about as far removed from being a stylist as you can get. I just fell into the whole styling thing actually. I had always assumed I'd go into research and maybe find a cure for something important but then I shared a flat with a girl I met online called Emily. Emily was a stylist and got great discounts on fashionable clothes and always seemed to be invited to celeb-filled fashion shows where people guzzled champagne like mother's milk. She regularly appeared on TV talking about the season's trends and every second day the postman would arrive with a parcel containing a bag, or a scarf or a bracelet or something nice. I used to hate the way the only post I got were brown envelopes and wished I could have a job like Emily.

Emily, despite her wonderfully glamorous job, was

quite a lazy thing though. Often she would hit the town after the fashion shows and wouldn't get home until all hours. Then she would be all hungover in the mornings, curled under the duvet with the curtains closed. She would beg me to go to the shop to get her some Lucozade and sweets, and then she'd bribe me to take clothes back to shops. Half of Emily's life seemed to be spent taking clothes from shops for fashion shoots and then delivering them back again after the shoots. Some of the shops were very strict about wanting the clothes returned to them the very next day. So if Emily wasn't feeling the best, she would ask me to go to the shops with the clothes and sign them back in again. After a while the shop girls started to recognise me and some even believed that I was the stylist!

Then one day I had to go to an upmarket boutique to give back a luxurious coat that Emily had borrowed for a photo shoot and the shop manager asked me if I would be attending their fashion show later that evening. I said I would love to but I hadn't received an invitation. Immediately she put my name on the guest list. I went along that night with my mother and we were put in the front row with a glass of champagne in our hands and treated like celebrities. I watched in awe as the glamorous models sashayed up and down the catwalk and I also tried not to get too excited as I spotted some high-profile celebrities sitting opposite me showing off their designer bags and shoes.

My head had been turned. The night of the fashion show had definitely been one of my best nights out so far and it had been completely free. Even better, on our way out, my mother and myself were handed goodie bags containing mini-perfumes, a snipe of champagne, some chocolate and a scented candle. We were like two kids after Santa had arrived, giggling on the bus home as we rummaged excitedly through the bags. I had been due to start work in a laboratory the following week but I decided not to take the job. I was going to be a freelance stylist just like Emily. I too wanted to start living the dream.

Soon afterwards I started approaching magazines and newspapers with ideas for shoots. The most important thing about being a stylist is that you have a contacts book because the shops, and especially the higher-end shops, are extremely strict about whom they lend their clothes to. But as Emily's unpaid 'assistant' I already knew a lot of the shop staff by name at this stage. I remained on their good side by always returning the clothes in impeccable condition without so much as a lipstick stain or a thread pulled and more often than not I dropped a little thank-you present, such as a box of chocolates, in to the staff afterwards. I didn't just sign the clothes in and out abruptly with no conversation either. Instead I took my time to chat to the staff and become friendly with them. That way I found out about all the upcoming style and fashion events. I started getting invited to more and more champagne events and I even got my photo taken at a few of them. When I started appearing in the social columns in society magazines I was chuffed with myself. Imagine! I could be spending all day in a lab wearing a white coat and goggles, but here I was being treated like some kind of celebrity.

But then one night I was out at a fashion show and I bumped into Emily unexpectedly. "What are you doing here?" she asked suspiciously, not looking one bit pleased to see me. "I thought you were supposed to be going out with your mum tonight?"

"I am here with my mother," I explained light-heartedly. "She's just in the Ladies' touching up her make-up in case we get our photo taken. It's a good night, isn't it? Did you enjoy the show? The clothes were fabulous."

She made a face and then nudged her friend who had pink hair and was wearing a fussy pussy-bow blouse, sequined hot pants and the highest pair of wedges I'd ever seen in my life. "This is Suzie," she said.

Suzie nodded at me but as her eyes were quite bloodshot I wasn't even sure that she could see me properly. I wondered how she was able to stand, never mind walk, in those ridiculous sky-high shoes she was wearing.

"She's my flatmate," Emily said to Suzie. "You know, the one I was telling you about," she added cryptically.

Suzie said nothing. She seemed kind of out of it. Then Emily linked her arm and led her away purposefully to the bar.

The encounter made me feel very uncomfortable indeed. Emily had made me feel like an annoying gatecrasher. I didn't really understand it. I mean, she had always been happy for me to carry the heavy bags of clothes back to the shops where I sometimes had to wait around for an age to get a staff member to check all the garments meticulously before signing them off. She was happy to ask me to take that brand-new designer shirt that had got make-up on the collar during a photo shoot to a specialist dry cleaner while she lay on the couch with a hangover, eating crisps and watching Jeremy Kyle, but she had never once invited me to any fashion shows, and now that I had managed to get invited to some myself, she seemed furious. I realised then that she had just been using me to do her dirty work. She wanted the name and the fame of being a stylist but she didn't want to do the horrible part which was carrying the bags around all day until you felt like your arms were going to come out of their sockets.

I began hiding my invitations as soon as I got them from the postman. It was ridiculous but I knew Emily was annoyed that I'd started going to glamorous events. As far as she was concerned she was supposed to be the one with the exciting job in the apartment and I was supposed to be the boring nerdy one.

After some soul-searching I plucked up the courage to approach a well-known women's magazine and offered to work as an assistant stylist. I didn't hear anything back for a week or so and then I phoned the editor to see if she had got my CV. I was afraid it might have got lost or something.

"Who is this?" The woman sounded harried on the phone. "Are you a stylist?" she asked, or rather barked at me. "I'm up to my tonsils right now. Are you free tomorrow to give a hand?"

I was so stunned I said that yes, I was free. I didn't have time to tell the woman that I hadn't had much experience and that I was just starting out as a freelance. Anyway, she didn't seem a bit interested in anything other than the fact that I was available to start as soon as possible.

She admitted to me that the in-house stylist in the magazine had just walked out unexpectedly, leaving chaos behind. Now there was nobody to organise that month's fashion shoot and time was of the essence. The theme was student chic. Did I think I could do that? Was I capable and confident enough to turn everything around at the speed of lightning? She said that I had to book a model, but that their in-house photographer would do the shots in his city-centre studio.

My head was spinning. Talk about being thrown into the deep end without a paddle. I found myself nodding in agreement to all her demands. Basically, I should arrive with a selection of at least eight different outfits. The shoot was to be a five-spread job. Think young and fun and preppy. Nothing too old or frumpy or stuffy. Think artistic yet slightly adventurous. Oh, and could I organise a make-up artist? Think minimum make-up. No false eyelashes or false anything. Forget anything that might be considered trashy. No orange whatsoever on any part of the skin. And could I also organise hair? Hair! At less than twenty-four hours' notice? Oh sure, no problem. Just leave it to me.

As I put down the phone I was almost shaking with a mixture of fear and excitement. I wasn't a real stylist, not by any stretch of the imagination, but I had just secured myself a booking for a high-end glossy magazine. This was a chance in a lifetime for me. It was surreal! Of course I had helped Emily out on many occasions but could I do it myself? And get paid for it? How much money should I even invoice for? Did I have the confidence to ask for the going rate even as a rookie? But then I didn't have much time to agonize over my new assignment. I had less than a full day to get organised. I needed to hit the ground running.

I rang around a few of the well-known hairdressers to see if I could get a hairstylist to come out to the studio for free. The first three salons were too short-staffed to help out but the fourth hairdresser said they would send out a junior stylist for free in exchange for a credit. I nearly jumped for joy. I knew from Emily anyway that magazines rarely pay for anything and expect to get everything for free, and my budget for this job was just two hundred euro for a model so I literally would have had nothing left to pay for extras. After a few more anxious phone calls I got hold of the owner of a make-up school who was eagerly looking for business. She said she would send a member of her team along to the shoot, and could we make sure to publish the email address and phone number of the school in the credits?

"No problem," I said, totally relieved.

I now began to feel guilty for having considered Emily lazy in the past. I had mistakenly thought that the tough part of the job was trudging around town with shopping bags pulling your arms out of their sockets. What I didn't factor in was the stress involved in co-ordinating a fashion shoot.

With only hours to go I had to find a suitable model. You would think in a city like Dublin I would have had no problem at all finding a suitable model. It would be easy, I thought. God, how wrong was I?

I went onto three different model websites and there were literally thousands of photos of models of all shapes and sizes. I didn't realise there were so many of them about.

Like, hello? Did every second female in Ireland aspire to be a model or something? Looking through all the pictures I began to feel overwhelmed. Some of the photos seemed quite old and out of date or they were too blurred to see what the girl really looked like. It was very important that my model was under twenty-one as she was supposed to be a student. I didn't want somebody too young-looking either. She had to look realistic and not a schoolgirl. I decided to hold a quick casting in town and bagged the use of a city-centre hotel for free for an hour. I then picked out a couple of girls from each website which wasn't as easy as just going onto eBay and clicking the Buy It Now button. First of all, when I phoned my preferred agency the girl on the other end of the phone told me that the two models that I had in mind were unavailable because they were on holidays. I then asked about another girl on the website.

"Oh Carla?" the girl said with a sigh, sounding rather bored. "Yeah, well, she lives in London now so she wouldn't be available at such short notice."

I found myself wondering why a model who lives in London and isn't available to work at short notice has a photo up on an Irish agency website. Then I asked for another girl that I liked the look of. She couldn't attend the casting unfortunately because she was five months' pregnant and was apparently only doing maternity fashion shoots at the moment.

At this stage I was practically pulling my hair out. It was the same story at nearly all the agencies. Nearly everyone I wanted to see was unavailable. The girls were either on holidays or sick, or lived abroad or had already been booked for the following day. One girl, whose picture on the agency site was stunning, turned out to be thirty years old so she was also a non-runner. Another girl had a whole arm covered in tattoos that you couldn't see in her agency shots. She wouldn't be suitable either.

Eventually I managed to get together a group of potential candidates that were available. I asked each agency to send the girls to the hotel for 4.00 p.m. so that I could make my choice. In all, twelve girls turned up for the one job. Now that might sound like I had a very tough time choosing one girl, but it wasn't like I was Simon Cowell on the *X Factor* with a pool of incredible talent to choose from. Okay, so I knew I wasn't going to have my pick of supermodels, and especially at such short notice, but some of the girls that turned up were so unprofessional that they beggared belief. A couple of them were chewing gum and looked like they hadn't even bothered washing, one was about the same height as me and I'm just over five foot, one was distinctly hungover and there was a whiff of booze and stale cigarette smoke about her, one had black roots halfway down her otherwise blonde head and the others simply did not have the look I had in mind. It taught me a very good lesson on not judging a model by the agency photos. I mean, obviously professional photos are going to make the subject look pretty fantastic but some of these images must have been Photoshopped beyond all recognition to the point of making crooked teeth into straight white ones and making cellulite, wrinkles, skin blemishes and spots completely vanish.

I was dismayed by what had turned up, but just as I was about to give up hope, one last girl arrived in through the studio door. She was a vision: tall, slim and fresh-looking with a megawatt natural smile. She was dressed simply in skinny jeans, a white T-shirt and a black blazer, and she was clean and healthy-looking with long wavy auburn hair cascading down her back. She was exactly what I wanted and I thanked heaven for sending her to me and saving the day.

Reena, as her name turned out to be, was professional, polite and utterly delightful to work with. She was patient and easy-going but also gave her all to the camera. Myself and the photographer, a seasoned snapper in his sixties called Luke, were completely bowled over by the lovely Reena. She even impressed us when halfway through the shoot she offered to go out and buy us sandwiches and coffee!

All the clothes looked lovely on her. She was so slim that everything we put on her fitted perfectly. She didn't even have to hold in her tummy! We took eight shots in total and then viewed them on Luke's laptop. It was pretty difficult to narrow the selection to just five. Reena really looked the part in all of the photos. But then she was a student herself so why wouldn't she have? She was perfect!

At the end of the day I was completely exhausted, I hadn't eaten and I was struggling to keep my eyes open. It had been fun but a very tiring day. The hairdresser, make-up artist, the model and myself had all been in the large unheated studio since 7.30 a.m. It wasn't at all as glamorous as you might think a fashion shoot would be. But it was still exciting to have been part of it all and I now felt like a real stylist rather than a mere pretender. I literally couldn't wait to see the end result in a real magazine on the shop shelves.

The best thing of all was that the editor phoned me later to say how pleased she was with the results of my photo shoot and immediately commissioned me to do another one for the following month's edition. The relief was enormous. I had been so terrified she'd think I was crap! I couldn't wipe the smile off my face for the whole day. It would be all systems go from now on. Yes, I was in business!

I remember so well the day the magazine was supposed to be out and I went to my local newsagent's first thing in the morning. I was almost shaking with excitement and anticipation as I scanned the magazine rack. But, alas, I couldn't see the magazine at all. The guy behind the till said it hadn't been delivered yet but they were expecting it in later that day. I must have made at least five trips to the shop on the same day but no luck. The magazine hadn't been seen at all. I was engulfed by disappointment. This was as bad as waiting for exam results. Actually it was worse, because when I was in school I hadn't particularly cared about exam results. Reluctantly, I accepted that I wouldn't see the magazine until the following day.

And then, when I eventually saw it the following morning, I stood in the shop with trembling hands, flicking over the pages frantically until I saw the shoot with Reena. If the magazine had been *Vogue* and the model had been Kate Moss herself I couldn't have been happier. She looked beautiful and the clothes looked amazing on her. I bought five copies, then headed off to the off-licence to buy a bottle of champagne to celebrate and hailed a taxi to my mother's house. My mum was really proud when I showed her my name in the credits. She said she was going to buy five copies of the magazine herself, including one for my grandmother. We cracked open the champagne, toasted my first ever solo shoot and then I treated my mum to a late lunch in a popular little Indian restaurant around the corner from her house.

"Well done, you! I'm so proud of you, my love," my mother said as we toasted each other again in the restaurant, this time with sparkling wine. "This is all just so exciting. How much are you getting paid for the shoot by the way?"

I cleared my throat awkwardly. "Eh . . . I'm not sure. I didn't like to ask, you know."

"What? Now, that's a mistake, Kaylah. You need to get over your shyness. If you want to work for yourself, and compete in the big bad world you've got to grow a pair."

"I know, and you're right," I said, looking down at the menu and flicking the pages absently. "It's just that I didn't want to start asking about money before I'd got the job done. I felt like I needed to prove myself. It's tough out there."

"It was always tough. Life is tough, and you have to fight for everything that's worth having."

"I'm well aware of that." For God's sake, as if I didn't know! "Anyway, the good thing is that I've been asked to do another photo shoot for the next month's edition of the magazine so I can't complain. I'm happy."

And I was happy. Walking on air. Until I arrived back

at my flat later that evening to find Emily waiting for me in the hall. She was holding a copy of the magazine in her right hand and her face was like thunder. "What the hell is the meaning of this?" She held the magazine up in the air. "I want answers and I want them *now*."

I was shocked by the look of anger in her face. I mean, I had just had a fashion shoot published and I was elated. It wasn't as though I had committed a crime or anything. But the way she looked at me accusingly was actually making me feel guilty. Maybe I should have told her I was doing it. But then again, she didn't tell me every single job she was booked for. Were we supposed to tell each other everything now? Were we now like a couple joined at the hip?

"There is no law against me doing this, as far as I am aware," I said, trying to speak calmly. I had no idea why I was being forced to justify myself. "I can't believe your reaction."

"This is my territory," she snapped, almost spitting in my face. "You are completely stepping on my toes here, Kaylah. It just isn't on."

"Sorry, Emily, but you are being unreasonable. It's not like there is a law stating that there can only be one stylist in the whole of the country. Lots of people are stylists just like there are lots of nurses and taxi-drivers out there. We're all free to do what we want. I'd have thought that you would have been happy for me."

Emily's eyes narrowed. "You obviously did not think I'd be happy," she seethed. "Or else you would have told me about this photo shoot! You went behind my back. What do you know about styling? I thought you were going to be a lab technician. You're trying to steal my life. You're like that character from the film *Single White Female*. This is outrageous!"

"But you don't even work for this magazine," I said, feeling the earlier effects of the day's happiness ebb away from me. "If you worked for them, maybe, just maybe, I would understand your reaction, but you don't!"

"I am a freelance, as you very well know," she said. "So I work with everyone and anyone that's willing to work with me. It's tough in this business to keep your head above water. I had been hoping to work for this magazine too before you came along and swiped the opportunity."

"What? That's utter nonsense," I said, defending myself. "It's not like they're only going to work with just me. Phone them up tomorrow and pitch an idea, I don't care. There's room in this town for us both."

"Yeah, well," she said, "there may be room in this town but there's certainly not enough room in this apartment for the both of us. I'm moving out. I can't deal with this any more."

I shook my head. "I honestly cannot believe you're being so dramatic."

"Can you not? Really? Well, to you this is drama, maybe. But to me, it's my entire livelihood. You learned everything about styling from me and from me alone. I trained you and you turned around and stabbed me in the back. I will never help anyone again because you get no thanks for it."

Close to tears at this stage, I nevertheless pointed out that Emily had been quite happy for me to be her practical slave for months, dragging bags around town and getting no thanks for it whatsoever. But she didn't want to hear that bit. When I was in the middle of talking to her, she started walking away from me. She disappeared into her room and slammed the door shut behind her. And the next day, true to her word, she packed up her belongings and left the place we shared together. And ever since, even though we both work in the same industry, see each other at various functions and a lot of time has passed since our infamous bust-up, we have never exchanged a single word.

16

Years ago, an auntie of mine called Kitty told me about a cruise liner she had once been on. She had taken a round-the-world trip with some of the money she had got from her husband's life insurance after he had sadly passed away.

"It was the most beautiful ship imaginable," Kitty told me, "and the service was second to none. Every cabin was assigned its own personal butler. It was actually embarrassing how much they looked after you. Nothing was too much for them. If you so much as sipped from your glass of water, the staff would top it up for you the moment you put it down."

Kitty had spent a lot of money on that cruise. No wonder the staff had been at her beck and call! She obviously tipped well too. I loved hearing the stories from the cruise and all about the characters that she had met on board. One lady on the ship was from California and had been on it for six months, probably because her family thought it was better than bundling her into a dreary nursing home. The Californian lady had been married four times but was a widow when she met Kitty. Kitty told me that the lady would arrive at dinner every night dripping in jewellery and would entertain fellow guests with wonderful tales about meetings with Hollywood stars. I was fascinated about it all, but especially about the private butlers whose sole job was to look after a single guest each. If the guest wanted the laundry done, he organised it; he made sure the cabin was full of fresh flowers; he would even come with you to the self-service buffet to make sure you didn't even have to serve yourself if you didn't want to. And he would dance with you in the evening if nobody else asked.

Now the reason I started thinking about Kitty's butler on the cruise ship was because it seemed like I had my very own butler in the form of Tanya. Okay, she didn't dance with me, but she more or less attended every whim. In fact, she was so attentive sometimes I had to ask her to take a step back. She wouldn't let me do anything. She was up well before me, and had all John's bottles made up and ready for the day, had the apartment looking like a brand-new pin, as well as having the coffee made and the eggs boiled as soon as I got up. Sometimes she would even bring me breakfast in bed. She was an absolute treasure. It was like having my very own butler although I wasn't wealthy – far from it in fact. I didn't know what I'd done to deserve this wonderful person in my home. In contrast to the last au pair who'd always looked like she was carrying the world's worries on her shoulders, Tanya smiled morning, noon and night. John adored her and I found myself feeling normal again after the whirlwind of my pregnancy and then the months since I had become a mother. I had wind in my sails now and I couldn't wait to go back to work. I knew I could trust Tanya with John and that I wouldn't be feeling guilty about leaving him behind. Well, hopefully not too guilty.

Anyway, going back to work full-time would surely help raise my self-esteem a bit. I longed to have a purpose again besides being just a mummy to John. I know that might sound awful but I really felt like I had lost myself somewhat. And while I was grateful for having found a new friend in Sheelagh, she was getting on with her baking business, and I yearned for office gossip and working to deadlines again. And I needed to get back in the office and in a position to hang on to my job. I knew that the recession had hit hard, especially in the media, and it wasn't the fun place it used to be to work. Magazines were worried sick about losing advertisers and readers, so keeping their in-house stylists happy was the least of their worries. We were very much a replaceable breed anyway. It didn't take a genius to work that out.

Tanya seemed to enjoy her nights off. She would go out late and stay out late but, no matter how long she stayed out, it never seemed to have any effect on her mood or her work the next day. She was always the same bright breezy bubbly girl from morning to night. She didn't drink alcohol, not even a drop. She told me she didn't believe that people should put their hard-earned money down their throat when all it did was make them act foolishly and then ensure they were ill the following morning. She said that her father had drunk too much when she was growing up and that he had been selfish, only thinking of himself. She said she didn't have to drink to have a good time.

The girls from the Secret Nanny Club all seemed to be great friends. Tanya never was short of company. She would spend all her evenings off with them. I told Tanya that she was more than welcome to invite the girls around to watch a DVD and have some supper for them one night, but she said that probably wouldn't happen because all the girls lived either in the city centre or the north side of the city and that Bray was a bit too far out for them to travel to. But she thanked me profusely for the offer all the same.

My father once told me that if something seemed too good to be true it usually was. And although I berated myself for it, I sometimes wondered how somebody as beautiful and as hard-working as Tanya was working in my apartment for mere pocket money. Most au pairs became au pairs to learn a language but Tanya's command of the language was excellent. She could have easily got a job in one of the top restaurants earning great tips instead of scrubbing my floors (her choice, not mine!) and changing dirty nappies. But when I said this to her, she shook her head and said she didn't want to be working in restaurants until all hours of the night serving drunks. She said she was happy living with me. She also said she liked living in Bray because of the sea and she would never be able to afford her own place in such a nice town. She told me that where she came from there was no sea, just a lake a couple of miles away, and it had always been a dream of hers to live by the sea. The way she explained it to me so simply made me wonder why I ever questioned her. I also wondered how on earth Joanne and her husband had treated this gem of a girl so badly. Really, how could they have been so cruel! Oh well, I thought, their loss would be my gain. I would treasure Tanya until the day she inevitably would want to leave and go elsewhere. I had already begun to dread that day.

Then for some crazy reason I found myself on the internet one night, looking to be distracted for a while before bed. I'm trying to stay away from eBay as it is so addictive and I always buy things I don't need from that site when I'm bored. I had gone off Facebook a bit too because people kept putting up all these inspirational quotes, and if I wanted inspirational quotes I'd spend my time visiting self-help sites. I'm not on Twitter either although everyone seems to rave about it. Maybe I'm missing out but I'm prepared to forego the pleasure. I've got an addictive personality as it is without tweeting about my mundane life to people who probably wouldn't be that interested anyway. But, for whatever reason, I found myself on this last-minute travel website and I saw a very cheap deal to the Costa del Sol for two adults – and an infant! Now I checked quickly to see if the room was a double or a twin and to my delight I saw that the deal offered a double room in a one-bed apartment and that there was a separate sofa bed in the living room. The flights were going out the following day to Malaga so I knew that if I didn't snap up the deal fast somebody else would.

My heart beating with excitement, I tiptoed over to Tanya's room and knocked gently on her bedroom door. I presumed that she was still up since the light was still on.

"Come in," she called breezily.

I apologised for disturbing her and sat down at the end of her bed. I proposed the holiday and she was initially surprised but then seemed over the moon at the suggestion.

"And you're sure you don't mind sleeping on the sofa bed?" I asked.

"Of course not! That's fine with me," she insisted. "I am looking forward to topping up my tan. I've never been to the Costa del Sol! This is so exciting."

I was over the moon. This summer had been a washout so far. I could barely afford it but I felt if I didn't feel the sun on my face soon I was going to have a breakdown. I needed to get away to save my sanity!

"Okay, I'll book it," I said. "Goodnight, Tanya. I'll chat to you in the morning."

I closed her bedroom door and then went back to my computer and booked the trip straight away. It really was an excellent deal and I was so excited about getting on a plane and escaping the dreary rain. Normally when you book a holiday you have to wait a few agonising weeks before actually going on it. But this was different. Within twenty-four hours I'd be somewhere hot. *Yippee!*

I was so glad I'd decided to get John's passport done a few weeks earlier. He looked very cute in his little baby passport photo. I placed it along with mine in my handbag. I was wide awake now and knew I wouldn't be able to go to sleep with all this adrenalin running through my veins. I took my old suitcase out from under my bed, dusted it off and started packing. Unfortunately I knew I wouldn't be able to fit into my swimsuit from my pre-pregnancy days but hopefully I'd be able to buy a nice new one over in Spain. I packed some sarongs and kaftans and a couple of pairs of elasticated gypsy skirts as well as some XL T-shirts. I packed some little T-shirts and light shorts for Baby John. Because he was under two and not taking up a seat on the plane (he'd have to sit on my lap), I wasn't allowed pack a suitcase for him too. It was a bit of a struggle trying to fit all of our clothes into a single suitcase – babies have so much equipment – but after taking out a pair of sandals and two heavy books I was finally able to push down the top of the case and zip it up.

I was so lucky that Tanya was coming on the holiday too as I don't think I would have had the courage to take John by myself.

That night I hardly slept. I was afraid that my alarm clock wouldn't go off at the time set. I had to be up early to get dressed and ready and get John dressed and ready and get us all to the Aircoach stop in Bray. We would have to allow for morning traffic so we'd need to leave ourselves a good two hours to get to the airport.

It started raining as soon as I locked the front door of my apartment. Just our luck! I pulled the hood over John's pram and we made our way to the stop. Fortunately a coach came by within ten minutes so we didn't get too wet. The driver put John's pram underneath, gave us our tickets and soon we were off. I was so ridiculously excited to be getting out of the country, away from the wind and the rain. It had been so gloomy and depressing recently. It would be nice to walk around the place in sundresses and vest tops.

The coach stopped and started a bit, picking up various travellers on the way but after O'Connell Street it was a straight run to the airport. We arrived in plenty of time and went to find our check-in desk. There were two fairly long queues of people for our holiday-operator desks but the check-in agents seemed to be going through the passengers fairly quickly and soon we were at the top of the queue.

"Aisle or window?" the friendly girl at the desk asked.

"Aisle, please," I said.

Normally, when I flew, I liked to be by the window to see out. I especially love flying into a hot foreign country when I can see the beaches on the approach, but today I had John and no doubt he would need to be changed at least once during the flight so I wanted to disturb the least amount of people.

"And could we possibly sit towards the back of the plane?" I turned towards Tanya and muttered under my breath, "There are two toilets down the back so the odds are better if we need to change John in a hurry."

She gave me a knowing wink.

It was a bit of a struggle going through security. It was normally bad enough anyway what with having to take off your shoes and your belt and put all your loose coins along with your mobile phone and laptop onto one of those tray things. But when you had a pram with you, it was even trickier. I breathed a huge sigh of relief when we had finally gone through. Now I wanted a drink!

In the past, any time I'd been at Dublin airport I had always felt as though I was on my holidays once I was past security and usually hit the bar straight away. But now as I passed the bar full of lively punters and their jars I felt a slight pang that I wouldn't be joining them. John needed to be fed and changed and I had to buy a few last-minute things in Boots such as nappies and Calpol. I had also managed to forget John's soother so I needed to buy another one as well.

I told Tanya that I'd meet her at the departure gate thirty minutes before take-off. There was no point us all hanging out of each other, and I was sure Tanya wouldn't mind browsing around the airport shops, the way I used to love to do before I became a harried mum!

After I had got John in and out of the changing area I wheeled the pram down to the boarding gate at my leisure. For the first time in my life I was well on time for a flight. Normally I would spend ages in the bookshops and time trying on perfumes, before knocking back a couple in the Irish-themed bar to soak in the atmosphere, and then rushing towards the boarding gate in a panic.

When I got to the gate even I was surprised to see I was the first to arrive. That was weird, I thought. Surely not everyone on our flight was in the bar or shopping for gifts? Then I checked the flight screens and my heart sank as I did so. Well, damn it anyway, our flight was almost three hours delayed!

There was nothing to do but wait. I got a can of Sprite out of a nearby vending machine and then sat down and sent Tanya a text to tell her the bad news.

She immediately replied saying that she knew, and

would I mind if she got her hair and nails done in the airport salon while we waited?

No problem, I texted back. I was surprised that she was treating herself. Then again, why not? She was going on holidays and I hadn't given her any notice to prepare herself. Mind you, I hadn't done anything myself apart from taking a razor quickly to both legs in the bath last night after confirming my booking. I had neither the time nor the money to buff and preen myself the way I used to!

An hour passed and when John fell asleep I wheeled the pram over to the newsagent's and bought a copy of *Hello!* to flick through the glossy pictures. I always justified spending money on magazines by convincing myself that I was doing research. I went and sat down and was halfway through reading a story on Victoria Beckham when I noticed Tanya sitting opposite me flicking through *American Vogue*. With her hair beautifully coiffed and her talons painted, she looked immaculate. I felt very shoddy in comparison in my old Dunnes Stores sundress, chipped nails and dull, lank hair – I wished that I'd got up an hour earlier this morning to wash and blow-dry it.

She looked up and smiled at me. "That was so relaxing," she said.

"I bet it was! You look great."

"I feel great. There's nothing like letting other people pamper you to make you feel like you are on top of the world. They are not very busy and we have still got a couple of hours to kill. Why don't you go off for a massage or a facial or something? I can mind John."

"Well, I think I'll just go for a little walk around the shops. Thanks, Tanya."

I took off my coat and left it with my little case and the pram. I headed for the make-up and perfume area, smiling to myself at Tanya's suggestion that I should go for a massage. Did she think I was made of money or something? Surely not? I had just about scraped enough money together for this last-minute deal for the three of us. My savings were depleted now and I wouldn't be able to get a massage for another, oh, ten years at least!

I had a fun time browsing around the MAC counters and having a look at all the new seasonal-coloured eye shadows. They looked fun but were too pricey for my purse. I tried on some new perfumes out of the sample bottles at the Elizabeth Arden counter and then I thought I'd go to Monsoon where I saw a 'sale' sign. Maybe I'd be able to pick up a cute little sunhat for John. It's funny but when you're a mum you will go without things for yourself, but rarely have to think twice about buying your child something new.

I found him a little blue-and-white cotton sunhat that you could tie in a ribbon under the chin. It was adorable and it was half price too which was even better! There were some very pretty dresses in the shop too that I would have loved to have tried on but, as I didn't have the funds for them, I didn't want to get depressed trying them on. I thought I'd better get back to Tanya and John. As I walked by the plethora of shops and bars, all looking so shiny and new and tempting, I heard my name being called.

"Kaylah?"

I swung around to face a very tall glamorous-looking couple, linking arms. I found myself squinting at both of them. At first I didn't recognise the tanned blonde woman, wearing skinny white jeans, a light blue-and-white-striped Ralph Lauren shirt and Missoni wedge sandals, but when she pushed her huge sunglasses off her face and broke into a smile, I saw immediately who it was.

"Oh, Lilly!" I threw my arms around her. "You look sensational!"

Lilly O'Dea is Ireland's top catwalk model with emerald-green eyes and thick wavy auburn hair. Her porcelain skin, with a smattering of cute faint freckles, makes her hugely popular with Irish brands. She is the current hot poster girl for all things Celtic.

She introduced me to her boyfriend, Greg. He gave my hand a firm shake. He was tall, dark and handsome and just the type of man I would imagine Lilly's boyfriend to look like. I would love a man like that, I thought fleetingly. Chance would be a fine thing.

"Are you going anywhere nice?" Lilly asked.

"Yes, I'm going to the Costa del Sol for a week," I said, suddenly feeling more dowdy than ever.

Lilly's eyes widened in delight. "Oh, really? That's where we're going too! Our friends have a place in Puerto Banus and we're going to stay with them for a few nights. We must meet you for a drink or maybe dinner some evening. Is John with you?"

I was so pleased she actually remembered my baby's name. So many people didn't and couldn't even remember what sex he was.

"I do actually. He's with my au pair at the boarding gate. Our flight is delayed."

"Oh no, how annoying! Our flight is going on time,

thank goodness. We're going Aer Lingus and hiring a car when we get there."

"Well, we're on a package holiday so we're on a special flight. It's my first time away with John so I wanted to go somewhere where there would be an Irish rep just in case. We don't have to worry about hiring cars or anything."

"Where are you staying?"

"In a hotel in Torremolinos. It's only about ten minutes' drive from the airport and it's near the sea. I don't think we'll be going out at night, but if we are I'll send you a text. Puerto Banus is a bit far though . . ."

"Yeah, it is a little far. By the way, I met Clive the other night in the Shelbourne Hotel. Himself and Jane are off to Majorca this week. He said he'd love to have taken John with him but maybe next time . . ."

She stopped when she saw the look of utter confusion on my face, followed by one of shock.

"Oh God," she said, "you didn't . . . I mean . . . Jesus!" Her hand flew to her mouth.

I felt like the entire departure lounge had started spinning around me. My head was throbbing. "Clive and your friend, Jane? Jane Dellany? The model?" My voice sounded so small and pathetic. I felt humiliated in front of this pair. There was pity and embarrassment written all over their handsome faces.

"Yes, sorry, I thought everyone knew."

I drew a sharp intake of breath and then exhaled slowly. "Not everyone. I didn't."

17

I locked the toilet cubicle door and sat down on the loo fully clothed. I was in shock. Clive had a new girlfriend? And they were going on holidays? I was absolutely shocked. I'd been thinking he couldn't pay any child support yet he was whisking away some model to the sun? Oh my God. I was so upset I was shaking. I wished I hadn't bumped into Lilly and her boyfriend. I hated the fact that they'd obviously felt so sorry for me.

They probably thought I was devastated because I still had feelings for Clive and maybe they thought that I harboured a secret notion that we might get back together in the future. But that was so far from the truth. If Clive was the last man alive I would never want to get back together with him. The thought of him touching me was enough to make my skin crawl. I couldn't stand him because of the cruel way he had treated me and his own baby son. I wasn't upset because I heard that Clive had a new girlfriend, I was upset because he hadn't given us any money for support, claiming near poverty!

Not only that, but he never even sent a text to see how John was doing. It was as though he couldn't give a rat's ass what happened to us.

I took a deep breath and tried to collect myself. I needed to calm down. I wiped an angry tear away with some toilet paper and went outside to the sink where I washed my hands in cold water and stared at myself in the mirror. I didn't like what I saw. I had got old-looking. I was haggard and unkempt.

I wondered whether Lilly and Greg had mentally compared me to Clive's stunning new girlfriend with her flat tummy and long legs. I was ashamed of myself in my elasticated dress which allowed me eat as much as I wanted to without any visible consequences. I had let myself go. I was a frump.

There and then I made a little pact with myself. I was going to take myself and my weight in hand. No more wine-o'clock once John had gone down for the evening, and no more late night snacking on things like crisps or crackers and cheese. I'd start when I got home from holiday. No more bags of home-made buttery croissants from Sheelagh – I knew she meant well but I'd have to tell her I couldn't accept them any more.

I was not going to let Creepy Clive ruin my holiday, I thought fiercely as I applied some lippy in the mirror. He had caused enough damage to my esteem already. He had ruined my pregnancy – a time which should have been a very happy one – and he had been nothing but nasty to me since John arrived. But by God, he wasn't going to be allowed to destroy my one week's holiday in so many years!

I walked back to the boarding gate like a robot. The world seemed to have blurred around me. But I wasn't going to crack. Hell, no. I had spent the last of my savings on this holiday. Once I went back to work properly it would be full on and God only knew when I'd get the chance to get away again.

"Not long now," said Tanya cheerfully when she saw me.

I was so glad she was coming on the holiday with us. If I had been going away with the baby myself I think I might have just cracked up altogether.

I sat down wordlessly.

"Are you okay?"

I turned to look at her, feigning surprise. "Of course! Why do you ask?"

"You look a little pale. Like you've seen a ghost?"

"Do I? Well, I am pale, I suppose. I'm Irish so I can't help it! But hopefully a bit of sun on my face can change that."

I picked up the magazine that I had left on the seat and started to flick through it. I needed an immediate distraction. John woke up whimpering and Tanya took him out of his pram and cuddled him on her knee. I continued flicking through the magazine but seeing nothing. I felt like I was in a daze and my mind was racing too much to be able to read.

About a hundred yards away there was a small bar with people sitting outside enjoying their drinks. I'd love a drink, I thought. Actually I need a drink, I told myself.

I looked at my watch. It was nearly one o'clock. I decided to get a drink and a sandwich. I'd just get a small beer. Or a cider. Just a half glass. No, wait a minute. I was on my holidays, I'd get a pint.

They had a good selection of freshly made doorstep sandwiches for sale. I went for the cheese-and-coleslaw one and asked for a pint of Heineken. Normally I wouldn't drink pints because I think it looks unladylike but I was thirsty.

Back at the gate John was trying to wriggle out of Tanya's arms. "He's getting restless," she chuckled.

"Oh dear, maybe we shouldn't have allowed him to sleep earlier. He'll drive us and everyone around us nuts on the flight!"

I put the pint glass of beer down at my feet after taking a large gulp. Then I took a large bite out of my sandwich. It was yummy.

"I'm sorry. I should have asked you if you wanted a sandwich, Tanya. Do you want one? They're delicious."

Tanya shook her head. "I'm trying to stop eating bread," she said, patting her stomach. "It's no good for me."

No wonder she was so slim, I thought, the self-loathing creeping back into my psyche. If only I had her discipline. Why was I so weak? I bet Lilly didn't eat bread either. Or Jane for that matter. I took another bite of my sandwich followed by another glug of beer. Why did I not have the willpower to throw the sandwich in the bin? I wasn't hungry any more. I was eating just for the sake of it.

"Are you sure you're not hungry?" I asked Tanya.

She shook her head. "I have an apple in my bag but I'm saving it for my flight," she said.

"How can you eat so little?" I wondered out loud. "I get so hungry. And once I start I can't stop! If I buy a fresh baguette I feel compelled to eat the lot. It's the same with a packet of biscuits or a bottle of wine or whatever else!"

"Of course you can stop," said Tanya. "It's just self-discipline, that's all."

That was nothing new. I knew about self-discipline. The question was, why didn't I have any? I gave a deep sigh. I had to stop feeling sorry for myself. If I needed to clean up my act and stay positive I was going to have to do that myself. Tanya wasn't going to be able to do it for me. Neither was Sheelagh or anybody else. I would start the diet tomorrow. We were going half-board in the hotel so I would just stick to fruit and vegetables. It was easier to be good when you were away. When it was really hot outside you just didn't feel like stuffing your face with fatty food. I'd just have to remember to lay off the ice-cream.

"I think they're going to start boarding soon," said Tanya, glancing at her watch. "If you like I'll start queuing with John and you can finish your beer in peace."

"Oh, there's no need. Save your legs, honestly. Our seats are pre-booked so it won't be like everybody will be fighting each other for the best seats. Relax!"

Tanya sank back into the seat. "I forgot we had arranged seating," she laughed. "You're right. There's no point in wasting our energy. We'll all get on board eventually."

For a moment I wished Tanya wasn't a non-drinker. I would have loved to buy her a beer. Then again, it was nice and comforting to know that my au pair didn't drink. It meant that I could enjoy another drink on the plane and she could be the sensible one looking after John. I felt momentarily guilty thinking such indulgent thoughts, but hey, I was on my holidays. I'd had the shittiest year ever being dumped by the father of my child and having to go it alone. And now he had found happiness with somebody else. Somebody with a flat tummy I would never have. I took another sip of my drink, enjoying the way that the bubbles were dancing into my bloodstream. I was already calmer, but I was still annoyed that Clive could be jetting off to the sun while he had led me to believe he was strapped for cash. Unless . . . unless Jane was treating him. She was a very popular model and as far as I could remember she still lived at home. She could easily afford to whisk Clive away somewhere hot if she wanted to. More fool her, I thought. Clive was just a complete user.

It looked like the flight was going to be full, I thought, judging by the queue that was getting longer by the minute. I finished my sandwich quickly and knocked back my pint.

"I'd better go to the bathroom," I told Tanya. "I can't get on a flight just having knocked back a pint or I'll be bursting. Mind my stuff, will you?"

"No problem," she said.

I raced off. I was feeling a little cheered up now with the beer warming my belly. I was going to forget about Clive. He wasn't worth a single thought. Why would I waste a week of my life or even a day thinking about somebody who didn't give a hoot about me?

When I got back I noticed that Tanya was at the top

of the queue with the pram and all of our luggage. I went and joined her. "How did you manage that?" I asked.

"Oh, they made an announcement calling for anyone with a buggy, a pram or a wheelchair to board first."

"Nice one."

We were the first to get on the little bus outside that was to take us to the aircraft. John was looking all around him with interest. It was so cute. He was probably wondering what on earth was going on, and who were all these people?

Once on the plane we settled down quickly. John began to shout a little and I noticed people glancing over in our direction with withering looks that said 'I hope he isn't going to start yelling'. I didn't blame them. After all, a few years ago that would have been me, hoping and praying I wasn't seated beside any boisterous, snotty-nosed youngster. Now I was the harassed mum terrified that my child was going to disturb everyone.

As luck would have it, nobody sat in the window seat of our aisle so the space was free. As soon as the Fasten Seat Belt sign was turned off, Tanya switched seats and sat beside the window and I put John in the seat in between us. At least we had a bit of room then. I couldn't have imagined keeping him on my knee for the entire two hours and twenty minutes of our flight.

When the drinks trolley came around, Tanya bought a black tea and asked me if I wanted anything.

"Not at all, I'll buy my own. I'm going to have an alcoholic drink anyway." Now that I'd had the taste of it I wanted more. It would help the flight go faster anyway. There was nothing more boring than being strapped into a seat for a couple of hours. Normally I would read on a plane or listen to my iPod, but I couldn't really do either of those things with John.

I ordered a vodka and orange juice and a tub of sour-cream-and-onion Pringles. I didn't want to keep drinking beer as it would bloat my tummy. And at least if I was drinking orange juice with the vodka I was getting a bit of Vitamin C into my body. At least that's what I was telling myself.

As Tanya entertained John by making his blue teddy dance on the seat rests, I slowly sipped my drink and munched on my crisps. I tried not to think about Clive but it was hard to think of anything else. The last time I had been on a holiday in the sun it had been with him. My mind jumped back to the first time we met. In sunny Croatia. I had fallen in love with him as we swam in the hotel pool, splashed in the sea and cuddled under the stars at night. Now he would be doing all that with somebody else. With a beautiful model no less. I, on the other hand, would be spending the last of my money taking his little boy and the au pair on a cheapy package holiday to Torremolinos. I would be the one putting the sun cream on John's little body every day and making sure he was kept in the shade. I was the one who would kiss him goodnight and make sure he was safe and well. I was the one who would comfort him if he woke during the night or mislaid his soother. Clive would be off clubbing every night with Jayne, probably drinking his head off, and telling her she was the most beautiful girl in the world as they made love. Just like he had done with me.

18

It only took us about ten minutes in the coach to get to our destination. The friendly Irish rep (married to a local Spaniard and sporting a deep mahogany tan to be envious of) told us that there would be a welcome meeting the following morning at eleven in the hotel lobby and wished us a good night. But we were dismayed when we took the lift to the fourth floor and found our hotel room stinking of stale cigarette smoke. It wasn't exactly the best welcome. I had to ask them at reception whether we could change and, after a lot of fussing and the man looking at his computer screen, we were eventually changed.

Actually, it was lucky that I had complained about the smell because our new room had a sea view instead of the view of the car park our original room had, and best of all we didn't have to pay any supplement for it.

It was still bright outside when we arrived and I was dying to sit outdoors somewhere and have a glass of wine.

"Can you give John a quick bath while I get changed?"

I asked Tanya as I dumped my suitcase on top of my double bed. "They should be coming around with his cot any minute now."

"Sure, no problem," said Tanya, taking off her jumper and hanging it up in the wardrobe that we would both be sharing for the week. "God, it is hot!"

"You can say that again. Thank goodness for air-conditioning. If we didn't have it I'd go out of my mind. The last time I was in the Costa del Sol it was August and I was staying in a little studio in Mijas Costa with a friend. It was about forty-two degrees and I remember having three noisy fans on in the room non-stop so I didn't get a wink of sleep the whole holiday!"

"It sounds like the holiday from hell," said Tanya, changing into a pair of denim cut-off shorts before turning on the bathwater.

"It was. And I remember having to take a shower about six times a night to cool down. It was one of those rare holidays where you end up counting the days until it's time to come home."

"I don't mind the heat too much," Tanya said while undressing John. "Luckily I have sallow skin, but you Irish need to be careful. I'm always amazed when I see people walking around Grafton Street in shorts and vest tops in the middle of March just because the sun peeps his head out."

"That's 'cos we're afraid if we don't make the most of it, it'll disappear for months. The sun doesn't visit us too much."

"But the good thing about Irish weather is you don't get mosquitos. Right?"

"Right, and we don't get cockroaches either. Actually

speaking of cockroaches . . ." I took a furtive glance around me.

"Don't worry, the room is cockroach-free. I checked already!"

"Phew! I honestly couldn't sleep at night if I thought there was one lurking about. Ugh! I'm terrified of the creatures!"

About fifteen minutes later we were ready to go out. I wore a light blue maxi dress that I had picked up in the summer sale in A-Wear. I knew that it was unlikely I'd ever get the chance to wear it with the dull weather at home so I was thrilled to be able to put it on without having to wear a cardigan over it. Tanya wore a funky black vest with diamante detailing down the middle. It showed off her amazing figure and as we walked along the street looking for a nice café she attracted more than her fair share of admiring glances. I envied her because she could wear flip-flops and her legs would still look fantastic, whereas mine would look like tree-stumps if I wore flats. I always had to wear high heels, if only wedges, to avoid looking like a little munchkin. Unfortunately combining wearing heels and pushing a pram was not always a good idea.

As we walked along the bustling streets of Torremolinos we came across a cute little tapas place which seemed to be busy, which was a good sign. If a place is busy with locals it's usually a positive sign, so we sat down at a table with the pram by our side. The wonderful thing about Spain is that families eat late at night and take their children out with them. So we didn't get any of the often disapproving stares that you got back home if you dared take a pram into a restaurant after hours. John was wide awake now which was surprising since he hadn't slept a wink on the flight. In fact he had been quite boisterous, climbing up on my knee and trying to pull the sunglasses off the people sitting in front of us. At one stage he even tried to slap one man's shiny baldy head which was mortifying. Luckily the other holidaymakers on the plane were in good spirits and seemed to think John was an amusing little baby. Thank God for that!

The young waitress at the tapas bar came quickly with the menus and bent down and gave John a big kiss on the cheek. The Spanish are very family-friendly and it really was a joy to be on my holiday at last. I tried not to think about Clive and Jane or the fact that I had no savings left in the bank now and would be taking a pay-cut at the magazine. I was going to enjoy every moment of my week away and when I got back I was determined to work very hard to make more money. I had worked three jobs as a student to make ends meet so I could do it as an adult too.

I would have liked to have ordered a bottle of wine but, as Tanya didn't drink and they didn't do half bottles in the tapas bar, I ordered a vodka and orange instead. Tanya had a Pepsi.

It was so nice to be able to sit outside and watch the many holidaymakers walk around leisurely with smiles on their faces. I sipped my drink and told myself that I should move out here. The cost of living was much cheaper than at home and everybody seemed to be smiling and in a good mood. Why did anyone ever leave? I wondered dreamily. This place was amazing.

The next morning I woke up early. At least, John woke

me up as he was shaking the bars on the cot. The sun was streaming through the window and I felt as groggy as hell. I was parched too and I had no water. Drat! I should have bought a bottle in one of the shops the night before.

I dragged myself out of bed and picked up my baby. I went out into the sitting-room area but the sofa bed was empty. That was weird. Where was Tanya? I checked the bathroom but she wasn't there either. She had her own key so maybe she went out for a walk and didn't like to disturb me. I hoped she would be okay. After all, she had never been in Torremolinos before and neither had I. Last night we hadn't seen too much so maybe she had gone to the beach this morning. The beach was about a fifteen-minute walk away. I just wished she hadn't gone without us.

Just as I was beginning to really worry about her, Tanya burst through the door with two bags full of groceries.

"Oh, my poor arms!" she said, placing the bags on the table with a thud. "They were so heavy!"

I was so relieved to see her and so delighted that she had gone shopping. I hadn't been this excited since Santa visited all those years ago. In the two plastic bags were warm croissants, fresh fruit, cheese, yoghurts, two huge bottles of mineral water and some freshly squeezed orange juice. My mouth parched and dry, I immediately reached for the water.

"Oh, thanks a million for this! I thought I was going to die of the thirst. You're an angel!"

I got a glass from the bathroom, filled it with water and knocked it back all in one go. Immediately I felt slightly better.

"I had a feeling you might be thirsty."

A wave of shame washed over me. I lowered my eyes, recalling last night. The measures in my vodka at the tapas bar had been especially generous and after that we'd gone to a karaoke bar where I'd downed a Sex on the Beach before getting up on stage and making a fool of myself trying to sing a Lady Gaga song. No wonder my head hurt this morning.

"You were funny though," said Tanya, laughing.

But I couldn't help feeling a little ashamed. That was no way to behave abroad. I wasn't on an 18-30 holiday. I was a mum with a baby. How could I ever have considered taking poor little John to a karaoke bar until 11.00 p.m. when he should have been tucked up in bed with his little teddy fast asleep? So much for my promise to turn my life around! Now that I was hungover, I knew I'd be stuffing my face with junk all day. I reached for one of the croissants and wolfed it down. It tasted so good.

"Listen, I was thinking of taking John for a little walk, maybe down to the beach? I saw a little shop when I was out earlier, selling buckets and spades. I know he's very young still but he might enjoy watching me making castles in the sand. What do you think? You could close the curtains and go back to bed for a little bit?"

Her suggestion made me feel even worse. I would feel like a right slob going back to bed to nurse my head while the sun split the stones outside. The weather was fabulous, without a cloud in the sky. Who knew? The following day it might be raining. I didn't come all this way and deplete the last of my savings to lie in bed with a hangover. I needed to snap myself out of this.

"No, I'll be fine. I'll just take the water in the bottom of the pram so as not to get too dehydrated. Wait for me a minute and I'll change into a vest and shorts. Is it hot out there?"

"It's roasting! Twenty-seven degrees already and it isn't even midday yet."

"Okay, that's brilliant. Will you give John a bottle and change him, please? Make sure you put all the Factor 50 for Kids into the bottom of the pram too, and a couple of changes of nappies, and wipes too. We need to be prepared!"

"Sure, no problem."

I squeezed into some navy cotton shorts and a white vest. I turned around so I could see what I looked like. Bad mistake. Huge! I was horrified at the sight of my bulging midriff and orange-peel thighs. Good Lord, I knew I'd become the new owner of unwanted stretch marks around my tummy and boobs since having John but I'd no idea that I possessed the dreaded cellulite too. Sweet Lord, I would have to invest in a full-length mirror as soon as I got home. I didn't have one in my apartment because I had foolishly thought I didn't have a need for one. Wrong!

Well, there was no point in worrying about my bulging tum now. There was nothing I could do about it except swap my shorts for a more suitable black-and-white sarong which I tied around my waist. At least I wouldn't look like a pale moving mountain now. We left our key at the hotel reception and walked outside into the sunlight. Immediately I felt uplifted. There is no way I would have stayed in bed like a lush and missed this.

We went to the little shop on the corner with knickknacks hanging outside it, including lilos and brightly coloured beach towels, as well as postcards and racks of English and German newspapers and magazine. I bought a cheap pair of sunglasses and a few plastic toys for John to play with on the sand. Tanya bought a straw basket and a hot-pink cap with *Costa del Sol* written on it. "So cheesy, I know," she chuckled as she tried it on in the mirror. "But it'll keep my forehead from burning anyway!"

The beach was down a steep hill and, although it was crowded enough, there was plenty of room for us to put out our towels. We could have hired deck-chairs but if we were to do that the expense would have added up over the week and I was trying to keep within budget. I had been naughty last night blowing money on a fancy cocktail, but at least I had got the madness out of my system and I wouldn't be partying any more during this holiday. I wanted to come home rested and relaxed after my week away, not needing another week to recover.

As I laid my towel out on the sand in front of the sea, I cast my mind back to a holiday to the Canaries I took when I was nineteen, with my best friend Gillian from school. We'd stayed in the heart of lively Playa del Inglés and had literally partied every night for a fortnight, recovering every day by sleeping. What an absolute waste, I thought now, although then I was thinking it was the best time ever.

"Water?" Tanya handed me the bottle and my book, the latest from Marian Keyes. It was a big thick doorstopper and I couldn't wait to get stuck in.

John, under the shade of his pram cover, slept soundly in a little vest and his nappy. I surreptitiously took my

194

phone from my bag and took a few sneaky photos of him. My heart nearly melted he looked so angelic and peaceful.

I read a chapter or two of the book, but it was so hot that I said to Tanya I needed to go for a swim. "Can you stay here with John?"

"Sure, no problem," she said, taking out her earphones. She looked so amazing in her black one-piece that I felt like a fright lying next to her. Still, being on holiday with a stick insect was what I needed. I knew I wasn't going to have any pizza on this holiday!

The swim was amazing and I felt so refreshed afterwards. The water had been warm and inviting and I could have happily swum about all day! Tanya didn't swim but ventured in a few times up to her waist and splashed herself to cool down. She said she didn't want to swim because she would only ruin her blow-dry from the day before! Eh, okay!

We went for dinner that night in the hotel. There was a huge buffet and you could help yourself to whatever food you wanted. I took this as a huge opportunity to fill my plate with as much salad stuff as I could. Tanya did the same. I declined the wine menu, but I cracked when it came to dessert. I just couldn't resist the dessert trolley!

After dinner we retired to the hotel bar and I put John down into his pram.

"We'll just have the one, maybe," I said. "I don't want to keep John awake too late and mess up his sleep pattern. We can sit outside by the pool area. It's nice at night when it's lit up and all the fairy lights are in the trees."

"Okay," Tanya agreed pleasantly as we took our seats outside. I ordered a brandy and Sprite and Tanya asked for a sparkling water. John was happy with his little teddy, playing in his pram beside us. None of the other punters took a bit of notice of us as they listened to a man in a tuxedo play the piano. I loved the way the entertainment at the hotel was low-key and they didn't have very loud music or flamenco dancers strutting their stuff in the evenings, like they do in some hotels. It was very mellow and just a nice way to wind down after dinner.

The waiter was quick with our drinks and gave John a little smile as he served us.

"Isn't it refreshing the way the Spanish are so family-friendly?" I remarked to Tanya after he had gone to serve the next table. "We haven't had so much as a disapproving look from anyone. And do you remember earlier on when I was trying to get the pram up the steps and about three Spanish men rushed over to help? I must say I'm very impressed."

"It's very nice, yes," said Tanya, fiddling with her long blonde ponytail.

She looked an absolute vision tonight as she took the sun well. She had a slight tan already and we were barely twenty-four hours in the place. I could only imagine the mahogany colour she would be by the end of the week! Tonight she wore a short black lace dress and black sparkly kitten heels. I thought she was a little overdressed for a three-star family hotel in Torremolinos but I didn't say anything to her. It was nice that she had made an effort to dress up and look her best and I was actually proud of her. She knew how to turn heads. I had noticed that on the beach and on the streets. People couldn't take their eyes off her.

We listened to about three golden oldies on the piano before John started acting up a bit, throwing his teddy out of the pram. I didn't want him to cause a scene or start shouting over the piano guy so I stood up. "I think I'll take John upstairs," I said. "I'd better do it before he gets cranky. But listen, if you want to stay down a little longer and listen to the piano, feel free, I don't mind."

"Okay," said Tanya, not budging.

I wasn't sure if that meant okay, she was going to stay down here, or okay she was coming upstairs.

"Will we see you later then?" I ventured.

"Probably not. I'm going to take a taxi to Puerto Banus and I'll go clubbing a bit there – meet some people."

She could have knocked me down with a feather, I was that surprised. Puerto Banus of all places!

"I didn't think you knew anyone on the Costa del Sol?"

"That's right, I don't," she said with a little smile. "But hey, I'll meet new people. Isn't that what holidays are for?"

And so we said our goodbyes. I headed upstairs to bath my baby and put him to bed while Tanya was heading to the port to mingle with the party people. No wonder she had dressed up to the nines that evening! Suddenly I felt very old and boring.

The next morning I got up fairly late. When I emerged from my room I noticed the sofa bed was empty again. I wondered whether Tanya had come home at all and I was a teeny bit worried. After all, I did feel responsible for her. Yes, she was an adult but I was the one who had brought her here on holidays, out of her comfort zone.

But I needn't have worried at all because the next minute she came bouncing in again with warm croissants and more water and juice.

"That's the second time you've missed the breakfast downstairs," she said, wagging her finger at me jokingly. "Tomorrow I must insist that we all go down together, at least to see what it's like."

"But they stop serving at ten," I protested. "I mean, who wants to set their alarm on holidays? Not I! Did you have a good time last night by the way?"

"Yeah, it was good. The port was packed! So many people. I met some guys who were having a party on one of the big yachts and I joined them. It was great but I was back here by two so I don't feel tired really."

The joys of not drinking, I thought sombrely. You could pack so much more into your life if you cut out the dreaded booze.

"Anyway," she continued, "I'm not going to join you for dinner in the hotel this evening as I've been invited for dinner in Marbella. You don't mind, do you?"

I was quite taken aback. This had come from nowhere. I didn't know what to think. "No," I said after a moment's pause, "no, of course I don't mind, Tanya. But it's going to cost a lot of money taking taxis to and from Marbella every night if you keep this up! You do realise that, don't you?"

"Don't worry. I have a lift for tonight anyway! One

of the guys I met last night is picking me up. He says he might even take me shopping in Puerto Banus. I do hope so. I discovered an amazing little Armani boutique on the port. I had a look in the window last night and saw the most amazing boots. They're to die for!"

I wasn't quite sure how to respond to that. "Okay, but stay safe. Phone me any time you need to, okay? But naturally your free time is your free time, so if you want to go out that's absolutely fine with me."

"Great – thanks so much!" she said, bright-eyed. "Now, will we go back down to the beach again today? Or will we take it easy and just sit by the pool? You decide. If you like I can take John downstairs to the kiddies' club in the basement where they have lots of soft toys to play with and a little ball-crawl. Babies can go in – as long as an adult stays with them, of course."

"Okay," I said. "Thanks. If you take John to the kids' club, I can do a few laps of the pool and maybe read some of my book in peace. I appreciate it."

"Hey," she said, "it's your holiday! This is all about you having fun and relaxing. Remember, this is all about *you*."

How weird, I remember thinking to myself as I went to wake Baby John up from his deep slumber. If it's all about me, then why did it really not feel like that at all?

19

Oh my God, I'm so broke after the holidays it isn't even funny! Not that I regret going on holidays even for a second. We had a wonderful time and it was so relaxing if a little bit boring at night. But hey, when you have kids you make sacrifices. Your life changes forever. Did I feel a slight pang of envy every night when Tanya went out clubbing in a different sexy outfit? Yes, a little bit, but credit where credit was due, her partying did not impact on her work one tiny bit, and she was great company for me. I honestly don't think I could have managed with John on my own.

But yes, I'm down to my last fifty quid now. *Yikes!* I am just counting the days until pay day. It can't come quickly enough. Okay, so I know modern mummies never have enough money, but this is the first time in living memory that I feel truly poor! Unlike our grandmothers who used to darn the family socks, regularly cut out savings coupons, and spend a week in a caravan in Ireland somewhere for the annual holidays, living economically does not come so easily to us modern Irish. My idea of saving the socks is not throwing them out every few weeks. That's what I used to do. The extravagance of it! Every now and then I would gather up a huge lot of odd socks, chuck them in the bin and then replace the lot with brand new ones. Now I wash the socks and dry them and put them back in the drawer. Mind you, I can't ever see the day where I will actually take out a sock from my drawer and start working on it diligently with a needle and thread. And I can't ever see myself fussing at the top of the check-out queue with discount tokens for the groceries either.

My granny, God rest her soul, lived through two wars. Her kitchen was always stacked with non-perishable goods such as tins of fruit. I presume that was because she feared the arrival of another war. She never wore her good shoes at home. She had slippers for walking around the house and the good shoes were kept in a box and were routinely brought to the cobblers when in need of maintenance. She never cooked without an apron. That was to save her clothes. I, on the other hand, don't wear an apron and can't think of a single friend who does. In my grandmother's house there was no fancy tinned food for the dog and as far as I remember he was happy enough with leftovers from the dinner. I don't ever recall him going to a beauty parlour either. He was washed down with soap and a bucket of water whether he liked it or not.

I suppose we could learn a lot from the way our grandmothers lived. They filed their own nails instead of going to nail salons and I doubt they ever messed around with streaky fake tan. During the summers they would swim in the real sea instead of spending a hundred euro on a seaweed bath or a mud bath in a fancy spa. They were healthier too. For a start they cooked proper meals from scratch and that's why their cooking was always so great. None lived in apartments so they had gardens to grow fresh produce. And very few were overweight as far as I can see from old photographs. Everybody always seems thin in old sepia photos. But I suppose back then they didn't have fast-food chains and people didn't drink wine with their dinner, and a glass of champagne was something only to be enjoyed at a wedding. Also, families were much larger back then so there wouldn't have been as much to go around. And because so few people had cars everybody walked everywhere and kept fit. There was no such thing as disposable nappies back in our grandmothers' day and cloth nappies were washed by hand as there were no washing machines. But, you know, no matter how bad the recession gets, I can never see myself doing this. God forbid! Nor can I ever see myself tending to the garden with a non-electric lawnmower, or swapping my beloved electric blanket for a woolly bed-jacket and hat. However, like everybody else, I must be realistic. I no longer order cocktails on a night out, I no longer buy shoes that are impossible to walk in but look nice, and I write a list when going grocery shopping, which is funny because I used to secretly feel sorry for people clutching lists in supermarkets as I would happily fill my trolley with wild abandon. Now I swear by lists. They save me indulging. Like once I realised that two small tubs of sun-dried tomatoes equalled a week's worth of nappies, the decade-long relationship between sun-dried tomatoes and myself came to an abrupt end. Oh, well. I don't think I ever really liked them anyway.

The morning I was going back to work I walked into the kitchen and caught sight of something so exquisite it almost took my breath away.

"Wow, what a stunning bag!" I exclaimed out loud.

I ran my fingers over the soft buttery leather beige Chanel bag sitting on my pristine clean kitchen counter and found them circling the interlocking double silver Cs. I have always wanted a Chanel bag and, heavens above, this was love at first sight.

"Oh, thanks," said Tanya with a smile. "I like it too!" She was sitting on the sofa with John on her knee, looking like a supermodel with her long blonde hair swept off her face, accentuating her high cheekbones. She wore skinny blue jeans, black knee-high suede boots and a floaty lace white top. She looked like she could be the wife of a jet-setting millionaire instead of a childminder. Once again I tried not to pinch myself.

"Where did you get it?" I asked. I knew the price of Chanel bags and I couldn't get my head around how Tanya would be able to afford one.

"It was a present . . . from a friend," she said, looking at John, not me. "Do you really like it?"

"Yes, I love it. It is a dream of mine to own a Chanel bag one day. But that day seems very far away right now, unfortunately. And this is one of the nicer ones. It's like a work of art."

Tanya sat John up on her knee and burped him. "Good boy," she cooed. Then she looked up at me and smiled. "You can borrow it sometime if you like."

"Thanks, that's very kind of you. I think I would be afraid to borrow it though just in case something happened to it."

"I would trust you," said Tanya. "Hey, you trust me with your baby and you have to admit he is a lot more precious than a handbag!"

"Well, when you put it like that," I said, switching off the kettle.

I decided I'd have a strong black coffee before catching the train to work. I couldn't eat breakfast. I was feeling too anxious. I wasn't quite sure what to expect. According to the emails Sally had been sending me via Facebook, tensions were high in the office and everybody was living on their nerves and, on top of that, while working in a magazine is usually considered to be a glamorous job, now the PR companies didn't send in half as many freebies as they used to.

I'll never forget my first ever Christmas working in the magazine. It was as though Santa was there every day, delivering goodies such as perfume, make-up, hair straighteners, anti-cellulite creams, funky jewellery pieces, cases of champagne, boxes of chocolates. The editor would tell the staff to take their pick after she had helped herself and could stuff no more freebies into the boot of her Audi. None of us had even needed to go Christmas shopping over the last few years thanks to all the free gifts we received. Now, according to Sally, the editor just kept all the goodies in her office, and only parted with the cheap rubbishy stuff that wasn't even worth selling on eBay. The recession had brought the whole office back down to earth with an almighty thud.

I had initially thought I'd be perfectly fine leaving John at home while I re-entered the working world. I had actually been counting the days until I was due to go back to work, so nothing could have surprised me more than the tears that escaped down my cheeks after I had left John in the capable arms of Tanya and waved him goodbye. Even as I sat on the train as it sped towards Dublin and looked out at the choppy sea, I was glad I was wearing dark glasses and that I had plenty of tissues to hand. I couldn't quite explain my immense sadness. After all, I had left Baby John with my mother on quite a few occasions when I was exhausted and needed a respite from my sleep deprivation. I hadn't felt sad then. No, I had just crawled into my own bed, thoroughly grateful, and relished my night's interrupted sleep.

But this seemed different somehow. Going to work made me feel like I was abandoning him. I kept picturing his gentle smiling face as I walked out the door with my umbrella and briefcase under my arm. I felt bad that I was going to be away from him for an entire day but it was comforting to know I was leaving my baby in good hands. And I would still be at home with him for most of the week.

Arriving at the office, I took the lift up to the fourth floor. I checked my appearance in the mirror and was less than pleased by what I saw looking back at me. I had applied my make-up a lot more heavily than usual to try and make myself look presentable. I wanted to hide the shadows under my eyes. Although Tanya was wonderful and helped me any way she could, it was me who had to tend to John when he woke up crying in the night. Last night he had woken up twice and needed to be comforted by his mummy, so I was tired. The pale-green suit that I had bought discounted in the July sales was more than a little tight on me too. Right, that's it, I told myself sternly. The diet starts today. I don't care how hard it is. If I don't shed these unwanted pounds, nobody else is going to do it for me.

Tina, the receptionist, buzzed me in when she saw me through the glass doors. "You look great . . . for somebody who's had a baby."

"Thanks," I said, looking around me with interest. Something had changed but I couldn't quite figure out what.

"They painted the walls cream," Tina chirped as though reading my mind. "Oh, and they've removed the water cooler in case you were wondering."

I raised an eyebrow.

"Cutbacks," she said with a sigh as she rolled her eyes to the ceiling. "Soon they'll be removing the loo paper from the Ladies'."

I smiled in spite of myself. Tina was a terrible moaner. Even in the good times she'd always had plenty to find fault with: the couriers were incompetent, the photocopier was dodgy, the place was too cold, too hot, callers on the phone were too rude and didn't speak slowly enough. I wondered how she had stayed so long in a place that was so truly awful.

"Is Sally in the office?"

"No, she's not actually – she was in earlier but she's gone to a function with Creea. Some champagne breakfast thing to launch a new collection. It's well for them, isn't it?" she added resentfully.

I knew better than to agree. The walls in that place had ears.

"Well, not to worry, I'll see them later," I said cheerfully, determined that Tina wouldn't see any disappointment in my face.

The truth was that I was surprised nobody was there to greet me and everybody seemed to have deserted the office knowing that I was coming back after a significant absence. Okay, I wasn't naïve enough to think that there would be balloons everywhere and that the staff were going to be gathered around to burst into song at the sight of me, but this non-welcome pretty much hammered home just how insignificant I had become at the magazine.

"I'll just go on through to my desk," I informed Tina. She didn't answer and had her eyes glued to the screen in front of her. She was probably on the website www.myhome.ie. Sally had told me that ever since Tina moved in with her new boyfriend she was obsessed with buying a new place with him, and kept annoying everyone in the office by saying that property was falling at such a fast rate. A couple of years ago she wouldn't have been able to afford anything in Dublin, but now that property prices had dramatically fallen she thought she had a good chance of purchasing a bargain. She was prepared to wait until they hit rock bottom.

With a slightly heavy heart, I pushed open the doors

of the open-plan office. I was about to go over to the desk in the far corner which had always been mine but it was occupied. A girl with long red hair and a floaty white cotton dress was sitting there with her back to me, chatting on the phone. There was nobody else in the office. I waited patiently for her to finish her call and then I cleared my throat.

She swung around and looked surprised to see me standing there. "Sorry, I didn't hear you come in. Kaylah, I presume?"

She wasn't so much friendly as polite. Even from the door she looked polished with nice make-up and nails. I also saw from the red soles on her heels that her shoes were Christian Louboutin.

"That's my desk," I said, and then nearly kicked myself for being so blunt.

The girl, whose name I later found out was Louise, raised a surprised eyebrow.

"Sorry, I meant that was my desk before I left to have my baby," I added, feeling flustered. "I'm not sure where my new desk is."

Louise was calm and collected as though she was a nurse dealing with a stressed-out patient. "Oh yes," she said, "you are completely right. Creea gave me your desk while you were absent. I am an intern here so I wouldn't expect my own desk. But, as you are working part-time and don't need a desk really, Creea has suggested we share this desk and the computer. I'm sure that's all right with you?"

I stared at her, dumbfounded. What? I didn't even have my own computer? How insulting! This was terrible. Surely things weren't so tight in the office that I couldn't have my own computer! It was unthinkable that I'd have to share my desk with a lowly intern.

I cleared my throat. "I'll have to discuss this with Creea when she comes back," I said, feeling hot under the collar. "As a stylist I need a desk with plenty of space to put all my bags on it. I can't even imagine sharing. There must be some sort of mix-up."

Even as I spoke I knew I sounded foolish. This was humiliating to say the least. I couldn't believe I was having this conversation with a girl who, although groomed to perfection, looked like she couldn't have been more than eighteen or nineteen years old.

"I totally understand," Louise answered. Her lips were smiling but her eyes weren't. "I hope you don't mind but I have a couple of urgent emails to send, so please excuse me."

With that she turned her back and left me hovering like a spare tool. I stood awkwardly in the doorway feeling as though I'd been treated like an unwanted smell. I didn't know what to do now. I couldn't just plonk my briefcase on top of somebody else's desk. Feeling hot and bothered, I decided to go back out to the reception area to get a glass of water to cool down. It was only when I got there I remembered that the cooler had been removed for economic reasons.

"Do they still have free tea and coffee in the kitchen?" I asked Tina who was now busy painting her nails a hot pink colour.

"Yes, but it's nasty stuff. They changed the brand. It's now the cheapest of the cheap. It would poison you so it would. You'd need to be hard up to drink it."

"Well, I am hard up," I managed a smile.

"Are you really?"

"Yes. Babies are expensive."

"Tell me about it. My sister has five under five. I think it's the reason I never forget to take my pill."

"Eh . . . can I leave my briefcase here with you? I'm going to sit in the kitchenette for a bit and read the paper. I won't be too long."

"Sure."

"Thanks. It's just I'm not sure which desk . . . I mean there's been a change in seating arrangements since I was last here. The girl with the red hair . . ."

"Oh, you mean Louise?" Tina raised her eyes to the ceiling.

"Louise? Is that her name? Well, she seems to think that we're sharing a desk."

"Does she? She has airs and graces about her that I don't know where she got them. She's a funny one, so she is."

"Funny?"

Tina lowered her voice. "As in odd, not amusing."

"Oh."

It really wasn't a good thing to be to be caught gossiping in the reception area with Tina about another member of staff. I glanced at the door anxiously just in case anybody suddenly walked in. But nobody was about. It was eerily quiet.

"I think I'll go and make my coffee even if it is nasty. Are you sure I can't get you one too?"

"Positive."

"Is there milk in the fridge?"

"Milk?" Tina opened her eyes dramatically. "Milk? Are you joking? Haven't you heard about the R word?"

"R word?"

"*Rrr*ecession," said Tina, doing a very bad impression of a French person. "Sure, how can we forget about the recession when we're reminded by Creea every single second of every single day? Invest in some warm heavy clothes for the winter, I say. It wouldn't surprise me if they turned the heat off."

"Right. Thanks for the tip." I found myself almost running off to the tiny kitchenette just to get away from Tina's gloominess. I hoped it wasn't contagious. But she called after me. "How is your little girl, by the way? I can't remember her name now."

I paused. And took a deep breath. "It's a boy," I said, turning around, "and his name is John. You sent a card on behalf of all the staff at the magazine. It was lovely."

Tina had the good grace to look embarrassed. "Oh yeah, so I did. I remember now. Congratulations."

"Thanks," I said before scuttling off to the kitchen. I badly needed my caffeine fix now.

Later that day I was in for a good old dressing-down by my boss, which was humiliating to say the least.

"You'll both have to share," said Creea firmly. "You'll be working from home most days anyway, Kaylah. If you're in the office and Louise is using the desk you can use my desk if it's available.

I felt so disheartened. No, I hadn't exactly been expecting balloons to welcome me back to work, but I certainly wasn't expecting this. Where was I supposed to put all my stuff? Sometimes I'd come back to the office with bags and bags of stuff.

Creea had an answer for that too. "We're installing personal lockers in the Ladies' tomorrow, so from now on everyone will have their own space to store their stuff."

Great, I thought. Now, not only did I not have my own desk any more, but I was to store all the expensive clothes, shoes and jewellery that I'd borrowed for glamorous photo shoots in what was the loo basically. I was so glad I'd come back to work – *not*.

Sally tried to make me feel better over lunch. "Look, I know it's not great having to share the desk with Louise, and I know she isn't the easiest person in the world to be around but at least you're still here." She put a slender arm around me. I noticed that she'd lost a lot of weight. Everyone in the office seemed to have shrunk since I'd last seen them. Tina and Creea looked sleek and slim but Louise was like a lollipop – straight body and big round head.

I found myself scowling at my cheese-and-coleslaw sandwich. I should have ordered a salad like Sally. "I feel like I'm obese," I said morosely.

"Hey, stop that! You've just had a baby," said Sally. "What an achievement that is. Come on now, don't beat yourself up for having put on a few pounds. It's the most natural thing in the world. The average woman would be happy with your size."

"Thanks. I appreciate it, but who wants to be average? Anyway, I just feel enormous today. Everyone else is so skinny compared to me."

Sally cut a lettuce leaf in half with her knife and fork. "But our office isn't normal," she said. "We work for a fashion magazine. I'm sure if you were working in an insurance office or something everybody would just look like regular people. We're bombarded by fashion images of skinny models every day. No wonder we feel guilty eating chocolate!"

"I suppose you're right," I said, forcing myself to cheer up slightly. I started tucking into my sandwich. The carbs felt so good. I could sense that Sally was looking at my plate longingly.

"Tina is on a strict diet at the moment," Sally said, eager to fill me in on all the gossip. "It's called the Heartbreak Diet. It's the most effective diet in the whole world."

"Heartbreak?"

"Yes, didn't you hear? She split up with her boyfriend a few days ago. She caught him in bed with another bird apparently when she arrived home early from work."

"What! Are you serious? That's terrible."

"Yes."

"Oh my God, poor Tina! She must have been devastated. So I guess they won't be buying a house now."

"I guess not. Well, not together anyway, Although she's still banging on about the fact that property prices are still dropping and have even further to go. It really annoys poor Annette from accounts who bought her house in the middle of the boom and is now drowning in negative equity."

"Well, she can be annoying all right. She just doesn't seem to know when to shut up and her mouth tends to start moving before her brain has a chance to engage. But she didn't say anything to me about the break-up."

"As if she would! Tina likes to pretend to everyone that her whole life is wonderful. I think the break-up was supposed to be a secret but she stupidly told Louise and now the whole office knows about it. Now she's starving herself in the hope of losing weight and getting her boyfriend back. No breakfast, black coffee all day, an apple at eleven, a half a tub of cottage cheese and some fruit at lunch and vodka in the evening. Apparently, she's lost a half a stone already."

"Wow."

"Yeah, and although it nearly kills me to admit it, she does look amazing. Bitch!"

I couldn't help wishing a little that I was on a Heartbreak Diet. Why does it never work like that for me? When Clive dumped me all I could do was stuff my face with sweets and cakes! I was so skinny when I met him and now I'm fat and disgusted with myself. How can these people simply stop eating over the loss of a man? I envy them!

I decided not to waste my lunch-break worrying about losing weight and I asked Sally about Louise. I mean, where had she even come from? And how long was she staying? Not too long, I hoped.

Sally popped a cherry tomato in her mouth and pretended to savour the moment. "Well," she said, "Creea took on Louise and another girl as interns, basically in order to save money by not employing a real person to do the work, and then the other girl left last week and Louise was kept on. I believe she's on a six-month contract, not that you'll hear that from her. That one wouldn't tell her left hand what her right hand was doing. She's a bit sly."

I raised an eyebrow inquisitively. "Sly? How do you mean? In what way?"

"Well, I'll give you a good example. The invitations came in the other day for the premiere of that new romantic comedy starring Colin Firth. You know the one everyone's raving about? So, the tickets were naturally like gold dust for that. Tina opened the envelope and left the tickets on her desk, but then she said she couldn't find them on the afternoon of the premiere. Myself and Tina had intended on going together and making a girls' night out of it but, as we had no tickets and it was too late to phone the PR people to see if we could get new tickets issued, we couldn't go. Anyway, the next day Louise came into work as usual and said nothing, and that afternoon I saw a picture of Louise and a friend of hers in the society pages of the *Evening Herald*! They had been at the film and the after party and they had even met Colin Firth. Can you frigging believe it? Her new Facebook profile photo is a photo with her standing next to him!"

"Oh my God, I feel sick!"

"Tell me about it! I swear on my life, myself and Tina were livid. Then when I asked her about the film tickets that had gone missing she said she didn't know what happened to them."

"Did Creea say anything to her?"

Sally shrugged. "No, of course not. Creea doesn't give a hoot about who gets to go to see what film. Now there's a woman who thinks she's carrying the weight of the world on her shoulders at the moment. And she's right to be worried. There are too many women's magazines in the current saturated market, all vying for the same advertisers. You wouldn't believe the amount of companies that are reducing their advertising budgets, even the staples such as the cosmetics companies and the hair-care companies. This is serious. And we're in competition with the internet now. People aren't really interested in magazines any more."

I knew she was telling the truth and, although I didn't say it, I was worried too. What if I lost my job? Okay, I knew I was being paid a pittance and I had little security, but I had a baby to support now. Where would I go if I wasn't here? Who else would allow me work half the week from home? Many employers were just not interested in mums with commitments. If I didn't have Tanya at home right now holding the fort, I'd be in right trouble. I felt uneasy about my future. The fact that I was being made share a desk with a newbie was definitely not a good sign. It undermined my status at work and it would eventually erode my confidence. Would the next step be out the door for me? I didn't even want to let my mind wander there.

The afternoon dragged on and on and on. It seemed like any time I took a call or phoned somebody, Louise would whip out her mobile and start talking loudly as though she were trying to drown out my voice. It was extremely difficult trying to work in such close proximity to somebody else. It felt at times like she was practically sitting on my knee!

I found myself looking at my watch a lot more than I

should have. I never remembered doing that before when I was at work. And I even found myself looking at photos of John on my mobile phone at one stage. Seriously, was that pathetic or what? I missed John. I mean, I really did miss him way more than I thought I would. I wondered if he was missing me. Then I chided myself, telling myself not to be completely ridiculous. Of course he didn't miss me. He was in the very capable hands of the lovely Tanya. She was like a second mummy to him almost.

For a few self-pitying moments I found myself wondering why I was sitting beside a hostile stranger in a cramped office space, doing a job that paid peanuts, when another woman was in my home not having to put up with any office politics crap and playing bunnies and teddies with the person that I loved most in the world. I fought back a lone tear. I didn't want to come across as pathetic. I wondered did all mums feel this bad going back to work or was it just me? Was I just a weakling?

When the time came to go home that evening I practically ran all the way to the train station. I didn't want to be a minute more away from my son than I had to be. There was a train parked in the station just as I came up the escalator. I rushed towards it, nearly catching myself in the sliding doors. Phew! I made it.

As I sat on the train, looking out the window so as not to catch anybody's eye, I wondered if I could do something else. Working as a part-time stylist was all very well for somebody in their twenties, living at home. Somebody like Louise, say. But was it really a proper job for a mummy who didn't have every second night off to go and schmooze at fashion shows? Maybe I needed to rethink my priorities. I mean, just because I was a stylist now didn't mean I had to remain one forever. Maybe I could still be a lab technician. Then again, maybe not. I had been caught by the fashion bug and I didn't want to completely opt out now. Anyway, I wasn't going to be pushed out by a youngster like Louise. I needed to get a grip.

The sun was shining when I got off the train and I had a skip in my step as I walked along the road, looking forward to seeing my baba again. You'd have thought I hadn't seen him in a month! I was feeling a lot more positive now. Why was I worrying about a teenager? She didn't have half my experience and I had spent the last few years gathering an impressive amount of contacts in the fashion world. I knew I could produce great, imaginative shoots. I'd done it before and I'd do it again.

Suddenly I spotted a very familiar figure walking towards me. She had a shopping bag in each hand and a child running along either side of her. She looked worn out and exhausted and far from her usual pristine itself. I nearly stopped dead in my tracks when I saw her, and for a fleeting moment wondered whether there was time to cross the road without being noticed. But then she looked up and stared straight at me. It was Joanne. And I had stolen her nanny!

20

"Oh hi, Joanne!" I said breezily, hoping like hell that she would be in too much of a hurry to stop and chat.

"Hello, Kaylah, how are you? Lovely day, isn't it?"

"Yes, it's lovely to see a bit of sun, but there's a strong wind."

"I suppose we should be thankful that it isn't raining."

"Yes," I agreed, feeling very uncomfortable indeed.

Did she know? I mean, did she know that Tanya was living with me? And was it the end of the world if she did know? I mean, why was I mentally beating myself up about it? People switched jobs all the time. Samira left me to work for another family and I had got over it. After all, it wasn't as though I had stolen Joanne's husband or got her fired.

"Are you doing much reading?" I asked.

Books were a safe subject and reading was something we both had in common. In fact, it was probably the only thing I had in common with this other mother who was at least a decade older than myself and, according to Tanya, had never worked a day in her life. Her husband was a senior bank executive who made enough money to afford her a nice comfortable life without ever having to worry about little things such as electricity and food bills. Tanya had confided in me that Joanne's life consisted of the book club, her Wednesday night bridge, her Thursday morning golf and the parent-teaching meetings at her children's schools.

"I'm not really reading much at the moment," Joanne said with a sigh as her two boys hung out of her, pulling each arm. "It's hard during the summer when the kids are off school. There really isn't five minutes to yourself when they're that age. It's been a fairly hectic summer and, to top it all, our nanny walked out on us with no explanation. Didn't even say goodbye."

There, she'd said it.

I found myself frozen to the spot. Shit! I felt like I'd been just caught cheating in an exam by a teacher. I'm sure I went the colour of beetroot. My mind was racing.

Hang on, I thought – no – it sounds as if she doesn't actually know. What should I say? Should I just come clean? Confess all? Would she forgive me? Then again, would I forgive her for treating Tanya so badly? After all, Tanya and myself had become good friends now. We'd gone on holidays together and she was almost like a second mum to Baby John. I felt almost protective towards her. She had come to this country to improve her English and experience a new way of life. Joanne and her husband had more or less treated her like a slave.

I opened my mouth. I knew I should say something but the first word was trapped somewhere halfway down my throat and I couldn't get it out.

"I . . . I know," I managed at last.

"Oh yes, I'm sure you know what it's like. It must be so tough being a single mum. I don't envy you."

So she definitely didn't know.

"How is your little girl anyway?"

"I've a boy actually – John. He's great." Why did everyone ask me about a little girl? "I'm back to work now. In fact, today was my first day back."

"And how did it go?"

"Oh fine, I . . ."

"Come *on*, Mum!" said one of the boys. Both her sons looked bored and sulky.

"I'd better go," Joanne smiled apologetically. "They've been promised ice-cream and they're holding me to it."

"Okay, well, I'll see you at the next book-club meeting, I suppose?"

"Yes, I'm not sure who's hosting the next one but I'll send a group text once the book and venue have been decided on."

I nodded my thanks. It felt like I was being scheduled in for a doctor's appointment. I really was not looking forward to the next book-club meeting which was a shame because I used to really enjoy the get-togethers. I bade her a quick goodbye, feeling delighted that I had managed to escape unscathed. Maybe I should have had said something. Surely it would have been better to just say it out and get it over and done with. After all, Bray was not a huge town and we lived in fairly close proximity to each other. I was bound to bump into Joanne again on the street. Next time Tanya might be with me and that would be very awkward indeed. And, of course, there was the book club – surely it was bound to come out there? They were bound to ask me and I could hardly lie.

I hurried along home towards the sanctuary of my little rented apartment. Soon I was there and putting my key in my front door. I could hear the happy sound of laughter from inside as I did so. My heart nearly melted. John sounded so happy and safe. His gentle chuckles were like music to my ears. I took off my coat and hung it up. Tanya had left the post neatly stacked on the sideboard. I quickly glanced at the small pile. Most of the envelopes were instantly recognisable and made my heart a little heavier. There was the credit-card bill, the waste-removal bill, a bank statement which would tell me exactly how little money I actually had to my name, a pink envelope which was surely from a PR company inviting me to a fashion show, and a white, formal-looking envelope which clearly stated *Private and Confidential*. I didn't like the look of that at all. I was about to open it when Tanya stepped into the hall with John in her arms. His face lit up when he saw me and it was enough to lift my spirits to the sky.

I reached over and took him into my arms for a cuddle. He was so warm and soft and his hair smelled fresh and clean. He gurgled at me in delight. "Did he just have a bath?" I asked.

Tanya grinned. "Yes, he had a wonderful bubble bath. He didn't want to get out he was enjoying himself so much. We had a great day. I took him to Dún Laoghaire on the train. We had lunch in Café Costa above Easons and then went for a walk on the pier."

"Oh, thank you so much, Tanya. I do appreciate that you took him out in the fresh air. It's important that he gets as much oxygen into his lungs as possible while we still have the weather. Once the hour changes and the evenings start getting darker there won't be as much opportunity. How much do I owe you?"

She stared at me blankly. "For what?"

"For the café?" I said. "And the transport."

"No, no," she insisted with a wave of her hand. "Not at all. We just had a muffin between us."

She refused to take anything from me. I made a mental note that I would have to provide her with a monthly bus and rail ticket so that she wouldn't need to spend a fortune of her own money taking John to nice places. I was so glad that she wasn't leaving him in his cot all day amusing himself, or plonked down for hours on end in front of the television.

"How was the first day back in work?" she asked, sounding genuinely interested. Tanya had a way of asking questions that didn't seem at all intrusive.

"It was okay," I said. "Just okay."

"Oh. That's a little disappointing," she said in an even voice.

I sighed and slumped down on the sofa. I wanted to put my feet up and watch *Come Dine With Me*. The thought of making dinner now was making me feel exhausted.

"It was bound to be a bit of an anticlimax," I admitted.

223

"I'd prefer to work from home all the time to be honest. At least I wouldn't have somebody hogging my desk here, which is what happened today. Hey, are there any pizzas in the freezer, Tanya? I'm just too tired to even think of starting to cook something now. If there's no food, I'll phone for a takeout."

"No need for that at all. The dinner has been made," said Tanya. "It's a vegetarian stew in a mild curry sauce and I think you'll really like it. It's healthy and full of nutrition. All I need to do now is boil the rice which won't take long."

I was deeply impressed and oh so grateful. "Thank you so much, Tanya. You're an absolute star."

"Wine?"

"You know me too well. Do we have any?"

"We do now! I bought a bottle of screw-top Chardonnay in O'Brien's off-license. Of course if you'd prefer a nice cup of tea, that's okay too . . ."

"No, I'll have the wine," I said with a smile. "I need it to relax. It's been quite a day. Thank you so much for thinking of me. You're so sweet."

"No problem. I'll put on the rice now and get John ready for bed as I'm waiting for it to cook. Do you need me to do anything else?"

"Oh Lord no, you've done more than enough. Even the place is looking so clean. I'm a bit overwhelmed to be honest."

"You deserve a little Mummy Treat," Tanya said, handing me the remote control. "I know you get up several times a night to tend to John and it must interfere terribly with your sleep. You should go to a hotel and have a good uninterruped eight or nine hours' sleep to recharge your batteries."

I once again had to refrain from pinching myself. How lucky was I to find this incredible girl!

"I wish!" I laughed. "But as we're just back from a sun holiday I can't justify taking another break!'

"But I am being serious. I know you were on holidays but you still had John and it's not really a holiday with a baby. Maybe you could go on a little spa break somewhere just for the night? I sometimes see really good deals on the internet with discounts. You get even more of a discount if you go mid-week."

I started imagining myself relaxing in a warm whirlpool. Or lying in a darkened room on a fluffy white towel while somebody massaged all the tension out of my back and shoulders. I wished Tanya hadn't put the idea in my head. I was sorely tempted to act on her suggestion.

"Well, to be honest," I said, "working in a magazine we often get the opportunity to stay in spa hotels for free as long as we give them a mention in the magazine. I'm sure my boss, Creea, wouldn't mind if I asked her. But I'd feel bad about leaving John here. I'd have to take him with me."

"No, it wouldn't be a rest if you had the baby. Try and get something and I'll take care of John for the night. Go on, you deserve it."

"Okay, I'll think about it. It does sound very tempting."

About fifteen minutes later I was halfway through my glass of wine and at the point of *Come Dine With Me* where they all start giving each other marks out of ten when, in a cloud of expensive smelling perfume, in came Tanya looking like a supermodel, with John in her arms. He was wearing his little *In the Night Garden* sleepsuit and he looked adorable. Tanya handed me the baby. I looked in awe at her slim enviable figure. Not many people I know could get away with tight leather trousers and a crisp tight-fitting shirt. Around Tanya's neck was a loosely-tied Fendi scarf, and her hair framed her pretty face.

"You look sensational," I exclaimed. "Are you heading out somewhere nice?"

"Yes, I am having dinner in town. I'm really looking forward to it."

"Lucky you. I hope you have a great time. Where are you going?"

Tanya shrugged. "I don't know. It's so long ago since I've been out to dinner. Well, say you could dine in any restaurant in Dublin, which one would it be?"

I frowned, casting my mind back. I wasn't a huge foodie but a couple of restaurants that I'd eaten in over the past few years had been particular memorable.

"Just thinking about that question is making my mouth water," I admitted as I cradled John in my arms. "I like L'Ecrivain in Baggot Street and on the north side of the city you have Chapter One which has won many awards."

"Should I try one of them?"

"Oh, no," I said, taking a sharp intake of breath. "I mean, they are great restaurants but it costs a good bit of money to eat in places like that. I would only go somewhere like that on my birthday or something. Are you meeting the girls from the Secret Nanny Club? I think Milano's might be a good spot? Good food at reasonable prices . . ."

"Not tonight. I'm going on a date so the price of the food is irrelevant."

My eyes nearly popped out of my head. "A date?"

"Yes," Tanya nodded. "He told me we could go wherever I liked so I wanted to choose the top restaurant in town."

"Well, if money is no object . . ."

"It isn't." Her answer was abrupt but not particularly rude.

"Then I would recommend trying out Patrick Guilbaud's which is a very fancy and renowned French restaurant in the Merrion Hotel. I remember going for a business lunch there when one of the magazine's main advertisers treated us. It has two Michelin stars, the highest out of any restaurant in Ireland. You would love it."

"Great, we might as well go there then," Tanya said simply. "Thanks for the recommendation. I'd better get my coat."

"Yes, it's kind of nippy out there and rain is forecast tonight so don't forget your umbrella in case you're waiting around in the rain."

"It's okay. I have a lift into town."

"Oh, you do? Oh. Right, well that's okay then. Have a great time so. I can't wait to hear all about it in the morning. Goodnight."

A few minutes later I heard a horn toot outside. Then I heard Tanya's footsteps in the hall, followed by the noise of the front door shutting. The curiosity was killing me and I was dying to look outside but didn't want to be caught prying. Well, wasn't Tanya the dark horse? Michelin-star restaurant, no less? In a way I was envious of her. It had been an awfully long time since I had been taken anywhere on a date.

Tanya had kindly left John's bottle made up on the kitchen counter so I just warmed it in a bottle of hot water and fed him while watching *Coronation Street*. I decided I might as well have an early night. It had been quite stressful going back to work that morning to find a junior plonked at my desk, and then meeting Joanne unexpectedly on the street had got my heart racing. I needed to put my electric blanket on, curl up with my latest Maeve Binchy book and hopefully before I knew it I'd have nodded off.

After changing John's nappy, I put him down into his cot with his teddy and smiled at him. He looked as snug as a bug in a rug and I tenderly stroked his little cheek. He smiled innocently back at me and once again I found myself thanking God that he had sent me this special little angel to share my life with. I loved him so much that I couldn't even really remember what life was like before him. What had I done with my time? With whom had I spent it? I recalled meeting girls I vaguely knew for cocktails to discuss men that had since vanished. I remembered not wanting to leave the office sometimes, wishing that I'd had a sleeping bag so that I could kip a few hours on the floor to save me having to go home and come back in again. I remember being absolutely fascinated by trivial gossip concerning staff members at the magazine. Now that I had John, all of that stuff seemed so unimportant. Being a mummy certainly put things in perspective. I certainly wasn't as career-focussed as I used to be, but I believe I was a more rounded person now. I was certainly more sensible and that was a good thing.

I don't really know what made me think of it, but suddenly I remembered that strange white envelope that had been waiting for me when I got in from work. I had been reluctant to open something marked *Private and Confidential* in front of Tanya. I thought I'd open it now. I took it to bed with me and opened it there. Then I wished I hadn't. It was a solicitor's letter from John's father, Clive, demanding access to his son.

I was astounded. Why was he suddenly looking for access after telling me in no uncertain terms that he didn't want to be involved with John? "You're on your own now," he'd said to me, with a fair amount of venom. So why the change of heart? And why couldn't he have contacted me directly instead of running off to a solicitor? This was all deeply disturbing.

21

Luckily Creea had loved my Christmas-party fashion shoot idea. Even though it was still September she told me to get cracking on it immediately. I decided on a big old-world country-house hotel in Kildare, about an hour's drive from Dublin. It was a former private house belonging to an earl, with magnificent high ceilings and beautifully sculpted mantelpieces. I organised with the hotel's PR and marketing team to have a roaring log fire in the drawing room which we intended on using, and they had given me permission to decorate it with festive candles and Christmas decorations. I even hired an enormous Christmas trees complete with fake ribbon-wrapped presents to put underneath.

The magazine works two months' ahead so time was not on my side. The shoot had to be in the November issue of the magazine and the pressure was on. The hotel had promised us the rooms to use free of charge in exchange for a credit mentioning their website and details of their Christmas Party nights and New Year's Eve ball.

My mother had kindly given me the use of her car to drive to Kildare, and the hotel had offered to put up myself, the photographer, the model, the hairdresser and the make-up artist free of charge. This was fantastic as it would save us getting up at five both mornings to get to the hotel on time. The hotel PR had told me there was no problem using the rooms for our shoots as long as the guests weren't disturbed too much. This meant that we needed to start work very early in the morning.

I had been so busy all week prepping for the Christmas shoot that I barely had time in the evenings to even cuddle little John. But I was glad to be busy because first of all it took me out of the office and, second of all, I didn't have time to think about Clive's nasty solicitor's letter. I tried to banish it to the back of my mind until I had decided what I was going to do about it.

The day after Creea gave me the go-ahead to put the Christmas-party fashion shoot together I held a casting in a city-centre hotel room. I had been going to do it with just the photographer, a lovely guy called Dave with whom I had worked in the past, but Creea had said it would be nice to take Louise along to the casting so she could have an idea how it worked. Reluctantly I agreed. Well, I could hardly say no to the boss, could I?

I had a clear image of the type of model I wanted to cast for this job. Usually when I dream up a shoot in the early stages I have a vague idea of the type of look I'm going for. By the time I see the girls and can envisage the end product laid out between the covers of the magazine, I am sure. I wanted somebody classy for my shoot. Tall, elegant, with high cheekbones. I wanted somebody with healthy-looking long dark hair and big, dark soulful eyes. I didn't want somebody cheesy covered in fake tan. In fact, I wanted the model to look pale rather than heavily-tanned. After all, it was supposed to be winter. After looking through several model websites, I made requests to see ten models.

It was great to see Dave again. I hadn't seen him since before I gave birth and he enveloped me in a great big bear-hug before planting a smacker on my cheek. "You look stunning," he grinned. "Motherhood obviously sits well with you."

"Thanks," I said. "It does. It's a tough but very rewarding job!'

Even as I uttered the words I was struck by a pang of guilt again. Here I was at work while a stranger soothed my child when he cried, fed him when he was hungry, watered him when thirsty and amused him with his toys. Stop it, I berated myself. This is just ridiculous! Millions of mothers go back to work. Millions! Stop beating yourself up for it.

"Coffee?"

"Oh yes, please, I'd love some. Actually, there's a great little deli on the corner of this street that does great takeaway coffees."

"Grand, so. Do you want something to eat too?"

I shook my head. I really had to cut back on my endless munching at every opportunity. I yearned to get my figure back. "No thanks, Dave. I'm fine with black coffee."

I had been about to ask him to get a third cup for Louise, but then decided not to as she hadn't even turned up yet.

The casting was about to start in ten minutes. Dave and I sat behind a large desk near the door. The models were going to wait outside and then come in one by one and show us their portfolios. Models' portfolios were like CVs to them. Ideally they would contain totally different head and body shots showing the client what they would be capable of in front of the camera. Sometimes the prettiest of girls just couldn't take a good strong photo, while plainer girls were more versatile and almost came to life in front of the camera lens.

"Right, Dave, it looks like Louise isn't going to show so let's crack on with the casting. You sit there and I'll go out and get the first girl."

I popped outside and the girls were all standing in a queue chatting among themselves. I asked them if they could come in one by one, starting with the first girl Helen. Helen was a willowy, sweet-looking brunette, a girl I'd worked with in the past. She was an absolute pro, always enthusiastic and professional and never late for a job. She had a reputation in the fashion world of being great to work with. Today she arrived in, bright and breezy, with her recently updated portfolio.

She looked Dave straight in the eye, extended her hand and smiled. "Nice to see you again, Dave." Then she greeted me in the same friendly, polite manner. We flicked through her portfolio, praising some of her recent shots, and then asked her to tell the next girl in the line to come in.

She thanked us and left. Dave and I looked at each other and immediately recognised each other's disappointment.

"Her skin," I said, feeling my face crumple.

He too looked disappointed. "I know. It's unfortunate."

"Her skin is usually flawless. I don't understand it."

Dave shrugged. "That's why it's important to hold castings. It saves time in the long run."

"You could always airbrush her face, I suppose . . ."

"I could. But it would be easier if I didn't have to."

Michelle was next through the door. I hardly recognised her as she had put on at least a stone since I had worked with her last. Her lovely cheekbones had all but disappeared. She was still slim. In fact she was a lot slimmer than myself and slimmer than most women you would see walking up and down the street, but the horrible thing about doing fashion shoots was that the samples that you were sent from the designers were almost always a size eight, making it very difficult to work with models who were of a bigger size. I wish it wasn't like that but there was nothing I could do about it. Michelle would not be booked for this casting.

"We'll let you know," I told her.

But I knew that she knew we wouldn't be contacting her. It was tough. Modelling was a tough game. Rejection was the norm, but still I hated to be the one rejecting. It was awful.

Next in was Lorraine Dyer. Lorraine is a very popular model. She isn't the prettiest model ever, but she has striking bone structure, and being closely linked to one of Ireland's top rugby stars has kept her firmly in the gossip columns for the past two years. She is probably in the papers at least twice a week, and will pretty much do anything from standing in a bikini on Grafton Street with a handful of lottery cards in her hand to sitting on a bike with an inflatable banana on her head. I don't think Lorraine has ever actually turned down a job, and although she will probably never end up on the cover of *Image* magazine, she sure is laughing all the way to the bank.

"Hey, you guys!" She beamed, flashing her pearly whites. She was wearing a tight vest that showed off her recent boob job, and dark skinny jeans. She gave us both a kiss like we were her very best friends. Lorraine is very full-on bosom-buddies with anyone that might help her on the way to the top. You'd have to give her full marks for her networking skills, no doubt about that.

She showed us her portfolio. It was mostly press calls, launching everything from fake tan to washing powder. Her book lacked classy editorials but you couldn't help being impressed by the sheer volume of work that she had done over the last couple of years. There were no flies on Lorraine.

We had to see seven more girls. As expected, some of them looked so completely different from their online photos that they might as well have been different people altogether. It was quite amazing.

And then, just as I was about to give up hope that we were going to find the right girl, Adrienne walked in. She was at least six foot, feminine and willowy with long, shiny, dark hair and legs that seemed to go on forever. She had nice straight white teeth, a clear complexion and a lovely natural smile. She was obviously very young.

She wasn't wearing a shred of make-up and it was easy to see how versatile she could look.

When she left, myself and Dave turned to look at each other, and smiled in unison. We both knew we had found our woman.

Immediately I phoned Adrienne's agency and booked her for the shoot. Her agent boss told me that she was new to the agency and hadn't actually done a shoot with any Irish magazine before. This made me doubly excited. It was every stylist's dream to discover somebody brand new, an up-and-coming star. Adrienne was from Latvia and her English wasn't perfect, but that was okay, I wasn't hiring her for her conversational skills. Then Dave and I went down to the lobby to have another coffee and discuss the concept of the shoot.

I'd forgotten what nice and charming company Dave was. He was very easy to be around. He filled me in on all the gossip around town. As a society photographer he could tell me who was dating whom, who had split up with whom and which models had recently invested in Botox and boob jobs. He even told me that a particular model hounded him day and night to make sure he airbrushed out any of her wrinkles in photos and demanded that she got a look of all photos before they were emailed in to the picture desks.

We both agreed that Adrienne was a rare find.

"Can you believe she's only seventeen though?" I said. "That makes me feel very old."

"Don't be daft, you're still hot, Kaylah. You'd be hot at any age."

To my absolute mortification, I found myself blushing.

I looked away quickly to hide my face. It was the first time in ages a man had actually paid me a compliment. I was so grateful I was almost overwhelmed. Dave's job was to photograph stunning women on a daily basis, and he told me that he considered me hot? I could have cried with appreciation.

"Thanks," I gulped because I genuinely couldn't think of anything else to say. And then, and I'm not sure if it was just because I knew he fancied me, I actually began thinking that Dave was very attractive. He had lovely eyes and dark wavy hair that was greying slightly at the temples. He had a really cute boyish smile too. Oh God, maybe I was falling for him.

22

The lovely country-house hotel in Kildare where we had arranged to do the fashion shoot was set in extensive grounds, with pretty manicured lawns and an abundance of exotic-looking flowers. It was stunning and I had such a good feeling about the shoot.

But when I walked into the foyer I was amazed to see Louise of all people already sitting there. Why the hell was she here? Was I dreaming? She was sitting cross-legged by a table with a cappuccino in front of her.

"What are you doing here?" I asked, genuinely stunned.

She looked up at me with a mock smile. "What am I doing here? Oh, didn't anyone tell you? Creea sent me. She thought it would be good for me to help on the photo shoot. Is that not okay with you?"

"But . . . but you don't know anything about setting up fashion shoots," I felt myself spluttering with annoyance. "You didn't even show up to the casting."

Louise looked suitably taken aback. "Yes, that was unfortunate," she said. "But I genuinely couldn't find the hotel. Listen, if there's a problem I'll just go back to Dublin and tell Creea that there was a problem with me being here."

She went to pick up the Louis Vuitton suitcase by her feet.

"It's okay, you can stay," I answered, probably a bit too gruffly. I needed to calm down and not lose my cool so easily with her. If she had been trying to get a rise out of me it had worked. "But listen, we're not here on a holiday, so I am warning you that organising a fashion shoot is not child's play. I expect you to be more of a help than a hindrance. Understood?"

"Yes, of course," she said, her voice almost a whisper. "So what can I do?"

"I'll let you know in a minute," I said, and then took a deep breath. Jesus, I wished she would just go away! Talk about stressing me out!

I was berating myself for showing my annoyance so obviously. I didn't want her to get the better of me. But really I was astounded by her cheek. Showing up here unannounced and expecting me to welcome her with open arms? Honest to God.

Adrienne arrived about ten minutes later with her little wheelie case, looking a million dollars. Her Bambi-like eyes were enormous underneath those long lashes of hers and her skin was radiant as though she had enjoyed a thoroughly good night's sleep. She wore a genuine smile as she came over to kiss me on both cheeks. I introduced her to Louise and then ordered us all coffees.

The make-up artist, Steve, and hairdresser, Diana, arrived together shortly afterwards. They always worked as a team and were a joy to have around. Dave arrived about two minutes after them. And even though it was a stupid hour of the morning, I admit that my heart did a little flutter as I saw him coming in through the door with his equipment, wearing jeans and a simple white T-shirt that showed off his impressive physique. I couldn't wait for this shoot to begin.

As Diana and Steve worked their magic on Adrienne's fine features, making her into a supermodel type, I busied myself sorting through the various outfits. I had picked out a few select beautiful, well-cut dresses and to-die-for high-end shoes to match. I had an array of Christian Louboutin, Jimmy Choos and Guiseppe Zanotti heels in different colours from which to choose. Some were shimmery, sparkly, sky-high and utterly bling, while others were kitten-heeled, satin and soft with bows. I coveted each and every pair and found myself thinking that if I'd won the lottery I'd take them all home with me. There is a myth in the fashion world that models and stylists get a load of free clothes from the designers in return for wearing and promoting their clothes. This is, in fact, not entirely true. Some designers don't even give you a discount, and make out that they're doing you a huge favour by lending out their precious designs to you. My greatest fear doing a shoot like this with high-end luxury clothes is that the clothes might get damaged. I have to make sure the clothes are returned in immaculate condition, meaning no make-up on the collars, no hint of perfume and no snags whatsoever.

I laid the dresses out on the sofa of the main drawing room where we were going to do the shoot this morning beside the huge log fire. It was a spectacular room with ornate ceilings and magnificent paintings. It really was a room fit for gentry. The dresses were like works of art. I had pieces by Versace, Stella McCartney, Alice Temperley and even a stunning black dress from Victoria Beckham's latest collection. Even touching the fabric of these beautifully designed dresses sent a frisson of excitement down my spine. I was in love with the sheer quality of them all. If only I were rich!

I spent a good twenty minutes meticulously taping up the soles of the shoes. As long as the shoes were properly taped up in shoots, there wouldn't be any unforeseen casualties. Taping the soles made sure that no matter where Adrienne walked in them they wouldn't get scuffed. The last time one of my models scuffed a pair of designer shoes it cost me a week's wages. And they weren't even my bloody size. I ended up selling them on eBay for a fraction of the cost. An expensive lesson learned.

By nine thirty everybody was ready and Dave started shooting Adrienne. Diana and Steve had done an amazing job on her appearance and she looked very like (a very tall) Kiera Knightly with her subtle make-up, razor-sharp cheekbones, translucent skin and willowy frame. As she posed and worked with the camera I genuinely could not keep my eyes off her. This was a genuine superstar in the making.

I still really had no idea why Louise was there. She looked completely bored throughout the shoot, filing her nails, yawning heavily and basically showing no sign of being at all interested in what was going on. She spent a good deal of the time going outside to chat on her mobile phone and took far more cigarette breaks than was necessary. When I asked her at noon to get some lunch menus for the rest of us, she seemed to look at me resentfully before reluctantly agreeing to do so.

She was much more of a hindrance than a help. It seemed to be hard for her to grasp the concept that fashion shoots were hard work, with everybody needing to pull together to get the shots done. Time was of the essence.

We slogged continuously throughout the morning, taking shot after shot in the drawing room and then later in the day moving out to the gardens to take some outside shots. We stopped only briefly for soup and sandwiches. By six thirty we had finally wrapped up. We were all exhausted and in need of dinner and a good night's sleep.

Everyone went to their respective rooms. Louise, who was the only one of us who wasn't tired, said she was going to use the leisure centre which was attached to the country house and that she had booked herself a massage. It was well for her, I thought. Where did she get the money to act like such a lady of leisure? All I was fit to do now was go up to my room, run a hot bath, and then kip for a couple of hours before it was time for dinner. I said goodbye to the others, went up to my room, kicked off my shoes and flopped down on the bed.

The first thing I needed to do was phone Tanya to see how she was getting on without me. The apartment phone rang and rang and rang. No answer there. They must have gone out, I thought. Maybe Tanya took John to the shops, or for a little walk on the beach. I tried her mobile. It rang out. How bizarre! Tanya always answered her mobile promptly, especially when she knew it was me calling. I found myself panicking ever so slightly and dialled her number again.

"Hello?"

"Hello, Tanya?" I found myself shouting. "Tanya, can you hear me?"

"Yes, I can hear you. Sorry, it's a bit noisy in here."

"Where are you? Are you in a pub?"

"No, of course not." Tanya sounded mildly offended. "I'm in café in Greystones with John. I'm meeting a friend of mine here."

It definitely sounded like she was in a pub and I found myself getting a little annoyed. I hoped she wasn't taking advantage of the fact that I was away for the night. Suddenly I began to wish that I hadn't left her in charge. Maybe I should have asked my mum to look after John just this once.

"Tanya, I'd really like you to take John home now. He's due his nap soon, and I'd also like you to give him a bath and wash his hair this evening after he has his tea."

"Of course, Kaylah. I understand. I'll take him home right away. Is there anything else you need me to do for you? Any shopping to do before you get back tomorrow?"

I felt myself soften a little. "No, no, it's okay," I said. "I was just ringing to make sure my son was safe and happy. Thanks, Tanya. I'll see you tomorrow. If there's an emergency you have my mother's number."

Maybe I was being way too over-protective, I thought. Tanya was always such an angel around John. Perhaps I was worrying unnecessarily because it was my first night leaving him with somebody that wasn't family. I'd had a pretty intensive day work-wise and tomorrow was going to be an early start again. I should really take myself to bed and have an early night.

I phoned Dave's room to tell him I wouldn't be joining him for dinner and that I was just going to order room service instead. He sounded a little disappointed but said he completely understood. Then I phoned Adrienne and the others to tell them the same thing. I didn't have the number of Louise's room so I just texted her to say I wouldn't be going for dinner and that she should book for dinner at seven for herself and the others. She didn't send me a text back but I didn't worry my head about her non-response.

I must have been very tired because, after I had ordered room service and eaten, I fell into a deep undisturbed sleep and woke up just before my alarm clock sounded the next day. I looked out the window, and it looked like it was going to be a fine day. Oh great, I thought cheerfully, the weather was so perfect for our shoot. Hopefully we might even be able to get a few good outdoor shots too. The sweeping entrance to the country-house hotel was rather impressive, like something from a vintage film set. I imagined getting a good shot of Adrienne in the doorway. As though she were the Lady of the Manor.

I waited for the others in the breakfast room. After a while I checked my watch anxiously. Where was everybody?

I had arranged to meet the crew at seven so I was surprised when not a single other person had showed up by seven fifteen. Had I got the time wrong? It was most unlike me, especially on the morning of such an important shoot.

I texted Tanya, wondering if she and John would still be asleep, but she responded saying John was awake and she had just given him a feed. She assured me that he was in great form, which put my mind at ease somewhat. He was the most important thing in my life and he was all right and happy and that was the main thing. However, my work was the second most important thing in my life and if I didn't come up with some mighty impressive fashion shots for Creea's all-important Christmas issue, my head was going to be on the proverbial chopping-block.

Just as I was about to seriously question myself and my timing, Adrienne arrived at the table dressed in faded jeans and a white T-shirt. "I am so sorry," she said, rubbing her eyes. "I slept it out."

She looked exhausted, as though she had been out on the tear the night before. There were dark shadows under her eyes. I was naturally alarmed. "Did you sleep okay, Adrienne?"

"Yes, thanks, I got to bed a little late though," she yawned.

My eyes widened in shock. "What do you mean you got to bed late? Where were you?"

"We were at dinner," she answered groggily, rubbing her eyes. "Louise booked dinner for us all for nine but by the time we finished up it was almost midnight."

"You're kidding me! Nine was far too late for dinner. I texted her and told her to book dinner for you all at seven. No wonder you're exhausted and the others aren't here yet. This just isn't good enough."

"I'm sorry," said Adrienne, looking genuinely contrite.

I was fuming and I could feel myself getting hot under the collar. I really was so annoyed about this. I knew what Louise was doing. She was trying to sabotage my entire shoot! The shoot that I had worked so hard on to make sure everything was perfect.

Dave was down next, yawning loudly. "Sorry I'm late," he said. "We didn't get to bed until quite late last night."

"So I heard," I sighed my displeasure. "Needless to say I'm not impressed. Come on, we'd better get moving. There's no time for a long breakfast unfortunately. Just get some black coffee into you, grab some croissants and let's start. Where are Diana and Steve?"

"I dunno. Diana went to bed the same time as I did, around midnight, but the last I saw of Steve he was doing shots in the residents' bar with Louise."

I felt the colour drain from my face, I was that annoyed. "Right. That's the final straw now. I'm going to kill that girl when I see her. What a troublesome little cow! She must think this whole thing is a joke but our asses are on the line here."

"I know," said Dave sheepishly. "They asked me to join them in the bar but I had enough sense to say no. I wish I'd ordered them to go to bed."

"So do I!"

My blood pressure was about to hit the roof. Our make-up artist was obviously hungover in bed and it was the one morning that we really needed him to make our model look alive. This was a complete and utter disaster.

"Come on," said Dave, draining his cup of coffee. "Stay positive. It will all turn out great. I'll go up to Steve's room and rouse him. Do you want me to wake Louise too?"

"No, don't bother," I muttered. "She is actually a lot more useful to us when she's in bed asleep."

Steve came down the stairs a few minutes later looking as though he hadn't slept for a week never mind a night. "My head," he said mournfully. "*Ouch!*"

"If you think you're going to get an ounce of sympathy from me you're mistaken," I said in the most disapproving tone I could muster.

"Don't blame me! That Louise one is a terrible influence. She could drink anyone under the table."

I hoped that he saw from the look on my face that I wasn't one bit impressed with his late-night antics. "Come on, Steve, forget the excuses. We're under pressure for time now."

There was no sign whatsoever of party-girl Louise as we set up for the second day of the shoot. Diana, little star that she was, did wonders with Adrienne's hair, putting it in a chic up-style, and today she had an extra pair of hands. Jenny, her assistant, had arrived to help. Jenny was from Galway and had recently moved to Dublin. She was so lively with lots of ideas. She was like a breath of fresh air on the shoot and I could see she would go very far in life with that abundance of enthusiasm.

Steve managed to make Adrienne's angelic face look even prettier with dark aubergine eye shadow, flawless foundation, false eyelashes that looked remarkably real and plum lipstick. We worked hard to get the photos done, and Adrienne worked hard, putting her all into the shoot and changing into the different outfits at breakneck speed. Six hours later when we paused for some well-earned lunch, Louise wandered into the restaurant looking as a fresh as a daisy and announced that she had just had a swim in the hotel leisure centre. I am still amazed my jaw didn't hit off the floor in shock. I had never witnessed such bad behaviour by anybody since I had started working as a stylist. She was an absolute disgrace.

Dave had obviously noticed my distress, because after we eventually wrapped up he gave me a reassuring hug and told me not to let Louise get to me. He told me she wasn't worth wasting my energy on. Then he surprised me by asking me whether he could take me out some day the following week to discuss some ideas for shoots. I could see it was his way of making up to me for being unwittingly involved in Louise's attempt at sabotage. I agreed to lunch. In fact, I would look forward to it.

23

Creea sat staring at the computer screen. I was trying to gauge her reaction to the photos of the fashion shoot but it was hard to read her. "The model looks totally different in the second set of shots. I don't know why. It's odd," she said, squinting at the photos with a frown on her face.

My heart was beating like crazy and I could feel the palms of my hands getting sweaty. This was nerve-wracking stuff. Did she even like any of them? It was so hard to tell. I badly wanted her to love them. This was my big chance to get back in the game of fashion shoots after a fairly long absence. If I blew it I would probably never get this kind of opportunity again.

I felt myself secretly cursing Louise for turning up and ruining things for me. She was like a thorn in my side. It was true that Adrienne didn't look as good in the second batch of shots. Even I couldn't deny that. And the reason? Well, that was because she had stayed up late, thanks to Louise. I was still racking my brains to try and find out why she had even bothered turning up, unless it really was to sabotage my efforts. Did she think working in fashion was all about the honour and the glory? It was one-per-cent inspiration and ninety-nine-per-cent perspiration. Anybody who thought conducting fashion shoots was a walk in the park was in for a big shock.

"This one is great," said Creea, and I nearly fell off my chair with joy. At last! A glimmer of hope. "Where did you get the dog from? It's genius."

My head nearly swelled with pride. "To be honest I'm not sure where he appeared from. It was just one of those random things. When the photographer was setting up the shoot he just walked around from the back of the hotel and sat at the model's feet. He stayed there until he had got his photo taken and then just wandered off again. He must have belonged to one of the hotel staff or maybe even one of the guests."

"Well, I hope his owner won't be contacting us looking for an appearance fee!" Creea chuckled.

I could feel myself relax. Phew! At least my boss wasn't going to admonish me for the terrible second set of pictures.

"And I like this one very much," Creea went on, pointing to an image of Adrienne pretending to play a grand piano. "It really encapsulates old-fashioned elegance. Brownie points to you for that one too."

I felt myself blush. I had been yearning for praise and now that I was getting it I didn't know what to do with it.

"But some of the shots are unusable." Creea's face

clouded. "I'm afraid they're not up to standard. I mean, look at that one for example. The model looks like she's about to keel over with exhaustion. There's nothing special about that shot."

"Oh, that particular one was taken towards the end of the second day," I ventured apologetically. "The model was tired. She had been up late the night before."

I could feel Creea bristle. She turned to look at me and I could feel her eyes boring into me, making me feel so uncomfortable. "Why? How?"

I sat up straight in my seat. I'd need to choose my words carefully. I wasn't sure what Louise had already told her.

"Well, the model and the crew had dinner late and they stayed up late as a consequence. I'm sure they had drinks."

Creea's face darkened. I could tell she was furious. No surprise there. "They were drinking? Including the model? That's pretty unforgiveable. I thought every model knew that you just don't drink the night before a fashion shoot. Let her drink by all means, but not on our money. The nerve of her! We'll never book her for anything again! Where were you when all this was happening?"

I began to feel very small indeed. It was quite obvious that I was getting the blame for this even though I had been in bed during the late-night hooley.

"I didn't have dinner with them. I went to my room early. In hindsight I shouldn't have relied on the others to go to bed early too. And I should have warned the model not to drink but I didn't imagine in a million years that she would. Or that she would stay up so late."

Creea's eyes narrowed. "But you were the one in charge."

"I know but I had left Louise in charge of the dinner arrangements."

Even as I spoke I knew I sounded petty and I was ashamed of myself but I really felt I was being scapegoated here and that it wasn't fair.

"Really? Louise never mentioned any of this at all. In fact, she said the shoot went very well and that everything went without a hitch. Now I find out you were all getting locked in the bar?"

I must have looked horrified by her accusation. "No, it wasn't like that at all," I insisted. "The others stayed up late but they weren't manky drunk."

Creea looked at me huffily. "I bet that photographer, Dave, coerced them all into staying up late. That man has a reputation for being a bit of a party animal. He can't be trusted. It's not fair to blame poor Louise as she's only new and learning. Look, why don't you leave these shots with me to mull over? I need time to choose the six best ones. At least we have a cover here and that's the main thing."

I slunk out of her office, feeling elated one minute and numb the next. Of course I was thrilled that one of the shots was going to be made into a cover. After all, it is every stylist's wish to get as many covers in her career as possible and it has great prestige but I was raging that Louise had got off scot-free with her bad behaviour and that Creea had turned against Dave as result. What an awful mess that was.

I peered through the window of the door of the

communal office. Louise was sitting at the communal desk with her back to the door. I just couldn't face making small talk with her. I decided I'd go out for some fresh air. I had bags of clothes, shoes and accessories to drop back to the shops so at least I could use that as an excuse to get out of the office.

I was in the lift with two bags of shoes that needed to be dropped back to Grafton Street when my phone rang. Sugar! It was at the bottom of my handbag and my two hands were full. Whoever it was would just have to leave a message. The phone rang out and then it started ringing again. Gosh, the impatience of some people! What could possibly be so urgent? Then a sudden thought struck me. What if it were Tanya? Suppose she had dropped John on his head or something terrible like that. I let the two carrier bags fall on the ground, and rummaged around my big handbag. Finally I retrieved the blasted phone.

It wasn't Tanya's number flashing, it was Dave's.

"Hello?"

"Hey, Dave, how are you?"

"I'm great thanks, and how about you?"

"Great," I answered, my voice full of false gaiety. I waited for him to ask the question I knew he would inevitably ask. I was dreading lying to him.

"Listen, Kaylah, I was just wondering if you knew if Creea was happy with the shoot we did? I've tried phoning a couple of times today but the receptionist said she was out at meetings."

"Oh."

"Yes, so I was wondering if you knew anything."

"Hi, Dave, sorry, you're breaking up on me . . . I can't

hear you too well. I'm on the street and the noise of the traffic is deafening."

"Sure, okay, I understand. Can I grab you for that lunch tomorrow? Can we meet, say, at one outside the main entrance of Arnott's in Henry Street and take it from there? I've a great idea for a shoot and I want to run it by you."

I felt my heart sink a bit. I had been kind of hoping that he had asked me for lunch because he fancied me and not just because he wanted to work with me. But I guess I had got that completely wrong!

"That's fine, Dave," I said. "I'll see you then."

And with a heavy heart, to match the two carrier bags that were threatening to pull my arms from their sockets, I continued my way towards Brown Thomas.

24

Dave looked very nice when I met him – very laid back, and was, if I were to be perfectly honest, quite sexy.

I took my seat opposite him in the Thai restaurant called Koh on the Millennium walkway just yards from the River Liffey. It was a vibrant, eclectic part of the city centre. I've always wanted to try the restaurant as I adore Thai food so when Dave asked me where we should go for a bite to eat, I suggested this place.

"You look lovely," he said, leaning forward to give me a kiss.

He smelled of strong, masculine aftershave. Mmm. Very nice. Considering we weren't even on a date he looked like he had made a bit of an effort. He wore a royal-blue Ralph Lauren shirt that matched his eyes, jeans and a well-cut expensive-looking blazer. He looked like the type of man any woman would be proud to be seen with.

"Thank you," I said, picking up the menu and glancing through it.

A waiter offered to show us the wine list.

Dave looked at me. "You're not driving, are you?"

"God no, I'm not," I said airily as though I had left the car at home especially for the occasion. I didn't tell him that I got the train to and from work every day without fail. I couldn't possibly afford either a car or the petrol to fill it up, never mind the parking charges on my miserable wages.

"Would you prefer red or white?"

"White would be great, thanks."

"Chardonnay, Chablis, Pinot Grigio?"

"Pinot Grigio, please."

I relaxed into my chair. I was looking forward to my lunch. It was a treat, even though it was business-related and possibly the only reason that Dave was tolerating me was because I could be very useful to him. I had the editor's ear. Or at least, I'd had it. I wasn't too sure where I stood now with Creea.

Getting straight to the point, before we had even ordered, Dave brought up the subject of the Kildare fashion shoot again. I could feel myself groan inwardly. I had really been hoping that the business talk could wait until at least dessert.

"I still haven't heard back from Creea, even though I sent her a couple of emails and left messages with her receptionist. I'm getting a little worried now. Do you know if she's terribly busy at the moment?"

He looked so anxious for good news that I felt a bit guilty now. I cast my eyes down towards the menu in my hand and bit my lip. Of course my boss was ignoring him and it was partly my fault. If I hadn't told her about the late-night antics at the hotel, Creea might still be in the dark. I wondered whether now would be a good time to come clean. Maybe not. Every fibre of my body seemed to be telling me that I should wait until we'd had at least a glass of wine each. It would be easier then. For me.

I decided to tell a lie instead. "I think she is busy. She's been wrapped up all morning." Okay, so it wasn't a complete lie. Creea had gone off to a well-known luxurious spa on a freebie earlier on and had been in such good form she'd told me to take the rest of the day off. No doubt she was wrapped up now. In seaweed or something.

"No worries," said Dave good-naturedly. "There's no urgency or anything. I was just wondering if she liked the shots. She didn't say anything, did she?"

Feck it anyway! My back was really being put to the wall here. I wished he'd just give it a rest and let us get on with lunch. Just as I was about to make up some other plausible answer, a waiter came to our table with the bottle of wine and presented the label to me.

"It looks fine," I beamed enthusiastically.

He was wondering if "madame" wanted to try some first. No, goddammit, just get on with it, I silently urged. I needed alcohol in me now!

But of course I didn't express such emotions. "Go ahead and pour, please. I'm sure it's just fine."

I took an eagerly anticipated sip. Ooh, that was lovely! So fruity and chilled. "Good choice," I said, nodding my approval.

He smiled at the compliment. He had lovely eyes, I

thought. They were kind and thoughtful. You could tell a lot about people by their eyes. They were the windows to the soul.

He picked up his glass and I did the same. "Cheers," he said, smiling. "Let's raise a toast to many more fashion shoots in the future."

Oh God, I really wished he hadn't said that. Now I felt I was being completely used. I could have looked like the back of the bus and he'd still be toasting the future of our work together. Oh, well – he probably had a girlfriend anyway. All good-looking men of a certain age had girlfriends, or at least a girlfriend. And Dave even had all his own hair which was an absolute bonus.

I nodded but I didn't vocally agree. I mean I'm all for toasting health and happiness, but toasting work? Forget it!

A delightful young waiter came around with the bread basket. Oh no – carbs, I thought dejectedly but as usual I tucked in regardless. To hell with the diet – it wasn't working anyway! The restaurant was filling up which was good. The atmosphere was building.

"So . . . like I said . . . I have an idea for a shoot," Dave said dreamily, toying with the stem of his glass. "I think it's something that you would be very interested in. Would you like to hear it now or later?"

Or never! I yelled internally. Now I knew Dave was very passionate about his work and took it very seriously but this was just taking the biscuit. Why hadn't he just sent me an email with his wonderful idea? Why this charade? I felt like flinging my napkin at him and storming off. But that would be way too dramatic. I couldn't be acting like a drama queen in his company. Hell, we weren't even on a date!

I took a deep breath and leaned forward, trying to look enthusiastic. "Tell me now," I said. Best to get it over and done with, I reckoned. Then I'd be free to enjoy the rest of the meal! I opened my eyes wide to look like I was more eager than I actually was.

He put his chin in the palms of his hands and looked me straight in the eye.

"I am thinking hazy summer days,' he said. "Bikinis, cocktails, high-end designer kaftans . . . oval swimming pools, blue skies . . . I'm thinking . . ."

And I'm thinking I need to top up my wine pronto!

I looked at him as though he had completely lost the plot. What was wrong with him? Why was he talking such gibberish? He must have been on another planet entirely! We were heading into winter and this was Ireland. We hadn't had a proper summer for a couple of years. You could hardly call three days in May and two days in September a real summer!

"I'm thinking sunsets and sand, sea and . . ."

And I'm thinking I need to rein you in!

I couldn't talk about fashion shoots any more. I glanced over at the wine bottle in its cooler but refrained from reaching for it and topping up my own glass in case I looked ignorant. I just could not get excited right now about a fashion shoot set on a sunny beach and I didn't know where the hell he was going with this fantasy of his. It was so out there. I wondered whether I should tell him straight out to forget about it, that he was no longer flavour of the month with Creea and that in any case she wouldn't dream of commissioning any fashion shoots set on a beach or anything daft like that in the middle of winter. And besides, what kind of a budget did he think the magazine had to play around with? We might all be living in Recession-land but Dave was clearly living in Cloud-cuckoo-land.

"I think it's a great idea, Dave," I said gently so as not to upset him. "But maybe at a future date. We work months in advance. Once we put this Christmas issue to bed, we'll be concentrating on Valentine's and early spring. I'll have to focus on all that and –"

"Wait!" he said, cutting me dead.

I didn't know what to think. Maybe he was annoyed that I wasn't jumping up and down with joy after hearing his rather bizarre idea. Perhaps he was beginning to regret wasting a fancy lunch on me.

"I'm sorry, Dave," I said awkwardly. "Maybe we'll talk about the idea again."

"But let me explain!"

I felt my heart sink a little. I found myself fancying him less and less. He was like a dog with a bone. I couldn't fancy somebody who was obsessed with doing bikini shots in the middle of winter in a cold rainy country like Ireland.

"Okay, go on then . . ."

"I wasn't thinking of doing the shoot here in Ireland," he said, actually looking quite indignant at the idea of it. "I was thinking along the lines of the Cyprus coast. Cyprus has warm weather all year around and has beautiful beaches. I think it would be the perfect location for what I have in mind."

Right, it was official now, I thought. Dave had finally lost the plot. Cyprus? God, as if! I could just imagine asking Creea for the money for myself, Dave, a fashion model, a hairstylist and a make-up artist all to fly off to Cyprus for a fun shoot. Instead of simply scoffing at the idea, she might fire me on the spot for being so crazy. And then Louise would be simply delighted as she'd have my desk all to herself.

Suddenly I wished I hadn't thought about Louise. A vision of her smirking face floating before my eyes made me wince.

"Creea would never agree to my doing it, so there's no point even going there!" I said firmly, not wishing to spend my afternoon talking about something which was so off-the-wall it wasn't even funny. "Honestly, I'm not even really in her good books at the moment." And neither are you! "And she seems to think the sun shines out of that new girl, Louise. I have no idea why she is sharing my desk or even what she does at the magazine only interfere with my work. I hope Creea wakes up and smells the coffee. Louise is totally surplus to requirement."

"Well, I don't care what Creea thinks of this idea as it wouldn't concern her," said Dave, lifting the bottle of wine from its cooler. "More?"

I nodded and was just about to respond when he spoke again.

"Anyway, there's nothing much you can do with Louise except put up with her. Creea is hardly going to fire the boss's niece, is she?"

The *what*? Had I heard right? The boss's niece? My jaw practically hit the floor in shock. I found my world suddenly tilt to one side.

"Is that true?" I gasped, once I'd finally found my voice again.

"You didn't know? Sorry. I just presumed you did. She told us that night in the hotel after you had gone to bed. Her uncle is Adam Wolfe, owner of the magazine. So Creea didn't tell you?"

I felt completely betrayed. Why should I have been the last to know? No wonder Louise had this permanent superior little smile etched onto her face. Oh God, I felt like a real fool now. I sipped a little of my wine. This was not good news.

"Funny how I was the only person in the dark. I'm actually annoyed about that now."

"Well, don't be. Let's be positive. Let's think of sunny Cyprus instead."

"I told you, forget Cyprus. Creea wouldn't let me do it."

"But I told you, this would be up to you – it has nothing to do with Creea."

Huh? I perked up. What was he talking about? How could he think Creea had nothing to do with it? Without her blessing there would be no fashion shoot anywhere, never mind Cyprus.

"I don't understand," I said, feeling confused.

"It's not for your magazine but for a travel magazine in the UK. They've commissioned me to do a Spring/Summer swimwear shoot, and they have a good budget. We'll stay in a five-star resort and . . . well, naturally I thought of hiring you to style the shoot."

I was gobsmacked. I really was. He was offering to hire me? Oh God, and all this time I thought he was just treating me to lunch because he was counting on me for work. I felt guilty as hell. Especially as it was my fault that Creea wasn't too pleased with him right now.

"But how will I take the time off?"

Dave was so laid back about it all. "You don't need to. We could shoot it over a weekend. You have a reliable nanny now, don't you?"

"Yes, I do, but . . ."

We were interrupted by the waitress coming around to take our orders. I chose the Phad Thai with tofu and Dave went for the Thai crab and mango salad.

As I watched him studying the menu I thought he looked gorgeous then. I found myself quickly changing my mind again. I did fancy him now. I really did. And I was so flattered that he had asked me to come to Cyprus.

"Are you sure we could do it in a couple of days?" I asked anxiously when the waitress went off with our orders. As a mum of a baby who couldn't yet speak, I couldn't just head off on a whim.

"Just a couple, yes," he said. "Max three. You could take a day off on the Monday. How about it? Come on, Kaylah. The weather's still lovely at this time of year. A bit more sun on your face would do you the world of good."

I smiled as I buttered some bread on my side plate. It hadn't been that long since I'd last been in the sun. But that had been a manless holiday hanging around a kid's club for most of the day. I looked up at Dave's expectant face. He was really selling it to me now. I could almost feel the rays of sunshine beaming down on my body. Creea wouldn't like it, especially as she didn't like Dave at the moment, but it didn't really matter about Creea because I would be doing the shoot in my own free time and it wouldn't interfere with my job at the magazine. Gosh, I was getting excited now. I could almost smell the salty sea air and sense the feeling of warm sand in between my toes. How could I possibly say no?

25

"Oh my God, What a stunning Louis Vuitton!" I found myself exclaiming as I admired the brand-new handbag sitting on my kitchen table. "How many designer bags have you got now? I'm losing count! This is the real deal, isn't it?"

"Of course it is," Tanya said, sounding taken aback at the very idea that somebody might even suggest that she owned a bag that was a fake.

"But that must have cost you an absolute arm and a leg!" I truly was astonished. I always had told myself that if I ever won the lottery I would buy a Louis Vuitton bag. I thought they were just so classy and gorgeous.

Tanya just shrugged in that way that she had. "It was gift," she said. "And besides, I'm worth it. By the way, John is asleep. He has been very good all day. I put him down to bed about an hour ago after his bath."

"Thank you so much."

"I think he's growing."

"I should hope so. He's certainly drinking lots of milk!" I laughed.

"He looks more and more like you every day, I think."

"Really?" Good. I was very pleased with that comment. All Clive had contributed to his son's life so far was a nasty solicitor's letter. He hadn't even bought him so much as a teddy or even one nappy. He hadn't baby-sat a single night nor even enquired as to how the child was doing. And now he was looking for a night's access every second weekend?

Yes, I know it was only one night but I couldn't see myself agreeing to that. Clive was a complete stranger as far as Baby John was concerned. He didn't know what his dad looked like. How could I just hand him out every second weekend to a complete stranger? God only knew what kind of company Clive kept. He could have lads around at the house drinking until the small hours of the morning. He might even bring one-night stands back after the pub. Surely I would be an irresponsible mother if I just loaned out my son one night in every fourteen just to ease the conscience of a guilty deadbeat dad who hadn't helped me one ounce since my kid was born? Even thinking about the letter from Clive's solicitor made me want to hold my beloved child close to my chest and never let him out of my sight again. I just loved that little boy with every single fibre of my being.

"So do you need me for anything else? I cooked a lasagne earlier on and it's in the fridge. You just need to heat it up."

I was gobsmacked. This girl never failed to impress me. The apartment was gleaming like a shiny new pin and the floor was spotless. And now she was telling me that dinner was made.

"Oh gosh, thanks so much, Tanya. I think I'll have some and then have an early night. I'm pretty whacked right now."

"Will I pour you a glass of wine before I leave?"

"Oh no, Tanya. Thanks for offering but I was out for lunch earlier and had a couple of glasses then. I think I'll stick to simple old tea this evening. You go off and enjoy yourself. Are you going out with the girls from The Secret Nanny Club?"

"No, I'm going on a date," she said, without batting an eyelid.

I smiled at her. "This must be getting serious."

She tilted her head. "Serious? What do you mean?"

"Well, this nice gentleman must be taking quite a shine to you."

"It's a different gentleman this time." She laughed at the look on my face. "Why not?" she shrugged. "Life's too short to waste it with just one man when there are billions of them out there!"

I continued to stare at her, open-mouthed. I honestly didn't know what to say. I had thought there was supposed to be a shortage of men in Dublin! Apart from my lunch with Dave, the only 'date' I'd even come close to in recent months was in a fruit and vegetable shop! In a way I suppose I admired her. She was a beauty and not only did she play hard she worked bloody hard too. I honestly didn't know what I would do without her.

"Anyway, I'd better go and take a shower and make myself presentable," she said as I got up to turn on the kettle.

As I waited for the hot water to boil I tiptoed into my bedroom to see how John was doing. He was fast asleep with his little arm protectively around his teddy's waist. I felt a little pang of guilt. He hadn't seen me at all today. I'd been gone before he'd woken up. Now it was dark and he was in the Land of Baby Nod. I bent down and kissed his little warm cheek. I'll never be poor as long as I have you, my angel, I thought, looking at his sleeping little body. I wouldn't have traded him in even for the EuroMillions lottery. He really was the best thing that had ever happened to me.

A slight knock on the door. "You in there?"

I could smell her perfume before I could see her. It was strong and musky. She wore black leather trousers, red heels, a white shirt and an expensive-looking blazer. She looked sensational. In fact she looked so hot I wondered, and not for the first time, why this goddess-like creature was working for me and not gracing the cover of *Sports Illustrated*.

"I just wanted to say goodnight to John," I said in a low voice as I patted his forehead gently. "He looks even more adorable when he sleeps."

"I agree," said Tanya. "John is especially gorgeous."

"Well, of course I would think that. But I'm his mum and all mums think their children are gorgeous."

"I love children. I love their innocence. It's best that they keep it as long as possible. Real life is hard enough."

I turned to look at Tanya. I couldn't really see her face

properly in the doorway but her voice had a trace of disappointment in it.

"Would you like children someday, Tanya?"

She shrugged. "Maybe, maybe not. I think I probably enjoy my freedom too much to want to give it up."

The sound of a horn outside had her making for the front door. "See you in the morning," she called out as she left.

I sat for a while on my bed in the darkness listening to my son's rhythmical breathing. The apartment seemed abnormally quiet apart from the sound of my stomach rumbling. I had a feeling deep down that all was not what it seemed with Tanya. She was almost too perfect. What other nanny looked like a film star, acted like Mary Poppins and had a wardrobe to rival a wealthy Dublin socialite? It didn't add up. Tanya never had friends around. I had asked her if she wanted to meet up with Sheelagh's nanny, Claudine and she said that she didn't want to particularly. Then when I asked her if Claudine could join the Secret Nanny Club she had cryptically told me that it was full now and not taking on any further members for the time being.

She never invited anybody back to the apartment for a coffee. But then again, was I simply nit-picking? Was I looking for faults where there were none to be found? Surely I should be delighted with what I had? Would I want my tiny kitchen crowded out with her friends all talking a different language to me anyway? Certainly not.

Feeling a little more positive I wandered back into the kitchen to make some tea and toast. As I did so I felt my phone vibrate in my pocket. Who would be calling at this time of the evening? I fished out the phone. It was Mum.

"Hi, Mum."

"Hello, darling. How are you? I haven't seen you in a long time."

Oh no! A mini guilt trip! "I'm fine, Mum. I've been busy though. Going back to work has turned my life upside down."

"I called over this afternoon. Didn't Tanya tell you?"

"No, no she didn't, she must have forgotten. That's odd. It's unlike her to forget."

"*Hmm.*"

"What's wrong, Mum? Is everything okay?"

"I'm just a little uneasy. About that girl."

"Tanya?"

"Yes, when I called around she was watching TV in the sitting room with a gentleman friend. She said you were in work and that John was asleep in his cot and it was best not to disturb him. She made me feel very unwelcome on the steps of my own daughter's home!"

Mum was clearly upset. I was shocked by her phone call. And what's more I was confused. Why hadn't Tanya told me she'd had a visitor? I didn't like to think of complete strangers wandering around the place while I wasn't there.

"I'm so sorry, Mum. I didn't know. Listen, have you eaten? Tanya has gone out but she cooked a lasagne today and left it in the fridge. Would you like to call around and we can eat together?"

Mum gave a little sigh. You'd swear I lived across the

city rather than just down the road. "Well, okay, then. I suppose I'd better."

I put down the phone. I had a hollow pit in my stomach. My mum was onto something. She had just made my niggling doubts feel not so unfounded any more.

"I'll say it again. I'm uneasy about that girl. I mean, who was that man anyway? He was much older than her."

"They could have been just friends, you know," I said, finding myself defending my au pair.

My mother dug her fork into the lasagne. "*Hmmm*. A bit unlikely, don't you think? I'm a lot older than you are and I have hunches about these things."

"Okay, whatever you say, but I'm still not searching her room. That would be a gross breach of privacy. You cannot just rummage through people's stuff because you have a hunch that they're up to something."

Mum sniffed her disapproval. "I just think that I would want to know exactly who was living under my roof and sharing a home with my child."

I said nothing. I wasn't budging on that one. I was not searching Tanya's room.

By the time she left my apartment I felt drained. The woman had managed to suck the life out of me, trying to convince me that Tanya was the wrong sort of girl. And even though I tried to dismiss her fanciful imagination I couldn't help wondering that maybe my mother was right.

My mind was buzzing and I knew there was no chance of me going to sleep early so I sat in front of the telly, my eyes glazed over and not really seeing anything.

As I propped up the cushions behind my back my hand hit something sharp. Investigating what it was, I discovered a silver necklace. It was truly exquisite with a small diamond locket. That must have cost absolute fortune, I thought. I had never seen Tanya wear it but it must have been hers. It certainly wasn't mine.

Well, here was a god-given reason for me to go into Tanya's room with a clear conscience. I got up and made for her room, glad my mother couldn't see me now.

I opened her door slightly and turned on the light. The bed was neatly made and the room was immaculate. Under the window she had two rows of shoes and boots, most of them spanking new. Even from the doorway I could recognise the labels: Jimmy Choo, Louboutin, Gucci, Manolo. I could literally count the cost of thousands of euro among the fancy footwear. It was none of my business, however, I thought. Who was I to say that my au pair couldn't wear any kind of shoes she liked? There was a pretty shell-encrusted jewellery box sitting on the bedside locker next to the bed. I opened the box and was intrigued by what I saw. There were at least ten silver and gold necklaces, charm bracelets and brooches. I spotted a Cartier watch and a string of very expensive pearls. I was about to set the necklace down among the other trinkets but then figured it best to leave it on the locker where she would see it when she came in – and where she wouldn't realise I had been poking into her jewellery box. I quickly snapped the box shut. I didn't want to snoop any more. No matter how much I was tempted to open Tanya's wardrobe I knew that I couldn't. I would just never be able to forgive myself for snooping.

I closed Tanya's bedroom door, went into the bathroom and started slowly removing my make-up with cleanser and cotton wool. I then ran the bath generously, adding in the bath oil. My head was frazzled and my mind was racing. I just wanted to get into that bath and let it soak away all my concerns.

Just as I was about to immerse myself into the inviting bubbles I heard my phone beep. It was Dave.

Hey. Is 18 next week ok 4 u? Leaving DUB Fri afternoon, arrive home Mon morn. Weather Cyprus 28 C. Dx.

Immediately I felt myself getting excited. Dave had given me the link to the Paphos boutique hotel we would be staying in. It was stunning with views overlooking the ocean. I wanted to go so badly and doing the shoot over the weekend wouldn't interfere with my work in the magazine. But there was one major problem. I no longer trusted Tanya to look after my pride and joy.

26

The woman at the end of the phone hung up. It was what I had been expecting her to do to be honest. I phoned again and after two rings I was cut off once more. So much for the Secret Nanny Club. I sat at my kitchen table staring, with my head in my hands. What was I going to do now?

My head was reeling and I was shaking like a leaf. Tanya had brought John down to the strand earlier, leaving her wallet open on the kitchen table. I couldn't help taking a quick peek. In it was a thousand euro in notes and a small bundle of simple black cards with *The Secret Nanny Club* in white lettering followed by a mobile number underneath. I just had to phone the number straight away. I knew it was dodgy. Jesus, even an idiot could have worked that out!

My phone rang, making me nearly jump out of my skin. It was Dave.

"Hey, how are you?"

"Oh, Dave, I'm fine. Well, as fine as I could be really considering . . ." I trailed off.

"What's wrong? You sound off. Have you just seen a ghost?"

I took a deep breath. "No, but I think I've just spoken to one."

Then I had a brainwave. I asked Dave to phone the Secret Nanny Club on his mobile phone.

"Tell them you want a non-Irish nanny who is slim and blonde. Make an appointment and then phone me back immediately and tell me what type of response you get, okay? I know it seems like a crazy thing for me to ask you to do but it's so unbelievably important. Please – please!"

Dave, being the dote that he is, phoned the number for me and then phoned back. My hands were practically trembling as I answered.

"Dave?"

"Yeah, it's me. I rang that number, right?"

"Yes?" I could barely breathe.

"And I made an appointment to see a nanny tomorrow. The woman said there were no blondes available, only brunettes. Is this . . .? Kaylah, is this . . . what I think it is? What the hell's up?"

"Dave, I will explain it all to you later, I promise. But please, I need you to do one more thing for me. Phone back again and this time you must insist that you really want a blonde. Tell the woman that a friend of yours recommended a girl called Tanya and ask when she's free."

"This is all mad. You do know that?"

"I know, but this really is terribly important."

"Okay, but you've got some explaining to do."

He rang back about five minutes later. "Tanya only works after nine in the evenings. She's more expensive than the others and she insists on choosing both the restaurant and the hotel apparently. The woman on the phone wanted to be sure I could afford her before she confirmed the booking."

"And what did you say?"

"I said she'd better be worth it."

"And?"

"Well, the woman said that no client of Tanya's had ever complained before."

"Thanks, Dave. I really do owe you one."

Then I put down the phone and then, after taking a few more deep breaths, I made my next call.

Joanne answered pretty much immediately.

"Hi, Joanne, it's Kaylah from the book club here. I wonder would you be free this afternoon. I really need to talk to you."

There was a slight pause and then she said, "Sure. Call around at two thirty if that suits you?"

"Thanks, Joanne. See you then."

Joanne showed me into the drawing room. I sat down opposite her with Baby John on my knee I was so nervous but I desperately needed to get to the bottom of this. I refused Joanne's offer of tea and biscuits as I didn't intend staying long.

"I'm having a pretty stressful day so far," I admitted. "Baby John's father has just sent a second solicitor's letter about access to him, I'm supposed to be going to Cyprus in a few days' time to do a shoot, and now I've just found out that Tanya isn't what she pretends to be . . ."

"Tanya?" Joanne looked astonished.

I felt dreadful. "Yes, Tanya came to work for me after she left you. I'm sorry. I wish I had told you."

Joanne's hand was covering her mouth. Her eyes were wide open. "Oh, my God!" she finally gasped.

"She's an escort, isn't she?"

"Yes, she is." Joanne exhaled loudly. "And a highly paid one by all accounts."

"Oh Lord, this is so hard to come to terms with. How did you find out? I mean, how did you know that she was . . . *is* . . ."

"My husband found her photo on a website called Secretnanny.ie after a tip-off from somebody. It has since been taken down. When he confronted her about it she said that a friend of hers had put it up as a practical joke, but we had been suspicious anyway . . . all the late nights . . ."

"The clothes, the shoes, the jewellery . . ."

"Yes, and the boots. I once saw her wearing a brand-new pair of this season's Fendi boots and asked her where she'd got them. She told me she'd got them from a friend. Well, as both you and I know, friends aren't usually that generous. I'm so sorry. If I'd known that she was working for you I would have warned you. I had absolutely no idea."

"It's my fault for not letting you know," I said awkwardly. "But . . . why didn't you fire her?"

"We didn't want a big scene at the time in case the kids got upset, and anyway we didn't have any concrete proof that she *was* a working girl. We were just hoping she'd leave of her own accord."

"And she did." I gave a hollow laugh. "She came to live with me."

I felt like an absolute fool.

"I wish that you had said something that time we met outside the shop . . . you never said a word."

I was looking at the ground now, mortified.

"She's very clever, you know," Joanne said. "I'm sure she said lots of untrue things to you about myself and my husband. 'Always be careful of people who gossip to you,' my mother once told me, 'because soon they'll be gossiping about you to somebody else.'"

I tried to speak but couldn't. I had been a gullible twit as far as Tanya had been concerned. And now I was deeply ashamed of myself.

She continued. "Before us she had worked for another family called the McKays. She had led us to believe that Mr McKay was making moves on her and that was why she'd had to leave. I met his wife out at a function one night and she assured me it wasn't true. It was actually she who tipped us off about the escort agency and then my husband looked it up online."

"Oh God," I said, wringing my hands in frustration, "what am I going to do? I won't be able to go to Greece now. My son is the most important person in the world and I don't trust Tanya."

"You need to be careful what you say to her. She's very convincing. She'll swear blind that it's nonsense."

"I know that now," I said with resignation. "When something seems too good to be true it usually is."

Back at the apartment Tanya was watching TV. The

place was gleaming as usual and she gave me a pleasant smile. "Hello."

"Oh hiya, Tanya," I said. "How are you?"

"I'm fine, thank you."

I put John down on his play mat. "Did you have a good night last night?"

She seemed surprised by the question. "No, actually, I didn't. My date didn't turn up. I was stood up."

I looked away. I didn't want her to be able to read me. "That must have been annoying."

"Yes, it's annoying when somebody deliberately wastes your time. Oh well, you can't win them all."

She spoke so casually, as though she were talking about a bingo game or something.

I remained calm too but inside I was panicking. I had a real-life hooker under my roof, albeit a very friendly, charming, kind and tidy one. I was very fond of Tanya but I could no longer have her living under my roof and in charge of my precious son. I knew I would have to confront her and not pussyfoot around any more.

So I took a deep breath. It was now or never.

"Tanya, tell me more about this Secret Nanny Club," I said, looking her straight in the eye. "What exactly is it all about?"

"It's just a group of girls, mostly foreign," Tanya shrugged.

"And do men pay to take the girls from the Secret Nanny Club out on dates?"

I don't know what kind of reaction I had been expecting, but Tanya's eyes never even flickered. "Yes, sometimes they do," she admitted in an indifferent tone of voice.

"Times are tough at the moment as you know, and childminding doesn't pay well."

"Do your dates pay for more than just your company?" I was practically shaking inside. I could hardly believe I was even having this conversation.

She didn't flinch. "Sometimes."

"I see."

I couldn't get an ounce of emotion out of her. I didn't know whether I wanted to cry or get mad at her. My brain was turning on its axis.

"I think I'll go and give John a bath," I said in the end.

"Do you want me to do it?" She jumped up.

"No, it's okay. I'll do it. Actually, I think I might stay with my mum tonight. I'll take John with me."

"Right."

"I'm a bit stressed."

"You look stressed," she said.

John was innocently playing with his bunnies and teddies, oblivious to the bizarre conversation going on around him. I picked him up and quietly took him out of the room. It was the last time we would ever see Tanya.

27

I hadn't met Sally properly for ages. She was always in a hurry these days, rushing in and out of the office. She was working on the Christmas gifts spread at the moment. It was no less than twelve pages long, almost taking up half the magazine.

Her eyes nearly popped out of her head when I told her I was going to Cyprus.

"Dave set it all up," I told her. "I didn't even have to do a thing."

"You jammy bitch," said Sally. "And Dave is quite a hottie too so expect temperatures to soar in Paphos! God, I'm so jealous."

"Well, I'm so glad I'm going away," I admitted. "I've been under enormous stress. Clive keeps sending me solicitor's letters about John, the nanny disappeared leaving just a note and –"

"Tanya's gone?" Sally sounded amazed. "Where did she go to?"

"I don't know. We had, er, words. I took John away to stay the night with my mum and when we came back the next morning she and all her belongings were gone. There was no argument or falling out or anything like that. She left the place spick and span and she even left me a card and a bouquet of fresh flowers to thank me for being so kind to her. She said she would miss myself and John. That's the really sad part because I knew she was telling the truth. And do you know what's even weirder? I really miss her too."

I picked up my coffee and to my horror a tear splashed down into the cup. Once I had started crying I just couldn't stop.

Sally was alarmed. "It's okay," she said, patting the back of my hand gently. "I'm sure Tanya had personal reasons for leaving."

I nodded. "Yes. She did have reasons. I just can't say what they are. I'd feel bad talking about her behind her back. She wasn't the worst of people, you know."

Sally was very sympathetic, if a bit puzzled, and handed me a tissue. "Shush now, dry your eyes. Think of Cyprus and all the fun you'll have. Is your mum going to mind John?"

I nodded. "She is, thank God. I wouldn't be able to go otherwise."

"Well then, at least you know he's in safe hands so you don't have to worry about him."

"It's my first time going abroad since he was born though. I might miss him."

"I'm sure you will miss him. That would be normal. But you'll be very busy too. And you'll be with hunky Dave which will be a welcome distraction."

"True," I admitted, blushing slightly.

"Anyway, just think of poor old me back in the office when you're away."

I laughed in spite of myself. "I will. You must look after Louise for me when I'm gone – that's a joke by the way."

"Louise?" Sally tilted her head. "Oh, where have you been, Missus? I can't believe you haven't heard the news?"

I sat upright in the chair and then leaned forward. "What news?"

"Louise has gone. She has been shown the door. Goodbye and good riddance!"

I could hardly believe it! At last some good news!

28

I was really looking forward to getting on that plane as I sat on the Aircoach on the way out to Dublin airport. I really hoped that I would get a seat next to Dave on the afternoon flight to Paphos.

It really had been a crazy few days. The model that I had booked to come out had developed some kind of face rash and had to cancel. This had meant me calling a last-minute casting in Dave's city-centre studio. Thank God I had found a suitable girl for the shoot. Clara was tall and willowy with sallow skin and dark blonde hair. She was also curvy in all the right places which was of the utmost importance for a bikini shoot. You couldn't have a stick with the swimsuit falling off her!

Jenny, Diana's assistant from Galway, who was also coming with us, would be a joy to work with, and this time we would hire a make-up artist in Cyprus for the shoot so as not to go over budget.

I arrived at the airport in plenty of time and decided to go into the Spar shop in the car park for a bottle of water and some crisps to keep me going while I was waiting. Dave had texted me a few minutes earlier to say he was nearly at the airport so I kept an eye out for him. As I came out of the car park I actually saw him getting out of a silver BMW. He was so tall I immediately spotted him. I was about to call out to him when something happened. A blonde girl got out of the driver seat and ran around the other side of the car to hug him. She was slim, blonde and very attractive and as he leaned forward to kiss her I found myself shrinking away. I definitely didn't want him to see me.

I turned back into the car park, and took the escalator up to the Ladies' room. I breathed in and out very slowly. It took me a few minutes to compose myself, I was shaking so much. Then my phone beeped.

"Hey, it's Dave. Wher u? At cust serv desk."

I smartened myself up and made my way back into the terminal. I had to remain professional at all times. Dave had never told me he hadn't got a girlfriend. He had never lied to me or led me down the garden path. I, as usual, had just happened to get the wrong end of the stick.

I made my way to the airline customer-service desk. Jenny and Clara were already there, chatting to Dave. The girl at the ticket desk said she couldn't put the four of us together so we'd have to sit in pairs. I offered to sit beside Jenny, so Dave and Clara ended up with seats together in another part of the plane.

Jenny was all excited about the trip and talked

incessantly about it throughout the flight. I had hoped her enthusiasm would rub off on me but it didn't really. Suddenly I felt exhausted. So much had happened recently and it hadn't even really sunk in yet.

On the plane, I had a couple of glasses of wine to relax. They say drink goes to your head much faster when you're flying and, you know, they're probably right. I found myself getting a bit tipsy and pouring my heart out to Jenny. I told her about Louise and how she had been fired after getting caught opening parcels that were addressed to the editor. When Creea had confronted her about the expensive items that had gone missing from cosmetic giants such as Lancôme and YonKa, Louise had broken down and admitted that she had stolen them and sold them on eBay. Creea had reported her to her uncle and he had quietly told her that things were obviously not working out for her at the magazine and that maybe she should pursue another career that was more suited to her.

Jenny, now that she was over her initial excitement of being on a plane, told me that in her mother's salon in Galway a receptionist had once stolen two thousand euro from the till over the course of the summer and that they'd had to install security cameras in the salon to try and catch her. Jenny also told me about a very good friend of hers called Darina, from Galway, who was working for a mad crazy family in Foxrock who gave her champagne to drink and could never keep an au pair for more than a month. She said her friend was desperate to find a new family, and that a nicer girl you could not meet.

I perked up when I heard this. I wondered if Darina would be interested in working for me. True, I would never be offering her champagne, but I reckoned I was pretty okay most of the time.

I decided not to tell Jenny about what had happened with Tanya, but I did find myself explaining to her that I was a single mum and that it was hard to cope sometimes. I confided that I had cried that morning saying goodbye to my beloved little man. I also told her that I had reluctantly agreed that Clive could come and visit John once I got back from Cyprus, so John could get to know him. I would see where it could go from there.

"I mean, no way do I want him to stay the night with Clive. But he is his dad and no matter how much I dislike him I can't deny John his own father."

Jenny was most sympathetic. "I know it will be hard but it's probably best in the long run," she said with a maturity far beyond her years. She told me that her parents were separated but that she loved both her mother and her father no matter what and she was glad they were civil to each other for her sake. "It's easier sometimes just to keep the peace," she said quietly. "Even if there is always an underlying sense of injustice that someone is feeling. I know my mam did everything for me, and made so many sacrifices for me, but I'm still glad I know my dad too."

By the time the plane had touched down in Paphos International Airport I was feeling a lot more relaxed. Jenny was a tonic and it was impossible to feel down in her company. If her friend Darina was even half as much fun, I was sure that I'd like her very much too.

The hotel had sent a courtesy mini-bus to meet us and

within half an hour we were at the ocean-front hotel. It was gorgeous, with a big airy lounge and huge window looking over the blue sea. It was so nice just be somewhere warm and sunny again.

As soon as we checked into our rooms, the manager phoned us each individually and invited us for cocktails on the balcony. It was fantastic to be able to sit around in the open wearing short sleeves and feel the warmth of the evening sun on our faces and watch it sink into the horizon.

We had an early dinner that evening at the hotel. I sat next to Dave and tucked into a delicious olive, tomato and onion salad with fresh bread. Clara, who was drinking only sparkling water I am glad to say, had the same dish and the others had haloumi with red peppers and capers.

"No nightcaps now," I warned Dave jokingly, wagging my finger at him as I retired for bed.

"Eh, no chance of that on this trip. I don't want to incur your wrath again, Missus – I'll be on my best behaviour," he grinned.

We agreed to meet in the morning bright and early for breakfast at seven. I ended up having a terrific night's sleep. I had left my window open and it had been so relaxing listening to the waves crashing gently outside all night long. I woke up feeling fresh and ready to face the world.

Clara was a joy to work with. She had a magnificent body but she was also lively and fun, open to suggestions, even coming up with a few great ideas herself. Jenny did wonders on her hair and Maria, the Cypriot lady from Limassol who had been hired to do the make-up was extremely sweet even though her English was somewhat limited. The hotel manager explained to us that the hotel was very popular for weddings and that Maria had tended to countless very satisfied brides over the years. I had been initially a bit nervous hiring somebody I had never worked with before, but her attention to detail was faultless and she had Clara looking like a goddess.

We did countless shots on the sand, on top of rocks, in the garden of the hotel, on the balcony, even some bikini shots around the pool area intriguing the hotel guests. We worked hard but it was so worth it. The shots we got were exquisite.

That night the manager arranged for us to have a special barbeque by the pool and the area was tastefully done up with fairy lights. We drank local wines and this time Clara was allowed to join in because she didn't have to get her photo taken the following day. Herself and Jenny were around the same age and had really bonded over the last day couple of days. So when Jenny suggested that they try out a recommended nightclub in Paphos to go dancing, Clara was delighted.

That just left Dave and myself. Neither of us wanted to go clubbing. Instead we sat in close proximity to each other in the bar, looking out over the ocean. He was really easy to talk to and I found myself talking to him about how upset I'd been about Tanya leaving, and about how guilty I'd felt spying on her. I told him about Clive and how he had left me when I was pregnant and that throughout my pregnancy I had cried into my pillow night after night until I thought that I'd drown in my tears. And when he put his hand over mine and squeezed it, I didn't budge. I wanted his hand there forever. In fact, I wanted more than that. I wanted to kiss him, and I wanted him to hold me, but he didn't.

After saying goodnight I went to my room and he went to his. I presumed he would be phoning his girlfriend to say goodnight to her too, and maybe tell her he was missing her. I wanted to phone Mum to see how John was, but it was very late now. I'd have to wait until morning. Instead I got into my bed and flicked through my phone photos in the dark.

"Goodnight, my sweet darling," I said to my baby, "Mummy loves you more than anyone or anything in the whole wide world, and I can't wait to see you soon."

The next morning it was just Dave and me together at the table that had been reserved for us.

"The girls obviously had a good night," he laughed as we tucked into our fruit and croissants.

"Yes, obviously they did," I agreed. "I'd say they had some fun fighting off the Cypriot men!"

"Oh, to be young again!" he said with a sigh.

"Ah, Dave, don't write yourself off just yet!" I said with mock horror. "You've a few years left in you."

We chatted easily over our coffee. Then Dave asked me what I would be doing for the rest of the day.

I said that I would see what the girls wanted to do first. Maybe they would like to go shopping?

"Oh right, yeah, fine. I'll just do my own thing then. I might do a bit of sightseeing."

We agreed to meet up later for dinner. I was a little disappointed that he hadn't invited me to go sightseeing with him. Maybe I should have offered to accompany him. The last thing I wanted to do was go shopping with the girls. I could have kicked myself for opening my mouth without thinking.

In the end I didn't go shopping, and Dave didn't go sightseeing.

I took myself down to the almost deserted beach with a book. I was reading the latest from Martina Conlon-McKenna. I sat down on a small rock, opened the book at page one and got stuck in straight away.

But before long I spotted Dave strolling towards me in a pair of white shorts with his sunglasses perched on top of his head. I had an overall warm fuzzy feeling at the sight of him.

"May I join you?"

"Of course. Please do," I said, glad that I had left my own shorts on. I wasn't sure that I was quite ready for Dave to see me up close and in a bikini. I'd never quite lost the jelly tummy since giving birth.

He lay his towel down very close beside mine. I could actually feel my heart beat faster as he did so.

"So you didn't go shopping in the end?"

"Nah. Too lazy."

"I didn't go sightseeing either. Too hot."

"Oh. We're both as bad as each other."

"Actually, I wanted to spend a little more time with you, Kaylah. We don't have much more time left here."

"I know. I'm going to miss this." My heartbeat was accelerating now. What was all this about? I suddenly felt myself getting very hot and it wasn't just because of the sun.

"I really like you, Kaylah. You're a very special girl."

"Oh. Oh, thank you. That's very kind."

He reached over and touched my arm ever so slightly. "I'm not trying to be kind, Kaylah. I'm . . . the truth is, I'm mad about you. Can't you see it? Isn't it obvious?"

I just gaped at him.

"I mean, if you don't feel the same . . ."

I sat up on my towel, brushing some sand off my thighs. What was going on? I was confused. "B-but what about your girlfriend?" I burst out.

He stared at me or at least seemed to. I couldn't see his eyes because of his sunglasses. I leaned forward and slowly took them off his face.

"I said what about your girlfriend?"

"I don't have one."

"But who was that girl who dropped you off at the airport?" I asked in an accusatory tone.

"In the BMW? That was my sister. You didn't think – oh, come on – did you really think I had a girlfriend? I'm bloody crazy about you, Kaylah. I've been crazy about you since I first met you. But I thought you had no interest in me."

Suddenly a million thoughts were running through my head. I wanted to speak but I just couldn't find the words. Instead I leaned forward and kissed Dave fully on the lips. They tasted salty, like seawater. I closed my eyes and savoured the taste. I would never forget that moment, not ever. I still remember it like it was yesterday . . .

Cyprus. She is a gorgeous girl who hails from Galway and she has a lovely temperament. When I offered the job to her she jumped at the chance to leave her old family. She said they were far too eccentric for her anyway, the final straw being when they asked if the cat could sleep in her room at night because he didn't like to be left alone downstairs and the children already had a rabbit hutch in their room and the parents had a pet parrot who hated the cat in theirs. I think she was very relieved to be able to move in with me. She's lovely company and she bonds well with Claudine too. In fact Claudine and Sheelagh came with us to the zoo the other day with the prams and we had a wonderful day out.

Baby John will be a year old tomorrow. My God! So much has happened this year it's scary. I feel like I am a completely different person than I was before. Dave has had such a calming influence on me. In fact, I'm so relaxed these days that I even find myself being surprisingly pleasant to Clive when he calls every second Saturday to take John off to spend the afternoon at his mother's house – a privilege I only agreed to after he made frequent visits to our place to make friends with John. They did make friends and now John always looks happy to see him which is the main thing. I love John a lot more than I dislike Clive so I just put up with him for John's sake. And there's a bonus to Clive's presence in our lives: he agreed to pay maintenance . . . after a little pressure from me.

John is growing at an alarming rate. In fact he's crawling around the place at breakneck speed and is eating me out of house and home too. Soon I won't even be able to call him Baby John any more. He'll just be plain John. I kind of miss him being a baby sometimes. When he was small he was easier to handle and I could just put him in the cot if I needed to do something. No chance of that now. I need eyes in the back of my head to watch him!

Dave asked me the other day if I had ever thought about giving John a little brother or a sister. Truthfully, I hadn't. Not until now anyway. But who knows? Maybe Dave is secretly becoming a bit broody. And maybe, just maybe, his broodiness will rub off on me too! But for the moment I'm just happy out.

If you enjoyed
The Secret Nanny Club by Marisa Mackle
why not try
Along Came a Stork also published
by Poolbeg?
Here's a sneak preview of Chapters One and Two

Along
came a
Stork

Marisa Mackle

POOLBEG

1

New Year's Day

1st Jan

Dear Brand-New Diary,

I am so hungover it's not even funny. I woke up this morning screaming when I saw a big black spider on my pillow. I thought he was dead because he was lying in a pool of blood. But then I realised that it was just one of my false eyelashes, which must have fallen off at some stage during the night, and that the pool of blood was actually the remnants of the large goldfish-bowl-sized glass of red wine that I'd brought to bed with me. Yes, Diary, how sad am I that I actually thought it would be a good idea to bring my glass of wine up from the residents' bar? But since I'd paid a crazy hotel price for it with my hard-earned money, I'd decided I was going to drink it come hell or high water. I hate to see anything wasted, what with the recession and all.

I stayed in a very fancy hotel last night. It was an old period house in its own grounds. Five-star with all the trimmings and – wait for it – Jo Malone products in the bathroom! Me and the girls, Vicky and Selina, stayed in a triple room. At least it was supposed to be me and the girls. And at the beginning of the night that's what it was but "we" soon became "me".

Yes, just little old me on my ownio. It ended up being more of a girl's-night out (singular) than a girls'-night out (plural) because the others met a couple of men (seriously not my type at all) in a bar in town early on in the evening and disappeared off with them into the night, not to be seen again for the duration of our, eh, "fun" weekend away. I thought it was quite mean of them not to say goodbye really. I was in a strange place and had to get a taxi back to the hotel all by myself, and because it was New Year and every other person in the town was also looking for a cab at the same time, I ended up in a queue outside a dodgy chipper in the rain waiting for one. I began to wonder why I'd forked out on such an expensive hotel when I'd ended up, not snuggled up in a lovely comfy warm bed rubbing Jo Malone products onto my skin as a treat, but on an unfamiliar street with some teenager vomiting all over my cute strappy silver sandals. Yes, it was really gross but let's not even go there right now as I'm trying to block that particular memory from my mind.

Anyway I was about to report my friends to the police as missing persons when I got up this morning and noticed that the other beds in my room were still not slept in but then I got a text from Vicky going 'Hope u got back 2 hotel ok. X'.

Hope I got back okay? Was she bloody serious? Well, it's a bit late to be worrying about me now, Missus, I thought to myself. She'd a bit of a cheek really. I mean anything at all could have happened to me in a strange town. I could have been murdered in the taxi on the way back to the hotel and she'd have been none the wiser until this morning. So much for the sisterhood, huh? But do you know what really gets my goat? Vicky is one of those girls who is always shouting her head off about stuff like girl power and women sticking together, but after a few vodkas if there's so much as a sniff of an available man, all that girlie-support lark goes straight out the window.

Anyway, Diary, I am just home now. Just in the door less than an hour ago actually, looking like something the cat dragged in backwards. My eyes look like two bullet holes in my sunken face, thanks to the smudged mascara, and supposedly waterproof liquid eyeliner that I'd borrowed from Vicky as I'd forgotten to pack my own.

The first thing I did when I got upstairs was to run myself a steamy hot bubble bath using the Jo Malone products I'd swiped from the hotel bathroom. Well, I reckoned I totally deserved the lot as the other girls hadn't even bothered staying in the room at all and probably hadn't noticed them. But, alas, now I've blisters on both my heels after standing in the taxi rank for so long last night. Oh God, it was freezing standing outside that chipper. Minus two degrees or something. My legs had never been so cold in all my life. They were numb until that idiot got sick on them and kind of warmed them up. Oh stop! Block it out, Diana. Block. It. Out.

301

The taxi home cost a fortune too. They really do screw you for having to work on a Bank Holiday, don't they? I should have driven, but then again I'd probably have been over the limit even today after all the booze we consumed last night, and the police always go a bit mad on special occasions such as New Year's Day trying to breathalyse people. Still, the taxi almost cost as much as the hotel which is kind of killing me because I'm smashed broke at the moment. I don't know why I'm always penniless. I'm single, I live at home, and I don't have too many commitments or loans except for my car loan. But I just never have any money to call my own.

Anyway, it was better to take a taxi rather than face taking two buses home across the city on New Year's Day when there are hardly any services running. It probably would have taken me about six hours to get home – same time as a flight from New York to Dublin.

Diary, dearest, I know it's not so good me introducing myself to you when I feel like someone is bashing my head in with a sledgehammer and my mouth feels like the bottom of a sewer, but normally I'm way more upbeat and together than this. I'd kind of forgotten how bad hangovers feel. It's funny how you forget, isn't it? The way you go "Never Again" and then say the same thing a week later when you've done the same stupid thing all over again. One of my many New Year's resolutions for this year is not to drink. Well, not as much as I usually do. Well, between two and three glasses, maybe. If you don't drink more than three glasses you're laughing. Hmm, DEFINITELY no more than five glasses. And lots of water in between. I'm going to stick to that. No, really. I know I'll have you to answer to the following day so I'm going to keep that in mind next time someone suggests a Jameson or ten for the road.

I'm twenty-nine now. It's not good for me to be behaving like an eighteen-year-old who's just left home and is going nuts away from the parents. And I'm known too. Yes, I mean this is a bit embarrassing and I don't want to come across as big headed, but as my Diary I can tell you anything so let me fill you in. I recently started writing a dating column in a magazine, which is really quite popular, and I get letters and emails in from people all over the country. I've a little fan club of my own going on. People can register as a member of my website and read my tips on how to get a man, how to win a man back and how to get that ring on your finger. Hilarious really, considering my own wedding finger is completely ring-free. But it's very popular all the same.

My photo always accompanies the column so now I'm a tiny bit recognisable too. I'm not telling you all this to be blowing my own trumpet but just so you understand that it is definitely not a good idea for people to see me staggering around some strange street not remembering where I am or what my name is. Because they will probably remember. And tell all of their friends. And it could get back to the magazine – and my boss, nice and all as she is, might take a very dim view of it all.

So, this is going to be my year hopefully. Yes. I really believe that this is the year that my career suddenly takes off and I become the success story I've always secretly dreamed of being. I know I say every year that this might be the year but this time I really, really mean it. No more messing around. It's now or never. This is the year Diana hits the big time and finally meets a nice man. Nice is nice. I don't care if nice is boring. I'll settle for nice. All the cars and fancy suits in the world don't do it for me. He can look like Brad Pitt but, if he's not a nice man, I'm not interested. Don't think I'm settling for less. You have no idea how hard it is to meet somebody who is simply a nice person!

Jesus, my head! My hangover's getting worse, not better. Right, that's about it for now. Sorry but I have to lie down. I thought I was fine but I'm obviously not. Please excuse me, I'm going back to bed.

D

2

2nd Jan

Dear Diary,
Hi again, it's me. I feel much better today. Like a spanking brand-new person. I'll start off with a compliment by saying you're so lovely and pristine clean and you even smell nice. I hate even writing on you because it almost feels like some sort of vandalism, but it has to be done.

My sister Jayne gave you to me. She doesn't give me much because money is always tight with her even though she still lives at home as well with Mum and Dad and is manager of the spa of a top five-star hotel. She hardly ever spends any money and blames the recession for everything. Nobody in Ireland has embraced the credit crunch more than my sister, who uses it as an excuse never to put her hand in her pocket these days. Would you believe, she doesn't even let Mum and me use the facilities of the spa because she says it would be abusing her position of authority and she might get into trouble with the hotel. But she does our nails and stuff at home when we beg her which is handy 'cos Mum and I are always broke. She charges us a fiver each for manicures and pedicures and ten euro for a full body-spray tan. Yes, I know you're probably really shocked that she actually demands payment from her own flesh and blood, but at least we don't have to fork out full price somewhere else. Anyway, I find it really embarrassing standing in a salon wearing paper knickers while somebody blasts my boobs with fake-tan spray while asking me in a chatty voice whether I'm going on holidays this year or not.

So although Jayne's a scabby so-and-so and only gave me a diary for Christmas, because of her we don't ever have to go to the beauty salon, except for leg and bikini waxes. I mean we wouldn't ask Jayne to do that. And she wouldn't offer.

But things are looking up. You see, because my column is popular with all the single ladies out there (I write the sort of personal stuff most laydeez would rather not admit to but secretly love reading!), I've been getting lots of other offers like radio interviews and TV appearances and stuff. My editor is really pleased with me because every time I'm on air I plug the magazine so it's great publicity for her too.

I write a lot about being mercilessly dumped and being two-timed and being hit on by sleazy married men (isn't there an octopus in every office?). Love rats are kind of my forte and, you know, the good thing is that I don't have to do much research because I have probably met more rats in my lifetime than the Pied Piper of Hamelin, the latest being Roger the Rat who dumped me for a girl a decade younger than me who has just finished school. He dumped me because he said I was putting pressure on him to commit. Obviously because the new girl is barely out of her school uniform and the ink is still dry on her Leaving Certificate exams, she isn't talking about babies and settling down right away, which in his eyes obviously makes her infinitely more attractive than me. Not that I am broody or anything. I mean, that's where Roger got it all wrong. Of course, he probably got the wrong idea when I asked him to come into Mothercare with me to have a look at the cute little baby clothes. It wasn't like I was dropping hints or anything but it's just that, ever since my brother's wife had a baby girl, I just love baby stuff and I can't pass a baby shop without wanting to run in and buy something for my little niece.

Looking back, I can kind of understand why Roger freaked a bit, but the way he ran out of the shop was a bit pathetic. It was like somebody had taken out a match and set fire to his balls. He dumped me soon after that. Well, he didn't actually have the decency to tell me to my face. Instead he did it the cowardly way: not answering his phone or emails or fax messages or texts or letters or answering his front door. Oh yes, I tried everything until I finally got the message that our relationship was probably over, and the only person in town who didn't seem to know it yet was me.

But I'm better off without him. Oh God, yes. Like, did he think he was some great prize or something? The nerve of him making out that I was this crazy woman with a biological clock the size of Big Ben! That was so not the case. I didn't even have a doll when I was a little girl for goodness' sake. I was more into kicking a ball around the place and robbing my brother's toy soldiers. I never dreamed of having a big brood. I mean, I adore kids in small doses and think they're really cute, but at the moment I'm far too busy progressing with my career to even contemplate giving it all up for a life of domestic bliss. I, of all people, KNOW that becoming a mum is the end of life as you know it. God, I was even an au-pair in Normandy back in the day and I never got a minute to myself. Even going to the loo in peace was a rarity because there was always some little fist banging on the door demanding that I come out and watch Barney speaking French. I actually don't know how mothers stay sane at home all day listening to that big purple eejit dancing on the telly. It's a long time now since I minded children but to this day I still can't stand the sight of Barney's silly goofy oversized head. Or the Teletubbies' annoying babbling. So you understand, I'm just not the maternal type. Love kids, just as long as I don't have to wipe their bums or noses.

Anyway, now that Roger is trying to relive his youth by hanging out of a teen, I'm back living at home with my parents and older sister Jayne, and when I'm not out and about pretending to be loving the single life as research for my column, I'm holed up in my room reading all these self-help books in an effort to get on with my life and not become a bitter person. I have even recently taken to putting little positive post-it notes around the house, like on the fridge and the wall opposite the toilet saying "What's for you won't pass you," and all that. Dad's going mad because when he went to the bathroom the other day one of them stuck on to his jumper and he was walking around Supervalu doing his shopping and he said people were staring at him and laughing and he couldn't understand why. I'm sure he was exaggerating though. I mean the post-it notes are so small that nobody could have possibly seen the "I am the most important person in my life" message stuck to his back. Not unless they were right up close behind him.

But, to be honest, I don't think there is such a thing as a quick fix for a broken heart. It's not like you can go out and buy glue to put it all back together. Only time, and lots of it, can help the Cupidly wounded. I know that for a fact. Like I look back on men I used to pine over and think I couldn't live without, and now I honestly with hindsight can't think of one reason why I fancied them in the first place. The whole "grieving" process roughly takes about two years which is a bit annoying but I put it down to the fact that my star sign is Cancer and I'm a crab. Crabs find it extremely hard to let go. They'll cling onto their past with every pincer.

So I know with Roger it's going to take time. But not forever. I'm going to deal with the break-up in a mature dignified way and I'm not going to indulge in irrational behaviour such as rushing to the hairdresser's to cut off all my hair, or dramatically losing weight in an effort to lure him away from his teenage love. I don't want closure. Feck closure. Too many people waste so much of their lives looking for closure instead of just throwing their hands in the air and going, "Hey, it just didn't work out." Look, life shouldn't be about getting closure. If you get fired, you might not be given the right reason for why you're losing your job, but you don't spend the rest of your life asking yourself why oh why oh why and asking your old boss to meet up in the hope of gaining closure. No, the thing is, you move on quickly and find yourself another job fast, and vow to be more punctual and work harder and not turn up to work hung-over with a ladder in your tights ever again. I'm going to take that same professional attitude when it comes to relationships. I mean, it's mad, isn't it? There I am with a dating column and often on TV being introduced as a dating guru, putting myself out there as some kind of expert with people phoning in looking for advice, and I myself don't have a clue! Jesus, I haven't ever been able to hold down a relationship for more than a few months! What does that say about me? After all, I am the common denominator in all my failed liaisons. So maybe, just maybe, the problem is mine.

Until tomorrow.

Diana xx

If you enjoyed this chapter from
Along Came a Stork by Marisa Mackle
why not order the full book online
@ www.poolbeg.com

POOLBEG WISHES TO

THANK YOU

for buying a Poolbeg book.

If you enjoyed this why not
visit our website:
www.poolbeg.com

and get another book delivered
straight to your home or to a
friend's home!

All books despatched within
24 hours.

POOLBEG

WHY NOT JOIN OUR MAILING LIST
@ www.poolbeg.com and get some
fantastic offers on Poolbeg books